D0403622

Poor Banished Children

A Novel

Poor Banished Children

A Novel

Fiorella De Maria

IGNATIUS PRESS   SAN FRANCISCO

Front cover photo: Steve Lewis/Riser/Getty Images

Cover design by Riz Boncan Marsella

ISBN 978-1-58617-632-7
Library of Congress Control Number 2010931310
Printed in the United States of America ⊗

CONTENTS

ACKNOWLEDGMENTS

There are many people I need to thank for sharing their advice and expertise so generously over the past two years. Firstly, John Ash for his information on piracy, ships, and life at sea, but most of all for inspiring me to write the novel in the first place; Paul Lunde and Caroline Stone for their information on slavery in North Africa and for introducing me to so many lines of enquiry; Rev. Timothy Finigan for his patience in answering my many questions about the Catholic priesthood and religious life; and my father for providing much of the material on Maltese folklore and medicine. For any mistakes in the text, I have no one but myself to thank.

Note

The events recorded in this book are fictional, but I have drawn as closely as possible on historical accounts of slavery and piracy in re-creating the world of the Barbary slave trade, through which hundreds of thousands of Christians and Muslims lost their freedom. Pierre Dan really existed, though I have taken some liberties with his actions and personality. Ibrahim Reis is based on the real-life pirate Murat Reis.

PART I

Dreams of the Dead

Death has come for me again. The others are already lost. I heard their screams as I was cast into the night; I heard them cursing as they burned or drowned before the roar of the explosion stopped up my ears and I fell into a world of silence. I am burnt by fire and stifled by the black, icy waters that drag me down. There is merciless darkness everywhere, which even the flames tearing the ship cannot pierce. I spin and struggle, raising my head for air as my blood freezes, and I know the sea will take me in the end.

The ship is gone now, and all that remains are burning fragments scattered like votive candles in the night. And I remain—the fragment of a human life, drifting to its close. I am not afraid to die, even though I will die unabsolved, but I am afraid to be alone. I fear the loneliness of the last journey down to the depths of the sea, where I will take my place among the dead, and no one will know that I came to such a pass. There will be no Requiem for me and no resting place, only a troublesome memory in the minds of a few old friends who believe that I died long ago, at the hands of another aggressor.

There are faces all around me; the spectral images of those I have loved dance around my head, taking their leave of me, whilst those I have lost gaze at me in silent accusation. I will die with so many lives to account for, so much blood I never meant to spill, but it cries out for vengeance nonetheless.

Death is so slow in coming that I find myself fighting. If I had desired death as I yearned for it once, I would not have run onto the deck when I knew the end was truly coming; I would not cling now to splintering driftwood, praying that it will hold me. The very motion of lifting my head to take a breath is an act of defiance. I feel no pain, the chill takes away all sense, and I feel only the weariness of death as it reaches out to me. I have died so many times and been returned to the land of the living that I could almost believe I am not meant to go down with the ship—but I am cold. I am cold and weary and cannot draw breath any longer. In the gloom above my head a single star shines. Stella ... Stella Maris. I am lost. Stella Maris. I call out to the Star of the Sea but cannot hear my own voice ringing out across the murderous water. Perhaps this is death, then—cruel death from which I can never awaken. I cannot hold onto the driftwood any longer. My hands grow limp and numb with the cold, so that I cannot feel my own fingers as they uncurl.

"Mother? Mother, I am dying!"

"Hush", says a voice I can hear. "I am holding you."

Dreams again, the dreams of the dead.

1640—The Devonshire Coast

A group of fishermen found her body at first light. She lay on the beach—her hands still curled around the driftwood that had carried her there, her hair covering her face so that they thought at first she must surely be dead. However, when they turned her over they saw colour in her face, and they were so struck by the sight of her that they carried her into the town to see if she could be saved.

She was unusually small and of such delicate build that Tom carried her in his arms with the ease he might have used to carry a child. "She must have been on that boat", he said, when they reached the tavern and Mary was prevailed upon to come down and let them in. "She's hurt."

They had been woken up in the night by the sound of a distant explosion and seen flames on the horizon when they hurried to their windows to look, but when they had made a search at daybreak she was all they had found. They placed her over a barrel and began striking her back to release the water from her lungs. "A lady passenger?" asked Jonathan, his brother. "She is clothed as a man. Look at her."

Her shirt and breeches had been burnt and torn in many places, but she was very definitely wearing a boy's garb. "Perhaps she was a stowaway?" Tom suggested, but there was no time to consider the puzzle any further. The tiny body began choking and moving; then quite suddenly she lifted her head, opened a pair of huge, piercing black eyes,

and shouted in a barbarous tongue they did not understand.
"You have nothing to fear", said Tom, reaching out to place
a reassuring hand on her head, but she could not hear him
and thought that she had fallen into hostile hands again.
"There now, we are trying to help you."

But she would not be comforted, struggling and shouting so violently that they almost feared her and Tom could
have been convinced that she was not a human being at
all. A nymph of the sea perhaps or some other fantastical
creature, she was so wild and so perfectly made—except
that she was wounded and only a real woman could bruise
and bleed as she had done. "What are we to do with her?"
he asked when she lost consciousness again, much to their
relief. "We cannot keep her."

Mary backed away. "Do not look to me for help; she
cannot stay here."

"You have room."

"Ay, for paying guests, not sickly strangers. I am not a
nursemaid."

"Oh, Mary, where's your woman's heart?"

"Buried with my husband", she snapped. She took her
shawl from around her own plump shoulders and covered
the girl, who was shivering in a feverish sleep. "You should
take her to Branton Hall. Lady Alice is a good woman, if
a Papist. She will take care of her. Who knows, she may
even understand the nonsense she speaks."

†

"Would it be impertinent of me to ask how this woman
came to your house, my lady?" asked Mr. Forbes, when
she had dismissed the servant from the sickroom and they
were at liberty to talk. As a physician and fellow Catholic,

he had attended the family for many years and was Lady
Alice's most trusted confidant, but never had she called him
on so strange an errand.

"Some men carried her here this morning", she said,
seating herself by the window. "They said a ship had gone
down in the night—they heard an explosion—and that she
had been found on the beach, half-drowned. Naturally I
took her in and ordered the servants to care for her, but
when they tried to undress her they discovered she was horribly injured and were afraid to do her any further harm.
I did not know whom to trust. Since she was evidently in
need of help, I sent for you."

"And you have no notion of who she might be?"

"None at all. Her dress was so strange; if she had been a
man I would have thought she were a pirate, but of course
that cannot be. And she is clearly not from these parts; look
how dark she is." Forbes moved away and knelt at the girl's
bedside. The servants had eventually been prevailed upon
to strip off her tattered, damp clothes and had dressed her
in a nightgown before putting her to bed. She lay now,
senseless and trembling, entirely unaware of their presence.
"My dear Mr. Forbes, I have hardly considered where she
has come from; I have been so worried she might not live."

He turned to look at her. "Lady Alice, you have reason
to fear. This woman has been tormented almost to the point
of death. I am quite astonished that she is alive and cannot say with any certainty that she will live much longer.
Look." He would never have shown her what he had found
if he had not known how strong she was, but he knew that
Lady Alice had been a prison visitor as a young woman in
London and there was very little she had not seen, including
dead bodies. "If you will forgive me, my lady—" He pulled
back the covering and turned the girl onto her front, then

slipped the vast, ill-fitting gown off her shoulder to reveal fresh dressings. "She must have had her back to the explosion if she was on the ship, but she is quite badly burnt. And there are older injuries I do not like. Here." He pointed at the exposed side of her face, where a livid patch had spread across her cheek. "That was a hefty blow some days ago, powerful enough to break the cheekbone. Then there are these thin scars all over her body—"

He was cut off by the patient beginning to move; he quickly turned her onto her back again so that he could look at her face more clearly. Her eyes were open and she looked at him in undisguised terror. "Hush now, do not be afraid", he said, but knew he was wasting his time. She clearly could not understand a word he said.

"What about French?" suggested Lady Alice, but she simply shook her head when it was tried. "Latin?"

To Lady Alice's surprise, a look of recognition came into the girl's face. "Puella sum", she whispered, pressing her wrists together. "Puella."

"A slave?" Lady Alice knelt by her side to hear her better. "Where are you from?"

Her breathing was becoming laboured again. She struggled to form the word. "Malta."

"And your name? Do you have a name?"

The girl's mouth opened and closed as though she could not remember her own name or could not decide whether to trust them with it; then her eyes filled with tears and she shook her head. "Leave her", ordered Forbes, placing a hand on the girl's forehead. "It cannot matter now. She has not had a peaceful life; she deserves a peaceful death. Ask your servant to bring me more water."

Lady Alice turned to leave but stopped in her tracks, hearing the unmistakable gasping and grunting of a dying body attempting to speak again. "Do not speak if it troubles you", said Forbes, placing a finger on her lips to hush her, but she pushed his hand away, hissing between her teeth. Finally, they both heard one barely distinguishable word: "Sacerdos."

Forbes let out a long sigh. Quite without knowing it, she had made the most dangerous final request she could possibly have articulated.

Into the World of Dreams

When I was a slave, my dreams took me back to the world of the free. I dreamed that I was back in the land of my birth again, wandering the streets of the Gozitan town I had once imagined I would never leave. My masters could not stop me from walking where I pleased then, and I could run and laugh and drink deeply. Cool, clear water, heady wine. And the voices of friends returned to me like a love poem, whispering in my dreams to give me comfort before the morning and its terrors began.

But now the world of dreams and waking have changed places. By day I find myself in a place without a name, among a courteous people who care for me though they do not know who I am. A gentlewoman comes often to my chamber and sits by my bedside with her needlework, keeping watch over me. I am warm and safe; my wounds heal behind dressings I could not have made better myself. I lack nothing except peace, but I know it can never be mine, even when death comes.

In dreams I cross the sea and find myself in Barbary again. I see him, a white-haired Frank being led out to die. All those people seemed like angels to me, so white and gold and delicate, so very unlike any person I had ever seen before. This one seems unconcerned for his fate and makes no attempt to struggle, as though despair or fear have worked their wicked magic on him and he has no will left to put up a fight. Perhaps it is just as well; he could not possibly release himself. His hands are bound, and they hang him by his ankles so that his head is some distance from the ground. Only at that moment, when there is not the slightest hope of escape, does he seem to come to life, and he calls out in his language so pitifully that we all know he is pleading to be released. But this is a place without hope, without mercy, and they drop him down so that his head batters against the ground.

I have heard so many people screaming and crying that my nightmares do not distinguish one from another; I simply hear a cry of anguish coming from the mouth of this tormented man that might belong to him or to the child some paces in front of me, screaming at the sight of a man being dashed time and time again against the earth until his bloodied head cracks open and he dies. Or it might be my own cries, since no injury I attended when I learnt the physician's art was ever so horrible as that sight. They cut down his body as though it were a mere carcass, the broken head so disfigured, so utterly destroyed that in death the man barely looked human. Yet I thought, *He is some poor woman's son. Perhaps he is himself a father of children.* But then I wake trembling and weeping with the smell of blood all around me and the sight of his face just before they let him go ... and he is only a ghostly memory sent to torment my rest.

There were so many of them, poor souls, more than I could ever count, taken from any country I could think to name: French, Spanish, Greek, English, Venetians, Genoese, Blacks, and my own people—a people no one ever recognised. To our fellow Christians we must have seemed neither one race nor another, with our dusky looks and Arab tongue, a stiff-necked Christian people who called God Allah and worshipped Christ, whose eyes looked always toward Rome. To our captors we must have seemed like renegades of a kind, too like them for comfort and yet too unlike them to be worthy of any respect. Poor souls indeed, the most unfortunate of all the children of Christendom, snatched from families who could never hope to pay the demanded ransom, a people whom none would call their neighbour—poor banished children of a suffering God.

I can hear again. The blast ringing through my head as I was thrown overboard stopped up my ears for just a few hours, thank God, before sounds began to return to me. I feared, to begin with, that I was trapped in a silent world from which I could not escape nor hear the comfort of another human voice, where the only noises would be those I was condemned to remember.

When I first heard the lady of the house speak, I recognised her language, though I did not understand a single word. I knew that I had heard it once before, coming from that man's mouth as he pleaded for his life. He was an Englishman then, the man they killed in that bloody manner. I never even knew what it was he was supposed to have done—made repeated attempts at escape, perhaps, or helped others to flee. I suppose I remember him so clearly because I cannot help imagining how easily I might have been put to death myself or caused another to suffer in my place. Dear God, let no one have suffered in my absence. Let no one else have suffered. I never meant anyone to take the blame in my place, but I can never know what the true cost of my escape was. And I see him still in my most chilling dream visions, dying over and over again when he himself is at peace now. I see him or those who were good to me hanging in his place, and I will always see them because I cannot know what harm I may have caused on the long, perilous road to freedom. I can never know.

A Most Extraordinary Confession (1)

"Are you a priest?" I ask the man who sits near my head. The lady of the house told me he was a priest before she left the room, but he is not clothed as priests were in my motherland.

"Yes", he promises; "you called for me. Will you let me hear your confession?"

"You do not look like a priest."

He smiles. He is an old man with grey hair that must have been almost black once and a face lined with anxiety, yet he seems quite at peace. "It is far safer than it was when I was a young man, but I am used to caution and do not dress as a priest here", he explains, reaching into his bag and taking out a purple stole. It hangs around his neck like a silken rope. I find it impossible not to flinch. "There now, do not fear to trust me. God has spared your life and brought me to your side in your darkest hour."

"Father, it has been so long; I hardly know what to do. Where I have been—"

"Where have you been?"

"Hell. I am a voyager from hell."

Poor man. He looks a little startled by my demeanour; perhaps he thinks me a little mad, and I declare that I may be mad, but not without cause. I defy him to call me a liar. I have been burnt by fire and tormented by infernal creatures; I have been dragged, screaming with terror, from the land of the living. I have known pain fit to drive a strong man to madness, which is why I say that perhaps I am a little mad. I have known shame and I have known despair. I have seen men and women beaten, starved, confined like condemned criminals until they begged for death to claim them. I have stood helplessly by and watched innocent children snatched from the arms of their parents. I have seen the devil himself at work in the bagnos and slave markets of Barbary, and I have stared him in the face.

"Father, I have been delivered from the hands of my enemies, though I have not deserved it, and now I ask you to deliver me from the greatest peril of all. I do not wish to return to hell."

"You need not go to hell", he tells me; "be of good courage. You must hold nothing back."

It is like hanging helplessly at the brink of a fall, with a man I do not know promising to catch me if I let go. "I swear before Almighty God that this is a true account of my life. May I forget nothing; may I withhold nothing and come at last to peace."

I am afraid, wearily afraid. I must know that I will not be lost before darkness falls again. Yet it is the priest who should be of good courage, if he only knew the journey he is embarking upon. I will begin long ago, with a death I did not cause but which shames me still.

1629—Two Deaths

He had died as though struck down by the hand of God. Ursula had been barely five years old when her mother had sent her to the fields to take him water, and she had still been a little way off when she had seen him tumble to the ground. It was the suddenness of it that she never forgot. One moment her father was turning to exchange a word with one of his companions; the next he was dead, and that was the end of it. No time to give him his water, no time to take care of him nor bid him farewell—no time even to call a priest.

Her father's unexpected death marked a kind of death for her too, though she did not know it as she watched them lifting his limp body out of the dust and carrying him home. Many years later, as she confessed the sins of her life, Ursula recalled that her journey into darkness had begun on that day, the day her father was struck dead, when she sat in the tiny room where they had laid him in preparation for his burial.

Perhaps she should not have been left alone with him, but as she kept her lonely vigil she became frightened by the darkness of the room. At that time she was still a fanciful child by nature, and in the gloom of the death chamber she began to imagine that her father's ghost was creeping about her, unable to escape because the few ways out were covered in black and it was too dark for him to find his way. A lost soul. Invisible hands brushed against the back of her neck, making her jump up and turn herself about to shake them off. A lost soul. She had heard the expression before somewhere and thought him lost, trapped, only because she felt lost and trapped herself.

In her panic, she pulled down the black cloth that covered the window, unable to bear the darkness any longer. This was the first unforgivable mistake. The room was filled with weary, forbidden light, and she saw him laid out as though asleep, cleaner and more precise than she had ever known him, dressed in his best clothes, but peacefully asleep. With the sudden invasion of sunlight her fears melted away, and she knew he was not floating around her or touching her anymore. She could almost believe, seeing him so clearly, that he was not even dead. Her pulse began to slow again, and she made her second unforgivable mistake. She did what any other child in search of comfort might have thought to do and could see no wrong in the action. She curled up next to him and fell fast asleep, her arm wrapped affectionately around his neck.

If she had not disturbed his eternal rest, her family would not have turned against her; she would not have fallen into the hands of Father Antonin nor been condemned to wander so far from her native land. So much rested upon those few childish blunders or on the failure of her family to forgive her, but Father Antonin had said that regret for events that could not be altered was folly. It had been ordained that her father would leave the world on that day—and in the flurry of fists and raised voices that greeted her when she woke, it was determined that she too would leave the world of her birth.

Yet she still wished he could have come to life and saved her from them. Years later, she could still see him, white and serene in death, lying unperturbed by the angry scene taking place on his behalf. Or perhaps she had felt a little grateful that he was dead or he might have turned on her as well, but the dead could do no harm. The dead could do no harm ...

A Mother's Lament

God forgive me, I never loved her. Even as a tiny baby, she seemed to me an unnatural creature sent to mock my declining years, always crying and fretting, always demanding my care. If any of my children were destined to interfere with their father's rest, it was that restless, flame-headed girl who could never be still. I can still see her sleeping figure next to a man who might also have been sleeping, and I wished—God forgive me, I could not help it!—that she was the one who was dead and my husband could be wakened from sleeping.

When my sons tore her from his body, I felt sickened by her; the stench of the dead hung about her, as his soul must have hovered at her heels, and I could feel no love for her. They forced her into scalding hot water and chafed her until her flesh was raw, but she still seemed dirty with the touch of the dead. I let her go, the child who might have grown to be the comfort of my old age, and I saw her as a mere creature to endure under my roof, like a rat or a cockroach—and God punished me for my neglect of the child he had given me, and he took her away from me forever.

I have prayed a thousand times that the years might roll back so that I could go to her and ask her forgiveness, bring her home if she could know it as her home after so long. Yet I know that what is done can never be undone. I have received absolution, but I can find no peace. I cannot bring her back, and I cannot give a memory the love that hurts my heart. In the searing heat of the day, I watch the sea disappearing out of my sight and think of her broken body sinking into the depths, far beyond my reach. And I believe that I would crawl along the seabed on my hands and knees if I were able, until I found her and brought her home to rest. But it cannot be. I have brought a curse upon my head to live and die without her, and it is well that I should suffer the consequences of such a sin. What sort of a mother would abandon her own child? Better if I had never been born. Better if I had been a whore selling my honour to the wealthiest customer than that I should have failed to protect hers.

How long the nights are! How long and silent. I never thought when I was raising children that I would long for the sound of a baby's cries to wake me in the night and make me feel loved, but it seems a lifetime ago that I lay in bed with a tiny body wriggling against me and the pressure of a hungry mouth suckling at my breast. She had black, wondering eyes that stared up at me with the trust of the innocent. Oh God, I can see her face close to mine in the darkness of the night, feel her beating heart. The only prayer I have to say is the only one that I know can never be answered. Even God himself cannot make the years fall away.

The Journal of a Priest-Physician (1)

It was a time of fear and uncertainty. There were none alive then who remembered the raid that all but destroyed our little island, the corsairs who came in their boats to pillage the land and steal away its treasures. We are a poor, humble people, and so they took the treasures they found— our men, women, and children. The women and children were the easiest prey, slower and weaker than the men. They came and pounced on them wherever they were to be found—in their homes, in their beds, in the church, fleeing helplessly through the streets. A few of them escaped to tell the tale of how their friends and kinsmen were taken away, poor innocent souls bound for a life of misery with little hope of ransom and return.

None remembered that cowardly act of savagery against a defenceless people, and yet all remembered. Years passed and the island was resettled by men from our brother island of Malta, and the tale of years ago was whispered in corners ever after. The natural world itself does not forget tears and bloodshed; the land and air felt tainted by the act so that we felt it everywhere we walked. And we feared that they would come again to enslave us once more.

Fear. It is little wonder to me that Christ commanded his disciples not to fear so many times; it is so human to be afraid. Nothing in this world is certain, particularly for our people. We could not say that the rains would come, that there would be a good harvest, that we would be safe from plague and pestilence and our enemies across the sea. Even the strong, protective walls of the citadel were not comfort enough in a world where nothing is certain as far as the next sunrise.

Perhaps it was her lack of fear that I found so attractive. There was a defiance about her, even as she cowered behind the altar with Giuseppe trying to force her out. That she had the impudence to shelter there at all was telling enough, and I knew that Giuseppe was right to be angry with her, but I found myself thinking that if I had ever had a daughter, I should have wanted her to have such spirit. It did not matter to me that she was dirty and wild; I saw the child she would be if only there were someone to show her the way. So I reached out and took her by the hand—I hope to God that I did not do wrong by her. She could not have had a more diligent and patient tutor, a gentler confessor, and yet I wonder whether my actions led her to Barbary. In my darker moments, I cannot help thinking that I was merely a selfish man, bored and lonely, who needed a pet to occupy my time, a willing mind to whom I could pass my beloved knowledge. I came to love her so that she seemed like my own child; I had the arrogant pride to give her a name of my choosing, as though that gave me the right to think of her as my own flesh and blood.

There was never time to ask her if she had ever wished that she had found some other hiding place that day, but it all ended as I should have known it would. She was taken without warning, and the question I had meant to ask her went unspoken and unanswered. I know she is alive somewhere though they all tell me she must be dead. When I reach the moment in the Mass to pray for the departed, I cannot say her name—not her real name nor the name

I gave her; the word sticks in my throat and will not be spoken. She lived that night; I saw the evidence with my own eyes, that I cannot for love of her share with her family—and I pray that she will return one day a free woman. And if God is merciful to me, I may live to see the day.

The Wanderer

The year that passed between the death of her father and her discovery of a new father was the loneliest and cruellest of her life. She could still say such a thing long after she had seen Barbary and knew what it meant to be sold like an animal at the market, because an enemy of a different race and faith can never hurt a person as much as his own family; this is the loneliest and cruellest time. After she was removed from her father's body, no member of her family ever touched her or spoke to her again if he could avoid it. She found herself the unwelcome guest at her family's table, quietly but determinedly ignored by her mother and three brothers until she could have believed that they could only see or hear her when she had displeased them.

However, like many children who discover that they are unwanted, she quickly learnt to return the compliment. To begin with she imagined that she had broken some rule she did not understand and would be forgiven after a few days, but when the first confused weeks after her father's burial were over, the horrible truth began to sink in that she was in disgrace forever. Forever, a little like being in hell—retribution without end, without consolation, without any possibility of making amends. So she stopped running after her mother to try to catch her attention and fled her presence at first light every day rather than risk provoking her anger. She learnt to think of home as the place she could expect a little food and shelter for the night, but nothing more than that, and she felt none of the usual loyalties to her home and kinsmen that might have been expected of her.

The lonely, selfish struggle for survival absorbed every scrap of her energy and passion, drawing her attention away from her mother's turned back and cold, self-pitying gaze. It was slavery of a kind if she had only known it at the time, but it seemed to her a brutal kind of freedom. When hunger ravaged her, she learnt to beg or steal to satisfy herself. She felt no guilt at taking scraps from the mouths of more deserving people because those more deserving people had nothing to do with her and would not go so far as to walk within arm's reach of her if they could help themselves. After being apprehended two or three times, she lost her sense of fear for the consequences and any vague notion she had had that she was doing something wrong. Whatever she did she knew that she would still be despised, and the spittle and foul names she endured as she roamed the streets formed an irksome but expected part of it all.

†

She sat in a corner of the cave and smiled. There was no sensation quite as satisfying as being warm and safe whilst the world went mad just a few feet away, and it was going mad, the rain crashing down in vicious great waves, hammering the earth to a muddy pulp. Ursula had been to this particular hiding place before and had built herself a little nest in the farthest corner from the mouth of the cave, which she snuggled into now like a mouse—safe and warm, with bread skilfully pinched that she could enjoy without fear of being disturbed.

She felt especially proud of the nest, which she had built out of scraps of cloth she had filched from various places.

The largest, thickest, and warmest piece had come from the church and had taken a good deal of patience and daring to steal, involving kneeling for an age until there was absolutely no one about, creeping up to the confessional and swinging on the curtain with all her strength until it came down. She had had to break the curtain's fall to stop it making a terrible thud as it hit the ground, then had to drag the thing along the floor and wrap it around her like a long, trailing cloak as soon as she emerged into the outside world to hide what she was up to.

It had turned out to be very much heavier than she had imagined when she saw it hanging there invitingly, and by the time she had dodged her way to the safety of the cave, she was bathed in sweat and the curtain was very much the worse for dust. It did not matter, she told herself, as she snuggled up in her nest with just her head poking out from among the folds of the confessional curtain. None of it mattered. That the curtain was far from clean did not matter. That she had caused a scene greater than she could ever have hoped for in the church when the curtain was missed did not matter. That it was pouring with rain outside did not matter. She was not hungry anymore, and she was not cold nor wet. She was free of every burden.

†

Freedom. A brutal kind of freedom in a coastal village that existed merely to provide Ursula with whatever she needed to stay alive. Her wanderings had more purpose to them than it first appeared, even to Ursula. She preferred the isolation of the surrounding countryside to the cramped confines of human habitation, which she tolerated only for as long as she needed. It was easier to bear the harsh solitude of deserted places, the craggy land without shadow, than the weird loneliness of a place where there were people, but a people who raised their fists or turned their backs to avoid the sight of her.

If she could have seen how she looked through their eyes she might have understood them a little better, but she had no interest in the ways and thoughts of others. She was always dirty, her clothes ragged and ill-fitting, her long hair matted and tangled with neglect. During the dry, hot summer it became bleached and dry like straw, and her skin was baked black by the sun; when the rains came she became covered in mud and hid herself in secret, dry places during rain storms, sometimes staying where she was for days at a time.

It was the dawn of her life, so early that when she remembered it as a young woman she recalled only fragments of memory: sitting in her cave with the smell of damp limestone and old cloth, the blistering dryness of a parched mouth, and no source of water anywhere to be found; the sense of cold, unfearing resentment as her eldest brother marched her home because she had been caught pilfering again and he had been sent for; the giddy delight of running against the cool breeze of the early morning until she could barely catch her breath. This was Ursula's world, where she was both queen and pauper, but it was not long before she became so wild and alone that she could not remember ever having had a name.

Warda

Father Antonin was on his knees in the coolest part of the church when he noted that something was amiss. He noticed Giuseppe poking about at the back of the high altar with a broom and assumed at first that he had discovered a small animal that he was trying unsuccessfully to remove. He knew Giuseppe to be a man of very little patience and was not surprised when he quickly tired of trying to nudge the creature out and started prodding it with venom, shouting: "Get out! Get out of here, you repulsive creature!"

Father Antonin got up to assist him, but it was as he walked toward Giuseppe that he heard an unmistakably human cry. "What are you doing?" he called to him, hurrying to his side.

"There's some filthy child hiding back here", he explained, deaf to the human creature's protesting cries. "I knew I could smell an impostor all the way through Mass."

"I should have hoped your attention was better employed", answered Father Antonin tartly. He peered into the cavity between the altar and the wall and saw a small child sitting with her arms hugging her knees and her head down. Quite like a small animal, she appeared to have curled up into a ball to protect herself from Giuseppe's attack. "Good heavens, it is a little girl."

"Of all the ridiculous sights", snapped Giuseppe. "I am sure the little thief has been here before. I always thought it was the mice taking my food." He began knocking the handle of the broom against her bony shins again, but she gave an indignant shriek and grabbed hold of it, glowering at him with a hatred that made even Father Antonin a little uneasy.

"Stop that, man; she's not hurting you", he said, stepping in front of him. "She will hardly emerge willingly if you keep doing that." He turned to the girl, who was still glaring at them both. "Come on now, my girl, come out of there at once."

She gave no answer but clearly had no intention of doing as she was told. She truly was filthy, he thought, but he was determined not to let her know he had noticed. "There, she will not listen", said Giuseppe triumphantly; "leave it to me."

"No, Giuseppe, I think not", said Father Antonin a little wearily. "I will get her out."

Giuseppe grudgingly moved away, leaving Father Antonin alone with her. He took a deep breath and scrutinised her again as though looking for the way to reach her. It would be easy enough to drag her out by force if the space she was squeezed into were not so small, but he would not be able to reach her without turning himself sideways, and he could hardly pull her out one-handedly. "What are you doing in there?" he asked gently, and he noted with some relief that her expression softened.

"I was trying to find the door to heaven", she whispered. "I thought it must be here."

Father Antonin burst out laughing, causing her to bury her head in her lap again. He knew he had made a terrible mistake. "There now, there is no call to be like that", he coaxed. "Forgive me, I should not have laughed at you." She glanced up, intrigued by his tone. No one had ever spoken to her with such respect before. He reached out a hand to her. "Come on now, will you not come out and talk to me properly? This is no place for a girl." She instinctively backed away from the open hand reaching out to her, but when she did not come to grief she looked back at it as though she did not understand what was being asked of her. "Take my hand", he said. "I will not hurt you; you have my word."

She hesitated, holding up her own hand with its black, broken nails and raw knuckles, then braced herself and did as he had asked. She could not remember afterward what she had expected to happen, but she felt his fingers curling around hers and a gentle pressure that forced her to scramble toward him, out of the dark hole until she was standing before him.

"*Marija Santa*, what a sight you are", he said in spite of himself. "Where are you from? Who are your parents?" She made no attempt to answer. Her glance was, he thought, cold rather than sullen, as though she did not understand that she was expected to talk to him. "What is your name?"

"How impudent you are!" shouted Giuseppe. "Answer the priest!"

She looked at him as though calculating the threat he posed, then glanced back at Father Antonin. "I do not remember", she said quietly.

"That is rather sad. What is your father's name, then?"

"He is dead."

"I see. Are you hungry?"

"Yes, I am."

†

"She is not fit to enter the house", protested Marija, when Father Antonin appeared in the doorway holding the hand of some dirty ragamuffin he seemed to have befriended.

"Come now, Marija, be charitable. She's hungry."

"Is she your wife?" asked Ursula. She could smell warm bread and felt almost giddy with hunger.

Marija glared at her, but Father Antonin chuckled. "I do not have a wife; I may not. Marija is a widow from the parish who keeps house for me." He turned back to Marija. "Do not trouble yourself. She can share my portion."

"She looks as though she has been rolling around in the dust for weeks", she declared.

Father Antonin sighed. "You are quite right, Marija." He turned to Ursula. "Go with Marija and she will clean you up; then you can have something to eat with me."

He smiled as the two females backed away from him. "Are you asking me to wash this creature? I would hardly know where to begin!"

"I am not hungry", said Ursula. She turned to run away, but Marija stuck her foot out and sent her sprawling onto the floor.

"Now then, there's no need to lie to me. Be a sensible girl."

She looked as though she were being marched to her execution as she stomped grumpily outside followed by Marija—equally resentful—brandishing a pitcher of water. He knew without doubt that she was doing what he had asked of her simply because of the promise of food, but he hoped in his naivety that it might have a salutary effect. Shortly afterward, he heard what sounded like a violent quarrel breaking out and foul language being shouted in the shrill voice of a small child, so utterly appalling that he wondered whether she might already be entirely out of control. She had clearly been badly neglected. She might not have a family at all, but he would have been surprised if such a young child were entirely alone in the world—yet she did seem to be alone.

The obscene language had been drowned by ear-split-ting screams by the time Father Antonin had finished his musings on the child's background, and he soon discovered why, when Marija came back inside looking wet and quite exhausted, closely followed by a girl he barely recognised. She had cleaned up very pleasingly. Marija had forcibly removed her ragged clothes and dressed her in a shirt he recognised very well indeed, the sleeves folded back many times and a cord tied around her waist to keep the ends off the ground. Her skin looked clean if a little chafed from rough handling, and her hair, which turned out to be quite a fierce shade of red, had been washed, mercilessly combed, and pinned back to reveal a thin, oval face.

"So that is what you look like", he said. She hurried past him and reached for the food, but he took hold of her wrist and held her back. "No, just a minute. I think you have something to say to Marija." He had used his severest tone of voice, and he could feel a pulse quickening under his hand, but she shrugged her shoulders as though she had expected him to talk to her like that and did not greatly care. "You do not use language like that to a lady. Not in my hearing."

"I do not like her; she struck me on the head. She *hurt* me."

"Well, that is hardly surprising after you said all those wicked things to her, what were you expecting? Since she baked the bread, you had better ask her forgiveness before you reach for it again."

She considered the situation for a moment, shrugged again, and turned to face Marija. "I am sorry", she said, tonelessly, and he thought she would have pledged her alle-giance to Satan if he had asked her to, as long as she was fed.

"Very well," he conceded, letting her go, "will you sit down?" She looked, not at him, but at the bread on the table and stepped forward. "There we are. Now, what am I to call you? What is your name?"

"I do not remember", she said.

"Nonsense, girl", cackled Marija. "No one forgets his own name."

"I do not remember", she said again, as though Marija had never spoken.

"What do people call you?"

She hesitated. "Filthy, thieving, godforsaken trouble-maker, mostly."

He smiled. "Oh dear, then I shall have to give you a name. I shall call you Warda."

Marija snorted. "She's a sight more pleasing than she was when she was dirty, Father, but she's no flower."

But that was the name he gave her, and from then on, it was the only name she ever used or answered to. And because he had been the one to name her and to take the trouble to win her trust, Father Antonin was soon the only person alive she respected. In searching for the door to paradise, she stumbled unwittingly into the path of a man who would show her the ways of knowledge and wisdom. But there would come a time when she would stop look-ing for the door to heaven, not because she was too old to search for such a thing any longer, but because she knew it would be locked and bolted against her.

A Most Extraordinary Confession (2)

I was the most fortunate of children. For a few short years there was no other girl in the country who had such a life. For the first time I could remember, I seldom went to bed hungry, and by day I found myself in the company of grown men and women who treated me with gentleness and affection. Father Antonin—may God reward him for his goodness to me—taught me about plants and animals, and how to read and write. As I grew older, he gave me the gift of languages and, what I came to crave more than anything else, his art of healing. I do not think he intended to do so much to begin with, but I was little better than an animal when he first fed me, and I returned to the place where my hunger could be satisfied the next day and the next and the next, until he came to expect my arrival and there would be a little portion of food waiting for me when I appeared.

But he was not content simply to give me what I needed from his table. I had always been a beggar and was content to be a beggar with a willing patron, but he said that I should understand that all things must be paid for and that it was an honourable thing to earn an honest living. So he began to give me little tasks to do to earn my bread. As I was very small and had no skills of my own, I fed his chickens and began to take pride in the thought that I was of use to somebody. I can still remember the smell of grain and feathers as the chickens hobbled up to me, pecking the ground around my feet, and the childish satisfaction when they began plodding toward me as though they were greeting an old friend.

When my hands were a little steadier, I gathered up their eggs every day, and that was when I first became curious. It was not long before I realised that Marija used only a tiny number to cook with and I never saw Father giving eggs away to the poor. So one day, when I went to the door of his workroom to hand him the basket, I asked him.

"I wondered when you would start asking questions", he said; "come in, and I will show you." He threw the door open wide, and I was standing in the cave of a sorcerer. Above our heads were plants in fat, dry bunches hanging from the ceiling, there were pots and jars of all shapes and sizes lining the walls, and thick, squat objects like slabs of wood that I was soon to discover were books.

"You have let your flowers die", I said, pointing at the sad, withered stems and leaves, swaying miserably in the draught.

"They are more useful to me dead", he chuckled, looking around for something to stand me on. He dragged what looked like an old box toward the table in the centre of the room and lifted me onto it so that I was high enough to see the surface. "I have been blessed with the two greatest callings in life—the curer of souls and the curer of bodies. I was a doctor before I was ever a priest."

I did not understand a word he was saying. "What is that horrible thing?" I asked, pointing at an open jar emitting an unbearably acrid stench.

"Turpentine." He brought out a bowl and a small vessel, which he placed beside it, then he took an egg out of the basket. "Watch this." He cracked open the shell on the side of the bowl and very carefully passed the yolk from one broken half to the other so that the egg white drained into the vessel. When he had drained it as well as he could, he dropped the yolk into the bowl and it broke. I watched as he added turpentine, then one or two other ingredients that looked like herbs of some kind, mixing them all together to form a thick, unappealing paste.

"I am not hungry", I said quickly, almost falling down in my efforts to escape.

"I am very glad to hear it. This is an ointment to heal a wound, you silly girl. Eat this and I'd have to bury you."

†

It was not long after I mastered the art of making such a potion that I found myself following him to a sick house and learnt how to clean a wound. I watched him pouring water and alcohol onto it to flush it clean, then applying the mixture I had made and binding it up with a bandage. We discovered that my hands were deft, and I soon began cutting the bandages and applying them myself. Before long, I was accompanying him on many of his visits, learning by observing his every move.

I was an accidental scholar. It was the way with everything I learnt. He would send me out looking for plants, but he would have to teach me the names and shapes of the plants for me to be able to find them, and so I learnt a great deal on this subject—the native names, the Latin names, the notion of different languages. In my wanderings, I stumbled upon the wonder of creation in the different healing properties of the many plants and flowers our beautiful earth had given us.

It became a greedy habit of mine. The more he taught me, the more I wanted him to teach me. As I grew, I became curious about the meaning of the symbols on the pieces of paper he gave me to take to people, and I asked him to teach me to read. How was I to know that the gift of reading would open yet more roads to knowledge that I would be compelled to run down to satisfy my curiosity? God forgive me, but I could not stop seeking. Like Adam and Eve, who could have tasted of every tree in paradise except the one they were commanded to leave alone, I filled my head with learning and found Father Antonin the most willing of tutors—how many hours I have spent at his side, assisting him as he attended a sick person or reading aloud to him. Before long I almost rejoiced that my family had abandoned me. I thought it the happy fault that had led me to this world of learning that I would otherwise never have known existed. Wickedness, or foolishness at least, for who knows what harm I would have escaped if I had kept to my proper place? Yet it is hard all the same to repent of any of it.

The Worst Dream

An infant rests her sleeping head on my breast. It is warm and trusting with little fine black hair and eyes tightly closed. There is an odour newborn babies have about them, a slightly sweet smell that warms the senses. I feel tiny fingers slipping into my hair as if to be certain that I will not abandon her as she sleeps. The small of her back rises and falls in short, gentle breaths as she slips through her own dream worlds, colours and sounds of the paradise she has so recently left, into which I cannot intrude.

The dream always begins that way. We are contented with one another, and I feel reassured by the weight of her limp figure on my arm, by the sense of safety she seems to enjoy through me and the protection of my body. If it ends there I will wake and weep, knowing that there is no baby for me to caress, neither in the land I have left nor the island from which I was taken.

But at least that way I do not live through the out-rage that always follows, that I know must come and yet always seems to catch me unawares—the sudden shadows all around and hands, not tiny and grasping like hers, but massive, tearing claws that drag us apart. I struggle—I always struggled—but she is torn from my arms and van-ishes from my side whilst I scream and protest.

I can hear her crying for me from some undefined point far away, but I am beaten back at every turn and plead for her. Her cries become weaker, and I can hear her frail life

45

trickling away because she has been taken from her nurturer—but I cannot reach her. The claws that snatched her from my body hold me down, and I will never have the strength to free myself.

And then I awaken, struggling and pleading, to find that I am being held quite gently by friendly hands, so that I will not injure myself in my dreamlike fit. But the infant is still gone, and I cannot hear her cries in the world of the dawn. Yet even knowing that she is nowhere near, they still see me covering my ears and pushing her invisible hands away, because at those times she feels so close that I could almost feel her heart beating against mine. The torment of a body, so palpable in memory that I can almost feel it, is impossible to bear.

A Most Extraordinary Confession (3)

I wonder whether Father Antonin is still alive? I never think of my family—they do not even wander into my dreams, but I think of my tutor all the time. I remember him as a quiet but forceful personality whom I quickly learnt to respect and who used his influence to train me first to conquer my own self before he could teach me anything else. I had spent too long living as I pleased and saw the laws of the world as my enemy, so he used rewards and reprimand to teach me the difference between right and wrong.

Not long after I began visiting him, he left me on my own in his workroom, long enough for me to slip into my sleeve a shiny metal tool that I thought must be valuable, but unfortunately he was not gone long enough for me to find some fitter place to hide it. He noticed that it was missing immediately and knew perfectly well that I had taken it.

"Warda, give it back", he said, calmly. I pretended I did not know what he was talking about. "I left a tool on that table", he said; "it was there a minute ago. Just give it back to me, and we will say no more about it."

"I did not take it", I said, looking him coldly in the eye.

"Do not lie to me." If he was angry, he hid it well. "I know you stole it."

"Perhaps someone else took it."

"Enough. No one else has been in here. Give it back, or I will force you to give it back."

"I should like to see you try."

He grimaced, seized hold of my arm, and pulled the offending object out of my sleeve with such little effort that I felt quite humiliated. "Do not try to steal from me or lie to me again", he said, and I found to my surprise that I could not raise my head. "You are quite the most impudent creature I have ever met, but not beyond redemption yet." I slipped to my knees through sheer force of habit and covered my head with my hands. "What are you doing?"

"I do not have so far to fall this way," I explained, "and I do not like people striking my head. It makes me feel a little sick."

"I did not intend to do anything of the sort", he said. "You have been beaten so often and you are so full of pride that it would hardly help matters. And if I did I would not touch your head; it is far too dangerous." He patted my shoulder. "Get on your feet."

I stood up and found that I was blushing. For the first time I could remember, I felt the awkward, nagging sense that I had done a person an injustice. I struggled to say the words. "I am sorry."

"I think you are", he said more gently. "Now I want you to do something to make up for it. Take that bucket over there and draw me some water from the well."

So I went out into the heat of the day to make my reparations, only to find when I arrived at the well that I could not do so. It was easy enough to lower the bucket into the dark, damp tunnel, but raising it again, full of water, was quite impossible for a child of my age to manage alone. I tugged and tugged at the rope until it began to cut into my hands, desperately applying every scrap of energy to drawing the water because I knew that this would make things right. It simply could not be done. In the end, I had to let the wretched thing go and burst into tears at the desolate splash of the bucket hitting the water. It was a long time before I summoned up the courage to creep back to the house and explain what had happened.

"There is no need to cry", he said. "I knew you would not be able to lift it. Come with me." He took my hand, and we walked together to the well; then he drew the water himself, and we carried the bucket back between us, with him bearing most of the weight.

"It was a trick, wasn't it?" I asked, when he gave me a beaker of water to drink. "You knew I would not be able to do it."

"Not a trick, a lesson. It is not sensible to challenge a person who is stronger than you. You need to know your weaknesses."

"I do not think that is fair!" I protested, glaring at him. "It is not my fault I am smaller than you."

"Not at all", he said; "just show a little humility. If you know your weaknesses you will not be enslaved by them."

I did not understand what he meant that day, but it was the cornerstone of the education he gave me. When I was a slave, I knew that if I had taken this knowledge a little more to heart, I would have come to far less harm than I did and might have reached freedom with fewer scars to show for it. But I did stay alive and I have come to freedom. And I will find peace, because it was the thought of him that made me ask for a priest, even though I imagined in my confusion that he would be the one to step through the door.

The Journal of a Priest-Physician (2)

Three years after she had first come to me, she made her first confession and received First Communion from me, and I am proud to say that my pupil understood better than most what she was undertaking. Just a year before, she had even asked me to teach her to read. She made the request quite suddenly, as she stood and watched me writing. "Will you show me how to read that?" she asked, and taken by surprise I found myself saying immediately, "If you wish, I will certainly teach you." Afterward I thought to myself, *Why should I not?* She had already shown such an aptitude for learning that it seemed no different from anything else I had ever taught her, but then I realised that my few books were all in Latin, so I had to teach her Latin as well. It was so marvellous to have a companion who could understand that most angelic tongue that I began conversing with her in that language, and it became a secret means of communication between us when I did not want my patients to know what we were discussing. She was such a natural scholar that I would often watch her going about the work I had given her to do and think to myself, *If she were only a man, what greatness might await her!*

Yet such was my foolishness that it did not occur to me how little she was in years, and I made a disastrous mistake. I gave her a knife, small it should be noted, but with a sharp blade encased in a leather sheath. I knew it would be useful to her, to cut the stems of plants cleanly, and I also meant to teach her how to bleed patients where necessary, as I was forbidden by the sacred canons to let blood myself.

She was delighted with the gift and promised to take good care of it, but it was with some trepidation that I watched her leave for home that day. Well founded, it turned out. She returned again in the morning, not as she usually did—with a smile and a spring in her step and a cheery greeting—but frightened and unwilling, accompanied by her elder brother. I should have warmed to him, as he looked so very like his father, God rest his soul, a man I remembered to have been honest and hard-working, but this young man's harsh manner unnerved me a little.

"Is this yours, Father?" he asked, handing me the knife I had so recently given to Warda.

"Why yes, it is mine."

Dear God, what has she done? I thought, but before I could enquire further, he had begun beating her about the head, shouting: "Thief! I knew you were a filthy liar!"

"Stop this immediately!" I shouted. "She did not steal it from me, and if she told you I gave it to her, I did so." He dropped her and looked up at me a little sheepishly. "When I said it was mine, I did not say that I had missed it. I gave it to her yesterday."

"She threatened me with it", he said, looking at me as though it were entirely my fault, which of course it was. "Forgive me for speaking out of turn, Father, but you should not put such objects into the hands of disobedient children."

I was gripped by a horrible fear. I had thought she had turned her back on her wild ways by then, but I knew in my heart that she might still have tried such a wicked act. "Is this true, Warda?" She bowed her head, unnerving me still further. "Look at me! Is this true?"

She nodded then began stumbling in Latin: "It was not my fault, Father; truly it was not my fault!"

"You will speak in your native tongue!" roared her brother. "I will not be deceived!"

"He is right, Warda; it is not fair. Let him hear what you have to say." But she hung her head again and refused to speak further. "I am very sorry that you have done this", I said. "Do you understand how serious it is?"

"I was not going to hurt him, Father", she said, looking up at me with great difficulty.

"That is another matter. You had no business threatening him." She buried her head in her arms, and I hoped she felt ashamed of herself. "Warda, I want you to go home with your brother." She looked up in alarm and began trying to converse with me in Latin again, but I cut her short. "Enough. Get up and go home where you belong. That knife was a tool, not a weapon. You will not misuse the gifts I give you."

†

I slept badly that night, tormented by fear at what I had done. A tutor is a creator of sorts, granted such power to form the next generation that such a man might allow human souls to slip through his fingers if he is a poor teacher and offers bad example. I feared that I had not been careful enough of little Warda's soul and that it might be slipping from my grasp, or that perhaps she had come to me too late. The case was hopeless. No sooner had I begun to feel guilty for being too lenient with her, I felt guilty for abandoning her to the wrath of her brother and the terrible recriminations that would surely have followed when they were out of my sight.

But then in the morning she appeared at my door again, nervous, hesitant, her eyes looking steadily downward; I invited her to enter. She crept inside like a frightened little dog, knelt at my feet, and kissed my hands. "Father, give me a penance", she said, with such perfect contrition that I knew she was up to no good. "And could I have my knife back, please?"

I laughed out loud in spite of myself and helped her to her feet. "All right, Warda, I want you to sit in the church until the Angelus and pray the Rosary."

"Could I have my knife ..."

"Not now." I watched her scurry away and hide herself in the quietest corner of the church for the long hours that stretched before her. And I felt again the guilt that had plagued me all through the night, this time the guilt that I was being too harsh, but I knew I could not relent now if I were ever to discover the truth from her.

A Brother's Threat

After the noonday Angelus, Warda hurried back to Father
Antonin in triumph, expecting her knife and something to
eat. She had been deprived of food since the evening she had
threatened her brother and confined to the house so that she
could not go out in search of anything to eat, leaving her
faint with hunger throughout the morning. "What are you
doing?" asked Father Antonin, sharply, when she appeared.
"I thought I told you to sit in the church until the Angelus?"

"I did", she protested. There was food on the table:
bread, oil, a little wine; she felt giddy. "I wonder ... I
wonder if I might have something to eat?" There were soft
lights all around her and the confused feeling of being hot
and cold and hot again.

"I meant the evening Angelus", said a severe voice far
away. "Go back immediately ... or you could sit down and
tell me why you threatened your brother instead?"

"No ... no, I will go back", she said, but the words slurred
on her tongue, and she felt as though she were being slowly
smothered by an enormous, heavy blanket. "I will go back
to the church ..." She tried to turn around, but the movement threw her off balance, and she felt herself falling.

God forgive me for being a monstrous tyrant, thought Father
Antonin, as he rushed forward to pick her up off the ground;
this I did not intend. He pressed a beaker of wine to her lips
but could barely bring himself to breathe before she opened
her eyes. "When was the last time you ate anything?" he

asked. "No, you are breathing too quickly. Breathe properly, that's my good girl. They starved you, didn't they?"

He helped her into a chair and placed pieces of bread into her hands, which she ate very slowly; she was too groggy to speak without difficulty. He waited until a little colour began to return to her face before asking again, "What happened?" She clearly had no intention of answering. "I know you did not draw that knife on him for nothing. What happened?"

She shook her head and filled her mouth with bread to stop herself from having to speak. "Warda, what can be so terrible that you will not trust me?"

She swallowed hard. "I swore an oath I would not tell", she said quietly.

"That was foolish. You should not make an oath lightly."

"I did not wish to make it at all. He forced my hand onto the holy cross and made me promise."

"A forced oath is no oath at all; you are free of it", he said, but she was clearly uncertain and remained stolidly silent. "I command you to tell me what happened. If there is any wrong in the breaking of that oath, let it fall to me."

She covered her face. "I cannot say it."

"I tell you to say it. You were compelled to make an oath. Now I am compelling you to break it."

"Father, I shall be damned!"

"God will not condemn you for this!" he exclaimed, and it was the first time she remembered such passion in his voice. "Now what in heaven's name is that brother of yours making you hide?"

She looked at him in utter panic, and he could sense that she was trying to decide whom she was more afraid of. "May I cover my face?" she asked.

"If you like."

She covered her eyes as though it somehow made him invisible and began to speak very quickly. "He was laughing at me, saying I was here more than I was at home, and I said that since I was not wanted at home it hardly mattered, and he called me—"

"Yes?"

"He called me a whore."

"*What?!*" Father Antonin leapt to his feet and tore her hands from her face. "Do you know what that means?"

Now she was completely terrified. "N-no, I do not," she stumbled, "but he said that was what everyone would think. That I was the priest's whore, always following him around everywhere."

"I wish you had told me this yesterday."

"I could not tell you without breaking the oath, and when I tried to warn you, you kept telling me to stop talking in a language he did not understand."

He sighed. "Yes, I did tell you that, didn't I? Did you tell him it was not true?"

"What isn't?"

Father Antonin wondered how he was to stop a scandal spreading throughout the town without Warda finding out the nature of it. "I will go and speak to him myself", he said. "He had a nerve coming here demanding justice from a man whose good name he is maligning."

"Wait, you cannot do that!" She got up and stood in the doorway as though she seriously imagined she could forcibly prevent him from leaving. "If you speak to him he will know I told you."

"What if he does? It is a serious matter forcing a person to take an oath."

"Father, *please.*" She covered her eyes again. "He will denounce you to the Inquisitor if you make trouble for him."

Father Antonin gave a deep sigh, as though he found the whole situation tiresome rather than threatening. He sat down beside her. "That is not a threat", he said.

"Of course it is!" she exclaimed, almost angrily. "You will get into terrible trouble."

"I do not think so, as I have done nothing wrong", he said. "I am not afraid of justice, and neither must you be. If I—or you when it comes to it—are called to account for our actions, there will be nothing to fear because we have nothing to hide. The worst that will happen is that your brother will be exposed as a liar and a gossip." He hesitated, not wishing to reveal too much. "There are ways of proving that you are not what he suggests if it ever came to that, but I do not suppose it will. I do not think even he is foolish enough to perjure himself before such a court."

"What ways?" she asked.

Father Antonin searched for a way to distract her and placed the knife back in her hand. "I think you may have this back." The ruse worked perfectly; she smiled and took it from him without any further prompting. "Please remember that in spite of what your brother has done, your actions were still wrong. Do not betray my trust in you again."

"Never, Father, I swear." And that, she would remember long afterward, was a promise she had made of her own free will—and broken many times.

The Journal of a Priest-Physician (3)

The months pass and life returns to its chilling monotony. The most terrible events of life always take us unprepared and leave behind the hardest of questions. The little town I serve lies within easy distance of the neighbouring town that was ravaged that night. The two settlements stand on either side of a small bay, and I have often walked through the brief wilderness to visit Warda or to attend to some patient there. That night, the pirates landed in that bay and made a choice—perhaps a quite arbitrary choice to turn on one settlement and not the other, calculating perhaps that there was not enough time to take both before help arrived.

They went the other way, and we were spared the horror our neighbours suffered. On the other side of the bay, the houses remain mostly empty—beds unmade, unclaimed food mouldering on tables, furniture overturned, unsettled dust, and cobwebs encroaching from every corner— as though trapped by some hideous enchantment. A few are filled by newcomers from the mainland, such is the certainty that those who were taken that night will never return. The few survivors trudge on with their grief and emptiness and with their disbelief. And I live with mine. Giuseppe tells me I must understand that she is dead and pray for the repose of her soul, but I know she is not to be found among the dead. Let him think me mad with grief, unwilling to imagine that a child I loved should have come to such an unspeakable end, but I know that she is not dead.

I want to remember her for a moment as a child, tumbling through my door making some merry greeting, her hair falling about her face like a lion cub. She grew far too fast, as all children do to indulgent parents who wish that they might never grow up and leave them. In such a little time it seemed to me that she began the irrevocable change from childhood to womanhood, and her days of mischief making came to their natural end. She still moved with an impish energy, but at my insistence she dressed modestly and covered her head like a lady, though I suspected she let her hair free the moment she was out in the open air and thought no one could see her.

God forgive me, but I was so proud of her. When I saw her moving purposefully around my workroom or sitting at her books, I remembered with fondness the day she had first entered my house. But it was that year, when Warda stood at the gateway to womanhood, that Marija warned me that I was making her into such a scholar she would never find a husband on this poor island.

There was a little envy in her words, I think, as she had found the girl sitting in a corner reading a book that she herself could not read. Warda said afterward that Marija had looked at the page and said, "So that is what our language looks like when it is captured on the page." And Warda had replied, "It is not our language; it is Augustine's", to which Marija had answered, "Well, you can tell Mr. Augustine that our language is good enough for any man." I reprimanded Warda severely for her arrogant laughter and made her ask Marija's forgiveness, reminding her that Marija was a good woman and deserving of her respect. Marija was too angry to be contented with a half-hearted apology, however, and when I had sent Warda out of the room, she began her tirade.

"You have made her too grand for her station in life", she protested. "What man would marry a girl who can read and write, who knows far too much for her own good? Had you not thought what would become of her when she was grown?"

The words stirred my conscience, and I knew she was right to ask such questions. If I had not been such a self-centred man, I would have cared for her when she came to me in such a way that would not have spoilt her for a simple man's wife. I would have taught her her catechism and let Marija teach her everything else—how to prepare food, keep house, sew, take care of children—but it did not occur to me to prepare her for the life she would surely be expected to live when she was grown. I saw instead a selfish opportunity to pass my learning to another, and she was as witty a creature as the best of men. But she was not a man, and now she was no longer a child.

"Will any man be so gentle, show her such respect and forbearance as you have done?" asked Marija. "Whatever is she to do? You are growing old; you will not be able to protect her forever."

I knew that I would not find a man who was worthy of her if I went searching myself. I imagined her married to some useless oaf and thought of how he would deal with a wife who spoke languages he did not understand and had read the Church Fathers, how he would seek to control her and only succeed by breaking her altogether. I saw the long years of miserable imprisonment that would follow such a marriage: keeping house with barely enough food to put on the table, bearing children who would be taken by disease, being trapped year after year in a squalid, unhappy world without friendship or learning, until plague or hunger took her to an early grave.

Then as I thought about it, I asked myself whether it was necessary for her to marry at all. Why should she marry a man to whom she was ill-suited and who would treat her badly, a man she could never give way to and who would think her worthless for lacking the skills and temperament he would expect of a wife? Far too many women were driven by harsh necessity into such unsuitable unions—why should she? Why should she be so wasted? There was no convent on Gozo, but I knew of a group of anchoresses in the neighbouring town, women who had spurned marriage and worldly comfort, among whom a pious, clever, and headstrong young woman with no prospect or desire to marry might find a happy home. All that remained was to pluck up the courage to suggest it to her.

†

"Have you thought to marry?" I asked her after Mass the next morning.

"Must I?" she asked, to my great relief, but she was alarmed. "Is there some man you are thinking of?"

"No, certainly not."

"If there is, my family will not give me a dowry, so I could not marry even if I wanted to."

"I have not told you to marry."

"I do not wish to marry!"

"All well and good then, for I have not asked you to!"

She stepped back and looked at me with great suspicion. "Father, why are you asking me about marriage? You have never spoken of it before."

"I wanted to be sure that you had no desire to marry", I explained. "You are growing up now and must think about your future. There are some people I would like you to meet."

I was afraid to tell her anything more. She was so wilful I knew she would never consider it if she set her heart against it at the first suggestion, but something told me that she would be drawn to the anchoresses when she met them. I had an excuse to take her there, as the three women had recently lost their servant and were in need of assistance.

†

"It looks very gloomy", commented Warda, as we came within sight of the chapel with its anchorholds built against it. Like our own church, it was a poor, simple building built by poor people, but she thought it gloomy without even stepping inside. Warda was carrying a basket of food for the good women and was clearly curious to see what these creatures locked away from the world would be like.

"You wait and see", I promised; "you will be surprised— they are cheerful enough."

Along one side of the little church there were four cells side by side, each with a narrow window covered on the inside by dark curtains. She paused at the first. "Is there a code I am supposed to use?" she asked, turning to me for reassurance.

"A simple good morning will suffice", came a sprightly voice from apparently nowhere, causing Warda to back away. The curtain behind the second window was thrown back, and Warda became aware that there was a person looking at her. "God bless you, my dear, and what is your name?"

"Warda", she said quickly, edging a little closer.

"I will not eat you; you may come a little nearer if you wish, then I can see you more clearly."

I watched in quiet amusement as this normally bold creature crept fearfully toward Chiara's cell, holding the basket out in front of her as though offering a libation to an invisible goddess who might or might not be on her side. I was not mistaken, thank God. Before long, Chiara had her laughing and chatting as though she had lived with them all her life, and I knew that they would soon become friends. Chiara was a well-to-do woman from the Maltese mainland, shrewd and intelligent, a widow of some twenty years who was supported in her vocation by the money her dead husband had provided for her. She would make a proper mother to Warda, I thought, witty enough to anticipate her actions, compassionate enough to understand her weaknesses and a commanding enough personality to ensure her respect.

Yet all the same, in spite of the ease with which her suspicions were broken down, my conscience nagged me again, and I wondered whether a little part of me wanted her to join them so that she would not go far away and would be free to continue her study with me. Well, it cannot matter now; she did go far away in spite of my very best efforts—because of them.

The End of Childhood

"What is troubling you?" asked Father Antonin, peering through the grille of the confessional. "There is something you are not telling me."

"It is not a sin", she said; "at least I hope it is not a sin."

"Will you tell me what is on your mind?"

She sighed. "I cannot make up my mind. The months pass, and I cannot make up my mind. I am adrift."

The months had indeed passed since he had first introduced Warda to the anchoresses. She had visited them many times, knew now what would be expected of her, and had told him often that she would far rather serve them than marry, but she wavered still, clinging onto a life she loved and did not want to have to leave behind. "Are you afraid to leave your childhood behind? You know there are girls your age married."

"I do not wish to marry!" she thundered. "I have never sought to marry!"

"Hush! Would you have the whole world hear you?" He paused, but she did not respond. "We have spoken of this many times. I can help you, but I cannot make the vows for you. Sooner or later you will be forced to make a choice— your family will not give you a roof over your head forever."

"It is all they have ever given", she answered, tartly.

"You must not be bitter."

"I am happy as I am, Father; I wish the time would stop."

"That is foolishness. Remember 'When I was a child I spoke like a child and thought like a child ...'"

"'... but now I am a man I must put all childish ways behind me.'" She quoted the words without any enthusiasm. "I wish I were a man; it would be much simpler."

"That is also foolishness."

†

The next morning, Father Antonin realised during Mass that something was amiss. As he stood at the altar he could hear faint breathing noises and was not surprised afterward to find Warda curled up behind it, shivering with the autumnal cold. "Sorry—I am sorry", she began immediately, before he could open his mouth. "I will do my penance later."

"Are you not a little too big to be hiding where you are not allowed to go?" he asked gently, reaching out a hand to her, but she ignored it.

"It was the only place I knew they would not find me", she said. "I cannot come out; they will come to you in search of me."

"Who is searching for you?"

"My mother and the man she intends me to marry."

Father Antonin hung his head. "So this is where childhood ends," he whispered, "almost in the place where it began." He reached out to her again. "Come out. I will not let them force you to marry any man."

†

When Marija had wrapped her in a blanket, Warda told Father Antonin how her brother had approached her as she had left the church the previous day and ordered her to return home with him, where she had found her mother waiting with a man she thought to be almost her mother's age. As soon as the realisation hit her that her mother intended him to be her husband, Warda turned on her heel and attempted to flee the house, only to be stopped in her tracks by her brother.

"Where are your manners?" he hissed, turning her around again. "Stay where you are!"

"Forgive her, she is a little startled", explained her mother, giving her the benefit of the doubt for the first time in years. "That is all."

"I do not wish to marry", said Warda quickly.

"Be quiet!" ordered her brother, who was still planted firmly behind her. "No one asked your opinion."

Warda swallowed hard, calculating her next move. Escape was impossible, but to stand there whilst arrangements were made for an event she could not countenance was insufferable. She turned her attention to the man who was sitting quietly in front of her. She recognised him of course, but men that age were virtually invisible to her, and she had never noted him particularly. He looked as they all did: dark, lined, hair thinning and beginning to turn grey, a little disgruntled. A proper husband for her mother, she thought, but not for her. The prospect of living with such a man filled her with an overpowering sense of disgust. "I am honoured that you should think of me", she said, as calmly as she could, but she was certain her tone betrayed the contempt she felt for him. "I am honoured, but I do not intend to marry any man. Please forgive me."

If he had anything to say in response, Warda never heard it. Her mother looked fixedly at the ground. "Take your sister outside", she said, tonelessly. "She may wish to consider what she has said."

Warda felt a hand grasping her wrist and was almost thrown through the doorway. Escape was not quite impossible after all, she thought, with enough determination. Desperation. She waited for her brother to release his grip on her for a second whilst he turned to close the door and made a run for it, fleeing into the encroaching darkness.

With only the shortest of head starts, he quickly caught up with her, knocking her down with such force that she was momentarily stunned. "Are you mad?" he shouted, when he tried to force her to her feet and she began kicking and struggling to free herself. "Do you want him to think you a savage?"

"He may think what he likes; I will not have him!"

"You may count yourself grateful that he will have you", he returned, catching hold of her hair so that she had to stand up if only to avoid the pain it caused her. "He will take care of you; he will give you a home. What more can you ask of any man?"

"Nothing more of a man perhaps," she acknowledged, but she was more concerned with seeking a way of escape, "but I have not asked for anything."

"Perhaps you would rather be without a home", he sneered; "you could always go begging to the priest for your bread."

Her unwillingness to make any response should have served as a warning, but Warda's actions were seldom easy, even for a clever man to predict. She allowed herself to be led back to the door, murmuring what sounded almost like, "Forgive me."

"There now, are you going to be a sensible girl and do as you are told for once?"

She was going to have to tell a wicked lie. "I have been foolish, and I am sorry", she said, and such was her dear brother's pride that he believed her. She waited whilst he opened the door, then she reached forward and slammed it shut, quite deliberately trapping his fingers. This time she ran as though pursued by a legion of devils, with the chaos she had caused ringing out through the night behind her.

She came eventually to the church, but was afraid they would search for her there, so she hid in the one place she could be sure they would not dare to look: in the narrow cavity behind the high altar. And there she remained through the long, cold hours of the night, drifting in and out of sleep, praying throughout Mass that no one would guess she was there until Father Antonin found her shivering and tortured by aches and pains.

"It seems to me that you would not feel trapped by a cell", mused Father Antonin when she had told her story. "If all that holds you back is your fear of growing up, I think you must enter without delay or the choice will be taken from you."

"I have been so happy", she said; "I cannot imagine having to be so *still*."

"You will still be free to move around where it is necessary", promised Father Antonin; "you will not be like those anchoresses who never leave their cells except to be buried, not to begin with anyway, but you are too old to run about the countryside now. Men will look on you differently now that you are grown. If you do not have the protection of a husband, you must have the protection of four strong walls."

"You will have to persuade my family", she said.

"I shall not fail to do so."

The End of Adventures

Warda knelt before the bishop. Marija had made her a new frock for the occasion; Father Antonin thought to himself that she looked quite grown up, dressed so nicely, with her hair scraped away from her face and hidden very modestly under cloth. "Are you promised in marriage?" came the question. He was a rather severe figure of a man, but the bishop seemed to have warmed to Warda, as Father Antonin had hoped he would, and he asked his questions in a considered, slightly hushed tone.

"No, my lord, by the grace of God", she answered impeccably.

"And do you desire to marry?"

"No, my lord, I do not. I choose to live a consecrated life for the good of my salvation."

"Do you choose this life freely and in full knowledge of its hardships?"

"Yes, my lord."

"And can you bear the yoke of a life of solitude, prayer, and self-denial?"

"Yes, my lord, by the grace of God."

He looked up at Father Antonin, who stood behind her. "How long have you known her?" he asked.

"Some seven years, my lord."

"And can you vouch for her character?"

"I can, my lord."

"I have heard reports that she is of an intemperate nature. Is it true that she once threatened her brother?"

Warda flinched visibly and opened her mouth to protest. "She did, my lord," he said quickly, "but she was much younger then."

"I repented of that act and did penance!" she protested, leaping to her feet.

"Hush, girl; who gave you leave to rise?" demanded Father Antonin, nudging her back down, but the bishop smiled.

"It is no matter, my son", he promised; "but I must be convinced that this child is fitted for such a life—for her own sake as well as that of the others."

"It is true that she has a wild spirit," conceded Father Antonin, "but it is tame now."

"Well, we shall see about that", he said. He turned his attention once again to Warda and began testing her knowledge of the Faith, starting with simple questions then drawing her further and further until she was quoting Thomas Aquinas at him in such flawless Latin that he thought she might put some seminarians to shame. "Thank you", he said finally, before turning to Father Antonin for an explanation. "You have been her teacher?"

"Yes, my lord."

"You are wasted here, my son. You should be teaching in Rome, not in this backwater, making a scholar out of a peasant."

"I hope that I have not done wrong", said Father Antonin. "I did not mean her any harm. She is a most diligent pupil."

"I have no doubt she is, but surely you must see that she is far too educated to marry a man who tills the soil—and far too poor to marry above her station in life. If she is not meant for an anchoress, I cannot say what she is fitted for, with such knowledge in her head."

"I cannot be rid of it now, my lord", she broke in, giving him a mischievous smile. To her surprise he returned it.

"Indeed, you cannot. My son, does she have a dowry?"

"No, my lord, her family have not provided for her."

"Is there place for her?"

"There is place, my lord, since Dame Lucia died—almost as though it were meant for her."

The bishop considered the suggestion. "Dame Lucia— God rest her soul—acted as servant to the others", he said. "She had made vows and lived a holy life, but she was the only one who was not fully enclosed. It might indeed be a fitting place for her." He motioned for Warda to stand, and she scrambled to her feet. "Daughter, you are far too young to renounce the world so completely."

"My lord, I promise that I am not!" she answered. "In my heart I am ready."

"Be quiet!" ordered Father Antonin.

"But I am!" She was beginning to wonder whose side Father Antonin was on.

The bishop raised a finger to his lips. "You are too young and too impetuous. Women who enter anchorholds are usually much older than you—older, wiser, more disciplined. It is a hard life, very much harder than any convent, to be confined to one small room like that, and you cannot know what it would mean." She opened her mouth, but a single forbidding glance from Father Antonin closed it again. "Now you will listen to me. Go and enter Dame Lucia's cell. It will be yours as of this day. Live as she did, coming and going to serve the others. She was supported by the small funds they had at their disposal, as you will be. Whatever else you should need, I will provide."

She broke into a broad grin. "Thank you, my lord. I will not be burdensome. May I make my vows today?"

"Hush. Live as I have asked you, and after a year, if your resolve is still fixed, I will return and you may make your profession—but only then."

†

So it was a little more quietly than she had hoped that Warda made the short journey, accompanied by Father Antonin, Giuseppe, and Marija, to the cell where she was to live and die. Warda was unusually silent, so much so that Father Antonin eventually had to ask if anything was wrong. "I wanted to take my vows today", she said. "I did not ask for a way of escape."

"You must be patient and trust those who are wiser than you", he said. "Make your vows in your heart if you wish." She nodded but said nothing. "Do not be sad. In a year's time, God willing, the bishop will return, and it will all be done properly."

"I am not sad," she said carefully, as the building came into sight, "even though I know this is not the way it is usually done. If I had answered better, he would not have asked me to wait."

"Do not reproach yourself. Your situation is a little unusual. You have nowhere else to go, but you are not ready for full enclosure yet. He acted prudently, and so must you."

"I will do as I am bid", she said; there was only the slightest edge to her voice, he thought. Warda went to the small window of Chiara's cell to present herself. The light of the day was so bright that when she looked in she could barely see the lady in question, but the voice that answered her was as bright and friendly as ever. "You are most welcome, child; we have been expecting you. Today you must rest and pray. Present yourself to me tomorrow, and I will tell you what you must do."

Warda walked to the door of the vacant cell and stepped into another world. The chamber was large enough to contain a bed and a small table and chair for the purposes of study. Next to the door there was a window like Sister Chiara's with a heavy black curtain decorated with a white cross to cover it when it was not in use, and another, narrower window on the opposite wall that allowed her to see the sanctuary of the chapel. She turned around and noticed that her friends had not followed her inside. "Will you not come in?" she asked; for the life of her she could not have explained it, but she felt afraid and needed them close to her.

"You have crossed into a place we may not follow, Warda", said Father Antonin simply. "Do not be afraid; this is a friendly prison. Now lock the door and stand near the window where we may talk a little longer."

But for a moment she could not move. She stood utterly still, looking at the man who had been her father and teacher for seven years; it seemed to her that she was on her deathbed, watching her short life unfolding before her for one last time: the death of her father and her banishment from her mother's heart; the wild, hungry months alone; her discovery by Giuseppe; and the joyous years of learning and companionship that she had thought could never end. She saw it all and took her leave of it. Then she stepped forward and pulled the door shut, turning the key in the lock.

Marija and Giuseppe stood back a little so that Father Antonin could speak with Warda privately through the window. "You stand behind a white cross", he said. "Red crosses are the emblems of the martyrs; black crosses are for penitents; white crosses are for the pure. You have not chosen an easy life. In other places, women come to this calling later in life, after they have lived some years in a convent or after a long marriage. Do you understand now why the bishop asked you to wait?" She nodded. "You are a woman now. I cannot call you by your nickname any longer. What name will you take at your profession?"

"You gave me a name when I had no name", she said. "If I cannot be Warda any longer, you must give me a new name."

He stopped to think. "Very well then, I will call you Perpetua. She was a spirited, courageous woman who became a saint. Perhaps you may do the same." He traced a cross in the air, then she felt his hand touching her head in blessing as it had done so many times before.

Perpetua watched until her three companions had disappeared from sight, then drew the black curtain across as though extinguishing a light. She turned to the window that revealed the sanctuary to her and focused her eyes on the flickering lamp near the tabernacle. Now that she was alone, she felt a weary peace descending upon her, and she slipped to her knees. *This is where adventures end*, she thought—and was almost glad of it.

A Most Extraordinary Confession (4)

"Are you in pain?" he asks, noting that I have begun clenching and unclenching my fists.

"Yes. Perhaps it is better that it should hurt after what I have done." A spirited, courageous woman who became a saint. I can almost hear Father Antonin saying it and feel such self-loathing it almost hurts. To think he had imagined I could *ever* come to any good. *Dear God, let him never know!* I know he was proud of me and loved me as though I were his own daughter—all to no avail. Let him never, never *know.*

"Tell me honestly," says the priest, "did you choose that life for the good of your salvation or because it was useful to you?"

I look away from him; I suspect he imagines that I am angry, though he could not guess what I am really thinking. "That is not a kind question."

"Maybe not, but I have asked it."

"There was little else for me to do, but when it came to it, I found myself better suited to it than I had imagined I would be."

There had been so little time for me to grow accustomed to my new life, but during those few short months of peace, I was quite content. I was not at all suited to a life of contemplation, but the life the bishop had chosen for me was a busy one. I had the other anchoresses to care for, their food to gather and prepare. I was permitted to continue my work as a physician to women; there was often a patient to be found seated in my cell awaiting my ministrations or standing at my window seeking advice. Father Antonin came often to counsel me and brought books and writing materials, encouraging me to write down the thoughts that came to me in prayer, so that I could continue to exercise my mind.

"I do not know how else to answer", I tell him finally. "The bishop made me wait to be professed because he doubted that it was a suitable life for me, but I never saw him again. I entered the cell on a bright, cool day before Lent had begun, and I was snatched away as the long, hot summer days began to make themselves felt. So I cannot tell you, Father, what sort of an anchoress I would have grown to be, because I never saw the year through to its end. I was never professed. I almost wondered afterward whether that was why I had been so keen to make my vows, because perhaps in my heart I knew that there would never be another chance."

"Be of stout heart", he says, "there must have been some other work for you to do."

"Or I was not good enough for such a life, and God took me away before I could bring shame upon it."

Father Antonin had told me years before that I should regret no misfortune that ever befell me, as all things happened for a reason and no suffering was ever in vain. But I wonder whether he had had in mind the terrors that were hanging over my head if I could only have known.

But "if only" was a regret. If only Assumpta had not given birth that night of all nights; if only Agata had not sought my help; if only I had not left the safety of the cell that had been built to protect women from the vices and violence of men; if only—but it had happened; it had all come to pass, and no longing for my story to have been written some other way could be of any consequence now.

"I squandered the time I was given. I realised afterward how much more I could have done, but it seemed to me that I had an eternity before me, all those long days. I could have helped more sick people; I could have taken better care of my sisters; I could have said more prayers and prayed more fervently. I was warned over and over again that death would come to me when I least expected it, and yet I was not prepared. I was not ready to meet it when it came."

I long for my past life. Lying in this quiet chamber, I find myself trying to imagine that I am lying in my cell, with the weak sunlight curling around the edges of that heavy curtain and no sound except for the natural world awakening in the still of the morning. The knowledge that even if I did not look out as indeed I should not, the world into which I had been born, with its dust-covered rocks and green plants and the whisper of the never distant sea, lay all around me.

"You are brooding", he says. "Will you not continue?"

†

The last day passed without incident, but I could hardly bear to think about it. I remember that it was unusually quiet; I spent much of the time praying and writing. If I had known what a day of endings it was to be, I might have lingered a little longer, watched the sun slipping beneath the horizon before I closed the curtain, but I had been warned not to waste time gazing out at a world I had renounced, and I let the moment pass. I put myself to bed without any unease, lulled into the calm of a dreamless sleep by the litany of prayers and invocations I had learnt so well by then.

"Jesu, if I could only have known! I went to my bed like a careless child! But if I had known, perhaps I would not have had the courage to go to that poor woman's assistance, and I would not have been fit for such a life either, if I had left her to die."

"You did not know", he says, putting a hand on my head to steady me, because I find myself trying to raise myself up. "Be still. You cannot reproach yourself for what you did not know."

And I remember how, when I went to bed, there had been a page of neat, small writing on the table that I had composed that day and not had time in the failing light to read over.

We live in a precarious world, where nothing is certain from one sunrise to the next, even in this cloistered life of bare walls and the flickering of a sanctuary light that never dies. In this cell, where little changes with the passing days and months, I cannot say when I lay my head down to rest what may await me when I awaken—or indeed if I will wake at all. When I said that adventures end here, I did not know that simply to live in this world of mysterious uncertainty is to embrace an adventure that ends only in death.

Into Endless Night

It was a desperately hot night, but Perpetua was not disturbed by it and only became aware of the prickling sensation of her nightclothes sticking to her when she was woken up by the sound of a young man calling at her window. She threw herself out of bed but took a little longer to arrive at her window than Sister Chiara, whose voice she heard shouting: "What is the meaning of this outrage? What business have you with us at such an hour?"

Perpetua pulled back her curtain and peered out. It was Pawl, a lad whose family she knew from the town, standing before them carrying a light. She knew him because his sickly older sister Assumpta, recently widowed, was with child and had suffered terribly during the long months of her pregnancy. She tried to remember, as she covered the window again and hastily dressed, how far gone Assumpta would be by now and noted that if labour had begun she was some weeks before her time.

"Please, Sister, come quickly!" Pawl exclaimed, the moment she appeared again. "She cannot deliver her baby."

Sister Chiara was clearly unwilling to let her go. "Is Agata not with her?" she demanded. "Surely she can provide help enough?"

"It was Agata who sent me", said Pawl hurriedly; "she declared there is something wrong with the baby that is beyond her skill to mend. Please, Sister, time is short."

"I think you must let me go", declared Perpetua. "He is right; there may be little time."

"Will you see that she comes safely back as soon as she may?"

"Do not fear, Sister", promised Pawl. "I will see her safely back before dawn."

Perpetua noticed as she bade goodnight to Chiara that the woman still seemed unwilling to let her go, but thought her simply a little too cautious because she felt responsible for her. And Perpetua was too preoccupied with thoughts about her patient to ask herself why, when Chiara had said goodnight to her, she had used a word that meant farewell, but a farewell made only at a final parting. It was an error perhaps or the gloom of the night making Chiara unusually melancholy.

Perpetua followed Pawl at great speed to his family home. She carried no instruments or remedies on her person except for the knife Father Antonin had given her long ago, which she still found useful for many purposes, from cutting bandages to making small incisions where necessary. More than that, she felt an almost superstitious need to carry it with her, as though she imagined that her mentor would be with her in spirit during difficult tasks if she carried his gift around with her.

"How is your sister?" she enquired of her companion. He was younger than she, scarcely more than a boy, and moved with short, nervous steps.

"Not well", he answered. "She is in very great pain."

"That is always so."

"But it is much worse than the last time", he persisted; "she cannot lose another child."

As they neared the house, Perpetua could hear the piercing screams of a woman in the final agonies of childbirth.

She broke into a run and threw herself into the dwelling, where the stench of female suffering hit her full in the face. It was the smell of sweat, urine, and, more alarmingly, blood. The woman must have been labouring violently for hours and lay on her back, struggling to catch her breath, barely able to follow the newcomer around the room with her eyes. As Perpetua reached Assumpta's side, she noticed her face twisting with mounting pain. As her agony increased, she was forced by the spasm onto her side and grasped the edge of Perpetua's shawl, pulling it so hard between her fingers that the cloth tore. The low guttural noise she had been making became a weary cry that grew louder and louder until, at the climax of the birth pang, she threw back her head and gave a tortured scream.

"Fetch water!" commanded Perpetua to Pawl, who stood flinching at his sister's feet. She turned to Agata, who had retreated from Assumpta's side when Perpetua arrived, as though afraid that the sister would blame her for the girl's condition. "Tell me all."

"She has been labouring all day, since before dawn", Agata explained. She was a small, timorous woman who had nevertheless aided the entrance of many an infant into the world. "The babe's position is bad. She has been screaming like this since the morning."

Perpetua turned back to Assumpta and brushed the damp curls off her face. "The pain is so terrible", whispered Assumpta, her voice hoarse from screaming. "In my back. The pain is in my back."

"Agata, wet her head", she ordered, as Pawl appeared with a pitcher of water. She placed her hand on the base of the woman's spine, causing her to cry out. She could feel a hard lump, which she knew to be the baby's head, and she could not stop herself from groaning—the baby was head down, but had turned so that the back of his head pressed against his mother's spine, causing unbearable, unremitting pain. "Pawl, leave the room."

She waited until the boy had left before taking a closer look at her patient. The baby's head was just visible, but when she slipped her hand around it she realised how grave matters were. The woman's body was ready, the neck of the womb open enough to release the baby, but the little one was well and truly stuck, the soft temple of his head suffering damage with every spasm, whilst the hard, pointed back of the head that should have been easing the baby's birth was causing his mother such agonies that she barely had the strength now to push him out. The woman's body began to shake with pain again; Perpetua withdrew her hand and took a deep breath as Assumpta screamed through another wave of agony.

"Agata, go out to Pawl and tell him to send for the priest", she said finally.

Agata looked up at her in horrified alarm. "Are you ... are you sure?" she stammered; "is there nothing to be done?"

"I may save one but not the other", she replied wearily. "Someone will have need of the priest before the night is out."

Agata gave the frightened squeak she always made in such situations and scurried outside, where Pawl was sitting anxiously, awaiting news. Perpetua returned to her patient, who was lying very still now, eyes half-closed, awaiting the next ordeal with weary terror. She was dying and seemed to know it. "Assumpta, listen to me", said Perpetua, getting on her knees at Assumpta's head. "The baby is trapped."

She hardly seemed to hear at first, but slowly her eyes moved to meet her helper's. "You can save him, Sister; I know you can."

"I can, perhaps, but do you understand the cost?"

"You must get him out", she whispered. "I cannot do it. I have no strength." She began to writhe and cry out again. Perpetua held her by the wrists to prevent her from harming herself in her despair. "For God's sake, help me!" she shrieked. "Take this pain away from me!"

"Listen to me, Assumpta. I cannot save you both. Tell me what I am to do."

Assumpta lay perfectly still, her face expressionless, but Perpetua knew that she had heard. Then pain overcame her once again, and she screamed for deliverance—any deliverance—whilst every birth pang caused the baby's temple to knock against bone. "Do you understand what I am asking you?" Perpetua knew the terrible choice she was demanding. Either the baby Assumpta had been carrying and nurturing in her body for months would be born dead and the terrible suffering she had endured to bring him into the world would prove futile, or she would die in terrible agony, without so much as looking him in the face.

"You know you must save the child", she whispered, but pain was taking her over yet again, and she screamed, "For God's sake, hurry! Do whatever it is you must do!"

Perpetua was used to this pattern: the swing between quiet resignation and aggressive outbursts brought on by unbearable pain and fear. She set to work immediately, steeling herself against the misery she was causing. The voice of hope told her that there was a chance she might save them both, a remote chance, whilst the cold voice of experience warned her that she could save one and possibly not even one life.

"Try to push once more", said Perpetua. "I know you are very tired, but one more effort might dislodge him."

No one could ever claim that little Assumpta did not use her last remaining scrap of energy trying to bring her baby into the world, but she was not quick enough. As she struggled with the final effort that was asked of her, she began to bleed. She had bled before, but this time Perpetua knew that she was bleeding to death. The hæmorrhage was so powerful that the most she could do was to cover up the lower part of the woman's body to try to prevent her from realising what was happening. She placed her fingers around the woman's pulse and felt it galloping with the desperate strain of trying to keep the body alive, but it was silent before Pawl and the priest arrived to give her comfort.

There was no time to think of how she had failed. "I need to perform a caesarean section", she said, without even turning to face Pawl, who had frozen in the doorway, too shocked to move. There was a smell of death everywhere, and so much blood that she could not hope to hide it. "Help me." She took out Father Antonin's knife and began cutting open the dead woman's womb. Behind her she heard a terrified cry. "Father, please take him away from the room. He should not be watching this."

She could navigate her way through a body easily enough even though she was not a surgeon, but the baby was already in the birth canal, and she had to drag him back by the legs. Her hands and clothes were thoroughly coated in blood, but she barely noticed; her only thought was how very difficult it was to keep hold of the slippery, limp body of a tiny baby who could do nothing to help himself into the world. "Agata, bind and cut the cord."

The baby would live if it killed her, she thought. She should not have felt like that; she should not feel that way about any of her patients, but something she could not name compelled her, and she could not resist. She cleared the baby's nose and mouth then struck his leg once, twice, three times, willing him to make a sound. Somewhere far away, she heard the priest ask, "Am I too late?"

She refused to answer, but so too did the baby. In desperation, she wrapped him in her mantle as though trying to force some warmth into his body. For those long silent moments she stopped being a physician and found herself behaving like a mother. It seemed to her afterward, never knowing what happened in her absence, that having lost the baby's mother—and it was not even the first time she had lost a mother in childbirth—that she found herself taking her place. It was like a taste of a forbidden love affair, the extraordinary sensation of having a tiny, helpless child placed into her hands who might open his eyes and gaze at her in adoration if she could only give him back his life.

She cradled his head against her breast and felt a tiny hand gripping her wrist, then the faint, painful sound of a birth cry. Behind her, Agata was cleaning up the carnage she had made, mopping up blood, covering Assumpta's body, whilst Pawl sat at his sister's head, still unable to speak or cry. Life and death in the same chamber, so close and so alike, tainted by blood and pain.

When the baby had been baptised, Perpetua knew that her work was over, but it was with something like grief that she settled the baby into his crib and broke the invisible chain between them.

"I am so sorry I could not save your sister", she said, as she walked with Pawl through the dark streets. He was quiet and withdrawn, and she knew that he must feel betrayed by her.

"You did what could be done", he said quietly. "I did not expect a miracle."

"The baby is a little small, but he is certainly a fighter—
God bless him. I will return again tomorrow if I am able."

Perpetua never knew which of them noticed first, but
the vision she saw as they caught sight of the bay imprinted
itself on her memory as one of the last images of her free
life. They were still a good distance from the church, on
a raised path overlooking the water's edge, and could see
lights blinking in the darkness farther along the shore.
A boat was landing, at least one boat, perhaps another,
and Perpetua's sharp eyes caught sight of figures hurrying
ashore and moving in a shadowy swarm into the town.
Pawl yanked her round the corner of a wall to ensure they
were out of sight, but they both jumped at the sudden erup-
tion—far too close for comfort—of chilling battle screams.

"Pirates!" hissed Pawl. "It's a raid; they'll find us."

There was no time to feel anything at all. "Pawl, go
home!" she commanded him; "you will need to protect
your household."

"What about you?"

She knew he wanted to go home; it was in the nature of
belonging to a family to want to protect the other members, particularly at such a moment. She thought of the tiny
baby she had fought to save whilst pirates ravaged the town
and only a priest, unarmed and of declining years, to defend
him. "They have more need of you than I have—you must
go!"

But he never left her company. The figure lurched at
them through the darkness, massive, terrifying, so unexpectedly that there was no time to escape. Perpetua was
aware of being thrown back against the wall, whilst Pawl
dropped instinctively onto one knee to draw his blade.
"Run!" he shouted, but he seemed to her to be more a
sacrificial victim than a defender, and she was paralysed

with shock, watching in growing despair as Pawl fought off their attacker. When it came to the test, he was simply too young, braver perhaps, but smaller and clumsier than his opponent, using a knife that was as useful a weapon as a stick. In his bewildered, grief-stricken state she knew he could not possibly win a duel against a skilled warrior, older, stronger than he, who was knocking him farther and farther back every time their blades clashed.

She turned to run as he had told her, but found that she could not bear to leave him to die alone and turned back just as the fight—such as it was—came to its bloody conclusion. She saw Pawl's head thrown back and his body falling onto the ground, then heard a heartrending cry—but it was not Pawl crying out. He had not died instantly, but the manner of it had made it impossible for him to make any sound at all, his head almost severed by the sharp, wide blade of the scimitar hacking across his throat. She was the one who was screaming.

Perpetua turned her back and ran blindly, but her heavy skirts held her back and it was too late; he had heard her and seen her when he first lunged at them and threw himself at her with the gleeful triumph of a man who knows he cannot be beaten. She turned toward him and struck at his face with her right hand, but he barely seemed to notice. He caught hold of her wrist and forced her effortlessly against a wall. "Let me alone!" she shouted, but the proximity of the man to her was unbearable. She was not used to this closeness; she could feel the man's breath in her hair and felt repulsed by the touch and stench of a man's body so near to her. She began kicking him, but he barely flinched and calmly placed the edge of a blade—still dripping wet with a man's blood—against her bare neck. She stopped struggling as he had known she would.

"You are a weakling", he said; afterward she could not tell whether she had understood what the man was saying or simply sensed that he would say such a thing to her, but the next sound he made was a shrill, wordless shriek. He had stayed still just long enough for her to slip a small knife into his neck; she felt the warm, unlovely sensation of blood pouring through her fingers for the second time that night.

"The weak shame the strong", she said without a trace of regret, but it was to her eternal shame that she felt no horror at her action as she stood against the wall, watching the man convulsing and dying, half-drowned in his own blood. Somewhere hidden in the back of her mind, there was the thought that this changed everything, all that had passed and all that would be. In a single terrible movement, she had crossed the boundary into some forbidden place, but at that moment she felt only the dull satisfaction of having conquered an enemy.

†

"It was an act of self-preservation", promises her confessor.

"I wanted to kill him", she answers brutally. "I rather think I enjoyed it. I had to kill him perhaps to save myself, but I should not have felt so triumphant when it came to it. *The weak shame the strong.* The shame of it."

"You are honest."

"I am nothing else." And she has somehow to confess how she thought she would be violated if she were captured and been so determined to preserve her honour that she tore off her habit and put on the clothes from Pawl's body. She had dishonoured the dead before and been cast out; she should have known she would surely be cast out again, but any horror she felt at doing the poor boy such an indignity or of wearing a dead man's clothes was overcome by her fear of rape. His ghost would not trouble her for this, she promised herself, as she ran in search of a hiding place, but she wondered whether she was being punished for her crime when she turned a blind corner and was knocked down, leaving her stunned and surrounded on the ground.

Of all the terrifying sights that were to greet her in the days that followed, nothing was more appalling than those shaven-headed, bare-armed men with their naked blades tearing the night air. Every muscle in her body tightened in readiness, but she felt paralysed with the shock of having killed and the prospect of being killed. She was no longer a visitor in a town of her beloved country; she had fallen into a hellish nightmare of demons and darkness where there was no way out and escape was an impossible dream.

"Come on, boy, have you no fight in you?" There was a good deal of laughter, but as she was hauled to her feet she felt too confused and disgusted to make any response. Never had any man presumed to hold her against his own body like this. The insult of a hand grasping her waist snapped her back to life, and she clenched her fists to retaliate, but she was startled by the sudden sound of a woman screaming at the top of her voice, so piercingly that she was audible over everything else.

Perpetua turned her head in the direction of the noise and saw a young woman struggling to stop her baby being forced from her arms. The mother screamed and struggled to hold onto the infant—struggled so hard she looked as though she would be torn limb from limb before she ever let go—but she could not hold him for long and must have realised it in those last anguished seconds. Perpetua watched as the wailing baby was pulled free and thrown quite deliberately against the nearest rock, whilst all the time the mother screamed and pleaded for the man not to let the child come to any harm.

Perpetua had seen death many times, but never violent, cold-blooded death as it had come to her island home that night—first Pawl, then the man who had died at her own hand, then a baby, fragile, broken, killed instantly only months after birth. She hung limply in her abductor's arms and allowed herself to be led away, unable to summon the strength to make a last backward look as she was taken to the waiting boat. She looked instead at her feet stepping across familiar ground and kept her head down until she reached the last fragment of shore. She hesitated, aware, albeit confusedly by then, that she was standing at the last point of her own world—then a heavy blow to the small of her back knocked the breath from her lungs, and she fell, half-dragged, half-tumbling, into the boat.

No, it was not a nightmare after all. She had merely stepped into the stories her people had told her once and become one of their unfortunate characters—except she doubted that she would be remembered. She knew that it would be as they had described it—she was being spirited away into a life all free peoples feared. In many ways she was already dead. To those few who knew her, she would simply disappear from their lives forever, and they might even say a Requiem Mass for her in her absence, so certain would they be that she would never return.

The bodies crammed around her bore familiar faces, but she could not bear to look at them. They were not compatriots anymore; they were bodies thrown together into the same unmarked grave. And there could be no kinship among the damned.

PART II

The Longest Journey

They tell me to lie still, but they do not know where I am. They see a body in a bed, tossing and turning with fever, but I am slipping into delirium again and can barely feel the touch of their comforting hands trying to pull me back into the land of the living. I am deaf and blind to this reassuring English chamber; I cannot see the sun streaming through the window or hear their quaint Latin words promising me that my troubles are at an end, because I am lost again. I am Perpetua the anchoress, the servant to good women who became a slave to a tyrant. I am thrown aboard the vessel again, hurled upon the water, and feel myself trembling with fear when they think I shake with sickness. The vessel that is to carry us across the sea to Barbary. It is an unnatural state of affairs, the ground lurching beneath our feet, and before very much time has passed, I can hardly remember what the luxury of being still had felt like.

We were pushed and beaten down into the cramped darkness below decks, so determinedly that our fear of such a loathsome, dangerous prison was chased away by our desperation not to come to any further harm. There were too many of us, yet they crammed us in as though we were bundles of linen or barrels of oil with no need for the light of day or air to breathe. I was one of the last to be captured and could not move quickly enough to escape hurt. There were many before me; I was caught between the crowd of terrified captives and those who had taken us, with their blades and fists. Oh God, if I could only have died in my anchorhold of some sickness before I came to such a pass, where I might have known the comfort of friends and the consolation of holy Church! I had fallen into some liquid world where nothing was stable or certain any longer, giddy, bewildered by the constant movement of the sea. Then came an unbearable feeling I could not shake off, a pounding of the head, a tightening of the stomach, and for more hours than I could ever record, I was violently sick, over and over again, until I felt as though my entrails were burning inside my body.

And in the acrid darkness there were people all around, pressing so close that there was barely space to breathe, let alone lie down and rest. I was a child of the outside world once, who had grown up out-of-doors in all seasons, and then a woman of the solitary space. Now that both freedom and blessed loneliness had been taken from me, I could not decide whether I was more frightened of being at sea in the certain knowledge that I would drown immediately if the ship went down or of being trapped below decks, surrounded by hot, sweating, fidgeting bodies and the growing stench as we were all overcome by seasickness.

Then as the hours passed, the long remorseless hours, some, particularly the children, found themselves forced to soil themselves where they sat, crippled by anxiety and exhaustion. We did not know it then, but it was the first of many humiliations we would be forced to bear. I knew in the depth of this misery that I had been mistaken. This was not a nightmare; it was not a story from the past. No, this was not death. We were not so fortunate as those of our compatriots who were struck down and killed trying to defend the town. The most degrading of deaths did not compare to a degrading life, and the dead were not forced to endure such indignities, even, I supposed, in purgatory.

Water. Oh God, I thought, *give me water to drink before I die of thirst....* A servant cradles my head and presses a beaker of water to my lips, little knowing how far away I am, but even I do not know precisely where on the dark sea we have journeyed.

I remember how I yearned for the cool, clean silence of my cell. Father Antonin had been very subdued, indeed, when he had told me that it was a friendly prison; it seemed to me in the choking darkness to have been a prince's court, airy and spacious where I could have danced with joy until night and its peace came. I told myself then that I might in truth still be there, fast asleep, overcome by some ghoulish dream sent to firm my resolve to pursue my calling in life, but no such illusion could attack the senses like that. I tried to imagine myself back home for a moment, chanting the prayers of Compline or Lauds, in harmony with the other women hidden away beside me. Just for a moment, for the length of a single prayer—but the groans and complaints and foul odours around me brought me always back to the hell I had been dragged to.

I was told afterward that we had been more fortunate than others who were dragged from farther afield, as our journey took days and not months, but every hour might have been an eternity when they stopped giving us water because there was not enough and we had long since stopped expecting food. Hunger and thirst I had known before, but never like this. Never the dry, dizzying ache for water or for anything, anything at all that could be drunk. I would have licked the moisture from the walls if I could have reached them and the wood had not soaked up the droplets of our breath. I became racked with cramps from close confinement and thirst; I retched but had nothing left to release. I tried to pray for the frailer souls among us who I supposed must be dying, but could pray only that God would have mercy on me and grant me the same deliverance of death. *My God, my God, why hast thou forsaken me?* The words rang in my ears, not in the graceful, eloquent Latin Father Antonin had taught me, but in my raw, earthy mother tongue. I reached for the rosary beads hanging from my girdle, searching for some diversion that would give purpose to this disaster, then I remembered that I had changed clothes with a dead man and my beads, along with my clothes, had been left behind. It was all gone, all of it, every aspect of my past life. In the act of stripping myself, I had discarded everything that had made me who I was, and I thought then how much I deserved to suffer. I thought of Pawl's poor murdered body, stripped and abandoned by me as though it were the carcass of an animal. In the midst of my fear, I had not spared a thought for a boy whose family I had known and attended, who had died trying to defend my honour. I had no right to feel affronted now if my captors, who did not know me, treated me as a chattel to be disposed of as they wished.

Agata and the priest must be on another boat, I thought, unless by some rare providence they had escaped—or the priest might have been killed on the spot if they had recognised him. And the baby. I knew they would not have taken the trouble to capture a baby—but that was more than I could bear to imagine. I struggled to breathe, as though the misery of the world was bearing down on me and stifling me to death. *My God, my God* ... and there was no angel there to comfort me.

A Gift Returned

"Did anyone survive?" demanded Father Antonin.

Giuseppe knew there was one particular person he was anxious for, in spite of the way he had phrased the question. "I hear they did not have time to break open the anchorholds—or they may not have realised there were people there. They will be among the few who were left alone."

Father Antonin and Giuseppe were walking together through the ravaged streets. An uneasy silence had fallen over the town, its inhabitants stolen away and the few survivors still in hiding. With his immediate fears gone, Father Antonin surveyed the scene as calmly as he could. The streets were strewn with debris: pieces of clothing, a shoe, a cloak, discarded in the frantic moments when escape had seemed possible; bits of broken furniture, no doubt stolen by the invading pirates and dropped when they became too heavy to carry; a few scattered coins here and there that had tumbled from purses and boxes. He noted black marks against the stone walls where fires had been started to spread fear and confusion; some houses had been razed and were still smouldering.

"Did they desecrate the church?" he asked Giuseppe.

"They broke the crucifix and smashed the Madonna", he answered, staring directly ahead of him. "Anything of value they could steal they took with them." He had not wept since he was a boy, and he would not be brought to such a pass now. "But they did not stop to break open the tabernacle. They took away the people who sheltered in the church."

"It is a wicked business." Father Antonin stopped in his tracks. "I wonder how many poor souls they carried away."

"It is not yet known, Father." Giuseppe hesitated. "They killed the priest. He was at a deathbed, poor man, little knowing it was he who needed the Viaticum. You will be needed."

"Take me to him."

†

The house still stank of blood when they stepped inside and saw not one but two bodies. Not just blood. The flies were already gathering at the smell of dead flesh, causing Giuseppe to retch violently when they stepped through the gaping door and the oppressive odour hit them. The old priest had been cornered and hacked to death. His body lay against a wall, slumped forwards as though he had fallen asleep sitting in the corner, but he had been wounded in such a frenzied manner that even Father Antonin, who was generally of a stronger constitution than Giuseppe, had to draw several sharp breaths through his mouth to prevent dizziness overtaking him. On a bed, covered in a blanket, was a dead woman. "Did they kill her because she was too sick to be moved?" asked Giuseppe, but he was too repulsed by the scene to step forward and see for himself.

Father Antonin pulled the blanket back momentarily then drew it carefully over the woman's body and made the sign of the cross. "No, she died in childbirth", he said; "someone has performed a caesarean section on her."

It was then that the baby awoke and began to cry noisily, demanding their attention. Father Antonin looked around for a cradle and found, tucked discreetly away behind his mother's bed, a makeshift crib where a newborn baby lay wriggling and crying. He fell to his knees and picked it up. "How on earth did the baby escape?" demanded Giuseppe.

"Either his presence went miraculously unnoticed," suggested Father Antonin, "or there was a little mercy, even from these black-hearted tyrants, and they did not stop to end his life."

What he did not know was that when the priest had heard the sound of the invaders approaching the house, his last act before he was cut down had been to command Agata to make as much noise as possible to hide the sound of the baby's cries. She had done as she was told and began screaming hysterically as their attackers entered the house, only to find that she could not stop screaming as she was forced to watch a frail, unarmed man butchered by an assailant half his age. She refused to be silenced until she had been dragged out of the house and knew that none were within earshot of it. Soon afterward, the baby, still a little groggy from the long, difficult birth, fell asleep and did not wake again until the raid was over and he was safe from harm. There had been some purpose, even in that long, tortured birth, but Perpetua would never know it.

"One life spared," said Father Antonin, "but he is alone in the world. He will need a mother. He will need food and shelter."

He could not pretend that it did not provide a welcome diversion from the horrors of the ravaged town to carry the infant to his home and instruct Marija to take care of him until a wet nurse could be found for the little child. He gave the baby a conditional baptism because there were none left alive or free now to say whether or not there had been time to christen him; he left Marija feeding warm milk into the tiny mouth, drop by patient drop.

†

It was as he and Giuseppe returned to their unhappy task that they heard the sound of women grieving, shortly before they came close enough to see them. Sister Chiara stood with another anchoress and an elderly woman whom Father Antonin recognised after a moment as Perpetua's mother. His stomach lurched with fear. Something terrible, something beyond his worst imaginings, must have occurred for the two women to do something as serious as to break enclosure without permission. Perpetua's brother, who had kept some distance from them, stepped forward to kiss his hand. "What has happened here?" asked Father Antonin. He noticed that the young man's hands were shaking.

"Ursula", he said, unable to lift his head; "she's lost."

"She was taken?" Father Antonin glanced sharply round at Sister Chiara, who had been talking to Perpetua's inconsolable mother but had looked up when Father Antonin arrived. "Sister, what is the meaning of this?"

Sister Chiara drew herself up and spoke with considerable self-possession. "She went to take care of a woman in childbirth", she said. "The brother—Pawl—came asking for her. Then we heard them coming. We huddled on the floor of our cells with the commotion all around us, but either they were distracted or they did not realise we were there, and they left us alone. But, of course, I knew she must be out there somewhere, and then she did not return, so at daybreak we ... well, there was nothing else to be done since there are so few people left to help. We were forced to break out and came searching ..." She trailed off, unable to continue.

"Has there been no sight of her?" He could feel a pulse hammering in his neck. "Answer me! Has there been no sight of her?"

"No," came the cold answer of a woman numb with shock, "but she is dead. We found her clothes."

And so they had. She stepped aside, and Father Antonin saw a sorry pile of cloth, torn and, he noticed on closer examination, heavily stained with blood in a number of places. "Are you certain these are hers?" he asked, begging for even a hint of uncertainty.

"Yes, Father. I saw her leave. Pawl's body was found nearby. He must have been killed defending her." She could not bring herself to mention that his body had been almost naked. He must have been stripped and robbed after he was killed, and the indignity with which his body had been treated could hardly be dwelt upon.

"He must have fought very bravely to have been killed", said Father Antonin; "a strong young man like that would have been worth a great deal to them alive."

Perpetua's mother burst into renewed, convulsive sobs. "This is a judgment!" she shouted, looking directly at him with such intensity that he wanted to shrink away from her gaze. "God forgive me, I never loved her. I never wanted her, and now God has taken her from me."

He felt a strange muddle of pity and loathing toward her. He hardly knew whether to try to assure her of God's forgiveness or to remind her that it was folly to weep for a girl she had never protected from rain or sun or hunger or violence. He knew that she was truly sorry in a way so many of his penitents never were, but the creeping, yawning grief that was overwhelming him left him with no words of comfort for her. "Sister, will you look to Perpetua's mother?" he said, but she was already leading the unfortunate woman away. "I will come as soon as I may."

The moment the wretched procession had disappeared out of sight, Father Antonin abandoned all pretences at fortitude, covered his face, and began to weep. The horrible spectre of her final moments hovered all around him: the fear and despair she must have known as she watched her defender killed in front of her; the dishonour, too terrible to imagine or speak of, that she must have endured before her death. It was more than he could be expected to bear: the thought that a child he had cared for and educated more diligently than many men cared for their own daughters should have come to such an unspeakable end. Yet he knew it would not do to say that she had not deserved such a fate when he would not have wished it on any other woman.

Giuseppe, who had never seen Father Antonin burst into tears before now, hovered awkwardly at his side. "Forgive me, Father," he said, laying a hand on his arm, "but you must lay aside your grief a little. There will be bodies to bury; there may be a few wounded. Come with me now."

"I cannot believe that she came to such an end, Giuseppe", he sobbed. "I could not have loved my own kinsman so dearly."

"You must not dwell on it now. Please, come with me."

But it was with an agonising effort that Giuseppe was able to persuade Father Antonin to get up and follow him. They had not walked far before they came across another dead body, a young man whose fist still grasped the weapon that had failed to save him. He stopped to take a closer look. "Leave him; he's an infidel", barked Giuseppe. "Would that our men could have slain them all."

But Father Antonin doubted very much that he had died at the hands of another man. He knelt near his head to examine the death wound and noted that he had been stabbed below the right ear, causing him to bleed to death. His billowing clothes were drenched with blood, and his face was almost impossible to bear looking at, unnaturally pale with the open eyes rolled upward. Whoever had stabbed him had either been extremely fortunate or known precisely where to strike, as the knife used had a sharp but small blade that would have done little damage had it penetrated many other places. He drew the knife out of the man's neck and took a closer look at it, but he had known whom it belonged to when he first set eyes on it, because he had given it to her himself long ago. And almost to ensure that he could be left in no doubt about the identity of the killer, he noted that the wound must have been inflicted by a left-hander.

†

It was the early hours of the following day before Father Antonin's work was done. In the event, there were few bodies to bury, only two other men besides Pawl, the old priest, and the woman who had died in childbirth. The community had been taken by surprise and snatched from their beds, leaving them too bewildered and too terrified to put up much of a fight. The body of the man Perpetua had killed was set upon by furious survivors and would have been horribly mutilated if Father Antonin had not pleaded with them to show respect for the dead. "What respect did they show to the living?" shouted a distraught man who had been separated from his wife and children as they attempted to flee.

"We are not like them", he had called back; "if they drive us to hate, we are no better than they are and the battle is lost." Easily said, he thought when many must have thought the battle already lost, at least for some of their number who would wear away the rest of their short lives chained to the oar of a galley or some other similarly terrible fate.

"There was no sign of Warda, I am afraid", said Giuseppe, as Father Antonin sat in silence at the back of the church, too distracted to rest in spite of his weariness. What Giuseppe could not see was a small knife, carefully cleaned, that Father Antonin held in his hand.

"But no body, either."

"Father, she's dead. You must believe it. They might quite easily have thrown her body into the sea when they had finished their sport with her."

"It does not make any sense. Our enemies do terrible things, but they do not violate and murder virgins; they take care of them and sell them to the highest bidder."

"Father, they must have done; why else would they ..."; he could find no kind or courteous way to say that it was the only possible explanation.

"My little one did not die last night", he said quietly; "she is stronger and more fierce than any infidel warrior."

Giuseppe shook his head and left his old friend alone, knowing that it would serve no purpose to argue with him now. And Father Antonin looked fixedly at the knife in his hand and thought, *But where are you now?*

The Death Prayer

There was always some greater misery awaiting her. On board the ship she had longed to reach dry land, even a hostile land if she could only leave behind the sickening motion and the stench of bodies crushed into the cramped confines of the ship. Yet when they docked and were dragged ashore she wanted to cling on for dear life and beg to be left alone. She could hear the ship's guns firing and sounds like the noisiest, most gregarious fiesta all around them, as though the whole town was in the midst of an uproarious celebration. She was too small to see over the heads of her fellow captives but could only guess that the townsfolk had come out to celebrate the safe return of the vessel with its rich cargo of foreign captives.

There was no sign of them going anywhere for a moment, so Perpetua fell down on her knees. The sun was still low in the sky, but the heat of the day was bearing down on her as she stood with her companions, shaking with fatigue. She looked up at them now, glancing from face to face and realised that she knew many of those who had been taken. They had placed the men and women on separate boats, and she had been placed with the men, but either none of them had noticed her in their confusion or they were going to some efforts not to ask her what she was playing at.

Whole families had been taken from their homes. Many of the little boys were still in their nightshirts, clinging to confused, frightened fathers who had long ceased their promises that all would be well.

And this was the land they were bound to serve. The ground beneath her looked little different from the barren, scrubby land on which she had been raised, but the city before them was too magnificent to belong to her world. Having only ever lived within a poor settlement, she could only stare at the vast, breathtaking, but quite, quite alien sprawl of dazzling buildings and what seemed to be fortifications, stretching as far as the eye could see. It was the stuff of dreams, the sort of place she had only ever visited in books, and yet now that she saw it, she simply felt afraid, as though it were the city itself that was out of place, not she and her unfortunate companions. The notion that they were aliens in some other people's land was too horrible for her to appreciate as they stood there. Exile was the most wretched punishment besides death, the fate the Israelites had lamented in Babylon. *We sat and wept as we remembered . . . as we remembered . . .*

"Sister?" called a voice she seemed to know. "Do you know what is going on? Why in heaven are you dressed like that?"

She raised a finger to her lips. "I mean to pass as a man; do not give me away."

"But why?" She was being addressed by a labourer whose arm she had once set and who must have imagined that she would be more knowledgeable than he on every matter. His face was bruised; she knew that he must have put up quite a struggle before being subdued. He might well survive if he had had the presence of mind to put up a fight. "There is blood on your shirt. They would have been gentler with a woman."

"It is not my blood", she answered a little tersely. "I cannot let them ... well, I have a vow to keep, albeit in my heart."

His face softened a little, as though reminded of the world they had so recently inhabited. "God keep you then, Sister."

"God keep us all."

Her companion did not have time to warn her that one of their captors had overheard their conversation and was advancing toward them. She heard a swishing noise a split second before a desperate pain paralysed her shoulder and a man began shouting in her face, too quickly for her to make out a word he said. She was too shocked to speak again and made no protest of any kind as she was chivvied to her feet and led with the others through the streets of the town so that the celebrating inhabitants could throw things at them—and spit in their faces and laugh at them and call them every hateful, disgusting name their language offered.

What a ridiculous sight we must be, thought Perpetua— *tired, dishevelled, filthy*—but she refused to bow her head in shame. Father Antonin had taught her at their first meeting that dignity and beauty were not diminished by outward appearances, which was why he had called her Warda, to prove the point to his housekeeper. She looked at a man several feet ahead of her who was trying to shield his son from harm, but they were both shaken by the hatred of the crowd and wept helplessly, causing even more scorn to be hurled at them.

Perpetua began to realise that this horror alone was having very little effect on her compared with her companions, but then, she had been hated and derided before. There was no insult, no act of spite these people could throw at her that her own people had not inflicted on her once. She

had accepted it as part of life when she was a child, to be
sneered at, to be spat upon and beaten, and she retreated
again into her child's mind that had blocked out all that
distressed her and allowed her to rise above it. Bring it all
on, she thought. If my own people could not hurt me, my
enemies cannot begin to try.

As a child she had imagined hell to be a fiery furnace
filled with monstrous demons, black as shadows against
the blistering flames. Her keen imagination, tormented by
too many dark hours spent in solitude, saw them creeping
across the smouldering rocks in a macabre, spectral dance,
torturing the chained souls who stood in their way. She
knew now that hell was painted in infinitely darker colours
than anything her mind could have created because she saw
it all around her—saw it, heard it, felt it, even tasted it in
the blood and dust that coated her lips.

Unlike some of the whiter captives, stolen from shores
farther away than her own, she was no stranger to the
stifling heat beating down on her head or the sensation of
crippling thirst, but never had it felt like this when she had
known that she could find shelter when she wanted it and
clear water when her errand was done. She imagined the
cool of the parish church, her head pressing against the cold
stone wall, or Father Antonin pouring water over her head
when she came staggering into his house, bareheaded and
sunburnt—*How many times have I told you to cover your head
before you step out of doors, my girl? It will be a fitting penance
if you sicken from too much sun!*—but it only made her the
more desperate.

"Where are they taking us?" a man walking a little
behind her asked, but she was still too shocked to speak after
the response she had received before. In any case she did
not know where they were going, and when they reached a

building that resembled a dungeon and were forced inside, she could not begin to guess why they were being kept there. It was only later she discovered that these places— bagnos, as they were called—were simply being used to house them until the next day's market. For the less fortunate men, condemned to a short life among the quarries and building works, this would be the place they were brought back to every night after many hours of crippling labour in the blazing sun.

At least I am not moving anymore, she told herself, searching for some minute reason to be glad; *I am not moving, and we are not shut up in the dark.* They had been crammed so tightly into the room that it was impossible to lie down, and she was forced to squat where she stood to take the weight off her feet. The place felt damp and putrid in spite of the hot, dry weather, and there was no roof or covering of any kind to protect their heads from the savage elements. Exhaustion and thirst had caused her mouth to become blistered, and in the hours that followed she was tormented with such unbearable cramping pain that she eventually abandoned any attempts at fortitude and screamed for deliverance.

She was not alone. It was so long since they had been given anything to drink that they were all near to madness; those who had the strength cried out for water, protesting that they would not last the night without it. When water was finally brought to them, it was slimy and brackish, but they drank greedily and could have convinced themselves that they had never tasted anything finer.

It was not the first time Perpetua had wondered whether death would be the quickest liberty she could hope for, and she prayed. Through the miserable, lonely night, too hungry, too distressed—too frightened, if she could only have admitted it to herself—to consider sleeping, she prayed that death would take her if there was no chance that she would see her native land again. Among the stories she had heard of this land as a child were gruesome accounts of executions so vile that the details could only be whispered: crucifixions, men's heads set alight by flaming crowns, bodies impaled, men and women beaten to death over a period of hours and even days. She did not yet know which of these accounts were true and which were fanciful, but even believing them all she told herself that it would be better to die the most horrible of deaths rather than live another day in such a godforsaken land. *My God, let it end*, she prayed. *In any way you choose, but let this end.*

She looked up at the night sky to remind herself that freedom was not so very far away, but the cold, sharp stars stared remorselessly back at her, offering no comfort at all. It was the most wretched single moment of her entire life.

The Life and Times of Pierre Dan (1)

When morning came they were given morsels of food to sustain them. They were so desperately hungry that the most extravagant of banquets would never have satisfied them by then, but none of them could guess when they would be fed again, so they ate whatever they could lay their hands on. Nevertheless, when they were ordered out, some protested that hunger and thirst and weariness had left them too weak to move. The response they received was so brutal that they quickly found the energy to struggle out—on their hands and knees if necessary.

Perpetua did as she was told, but she was still thinking about death as they approached the market. She told herself that Father Antonin would want her to surrender her life as a martyr if it came to it, but he had not educated her to be a martyr; he had educated her to be coldly rational. It was nonsense to think of such things. More than anything else she could say of him, Father Antonin had not and could not have educated her for such a life as this.

†

Another priest, younger than Father Antonin and with a fair complexion that betrayed his Northern lineage, stood some distance from the marketplace and watched help-lessly as the latest crop of captives was herded there like livestock. Having endured the triumphant cruelty of the locals, they were as quiet and compliant as sheep and stood in mute despair awaiting the next ordeal as though they did not care for a moment what happened to them. They were all ragged, he noted, eyes glazed with exhaustion and hunger, and some of the more spirited ones were bruised and bleeding. As to their origins, the latest arrivals almost all looked too dark to be European, and he could not immediately guess their race, whereas the others who had come in shortly before were clearly Northerners.

In the long years Father Pierre Dan of the Trinitarian Fathers had spent ransoming and ministering to captives, there remained no more horrible sight than that of an innocent human soul being sold to the highest bidder. Even a bloody execution for all its cruelty and pain ended in an act of liberation for the poor unfortunate, but being sold was the most demeaning and the most hopeless of situations. The more valuable the slave was deemed to be, the harder he was to ransom and the more of a drain he was on the Order's meagre funds. The higher-ranking slaves might be ransomed by their own families or influential friends, but the poorer ones had no other hope than the Trinitarian priests of being bought out of slavery. Skilled slaves would fetch a higher price than the unskilled, women, particularly very young girls, a vastly inflated sum that might compare with the wages a man earned in a lifetime.

He had never doubted the importance of the work he and his brothers did; ransoming slaves was as old a work of mercy as Christendom itself, but a sense of struggling against a relentless enemy haunted him wherever he went. His friends would have reminded him that there were limits to every human act, but he had only one response to that. There are limits to me, to my strength and to my resources, but there is no limit to the need. The ships came and went, returning with their cargoes of people, more and more with each passing year, and for every soul they redeemed, thousands were left languishing in the bagnos of the city, doomed to a brief life of misery and despair.

He watched as a group of men were paraded before potential buyers. The men were stripped naked so that their every muscle could be surveyed and examined, and they were forced to run and jump around to demonstrate their agility. The accepted purpose was for buyers to be given the chance to check a slave's fitness, but in truth it was as much an act of ritual humiliation as anything else. The banter used to encourage a sale was reminiscent of a vegetable market: "Come and buy! Look at this fine figure of a man!" All meant to demean; all meant to instil the belief in these people that they were worthless and undeserving of any respect.

He tried to calculate, by looking at each of them in turn, how long they would last in the galleys or quarries before they succumbed to illness or exhaustion. The younger ones might have some years in them, but a few, taken from poorer areas, already looked a little too thin for safety. It was all too easy for a judgment made at a distance to be mistaken anyway. He had once tried to raise a ransom for a young merchant who had been of such powerful build that he could have carried Father Dan on his shoulders, and Father Dan was by no means a diminutive man. But by the time he had collected the necessary funds, the man was skeletal after months of starvation and did not have the strength so much as to sit himself up when the priest had entered the room. He had died two days later, still a slave. In his own words, there was little purpose in redeeming him by then.

In another corner of the market, a young boy was being taken away from his father. They had almost inevitably been sold separately, and Father Dan knew that it was unlikely they would ever see one another again. There was a good deal of shouting and protesting from both of them, the father trying to hold onto the boy's arm whilst striking out uselessly at his abductors with the other. Father Dan found himself looking away as the child was yanked out of his father's grasp and hauled out of sight, screaming until the sound of his voice was drowned by the noise of the market.

Father Dan began to move toward the man, who had thrown himself into the dust and begun howling like an animal, but his way was blocked, as it so often was. The child was dead to him, thought Father Dan, and perhaps he knew—or at least guessed—the purpose for which the boy had been bought, how he would be abused and broken in the days that followed. In ten years' time, if either of them lived so long, they would not recognise one another even if they met, but for the moment the father was a distraught wreck of a man with the smell and the touch and the sight of his son still hovering around him.

Father Dan looked around for a distraction and saw what appeared at first to be another boy about to meet the same fate, though this one was alone. Like the others, he was dishevelled and had sustained minor injuries, but there was something striking about him that singled him out. His hair had an unusually strong strain of red in it, which made his face look as though it were framed by fire, but it was more his demeanour that attracted Father Dan's interest. He wore a look of cold defiance that somehow did not match his passionate colouring, but it gave him a quiet dignity, as though no crass act against him could really

touch him. It was only when they began trying to force
him to remove his shirt that he became actively resistant,
and it soon became apparent why.

The boy was a young woman who must have disguised
herself in male dress to escape violation, not realising in
her innocence perhaps that a boy might be bought for the
same purpose. The men howled with laughter all around
her, but she quite resolutely hung on to her self-possession,
refusing to react until one of them became impatient with
her and pushed her backwards, sending her tumbling onto
the ground. He marvelled that she could still retain such
grace, sprawling in the dust partially undressed, but she
seemed quite determined not to be broken. She has the
armour of a survivor, he thought, if she only knows how
to fight to her best advantage.

†

Perpetua felt herself being hauled to her feet, though she
was in such a trancelike state by then that she could scarcely
be sure she was still alive. She had been so frightened
and appalled by the slave market that she had tried to put
the horror of the scene from her mind. Father Antonin
had taught her to do that, if she found herself confront-
ing a particularly horrific accident or disease. The trick
was to concentrate on the necessary detail of that precise
moment: the broken wrist, not the whole mangled, broken
body; the bleeding woman, not the baby born dead and
the frightened family occupying the dark, squalid room.
As other captives, many of whom she knew, were similarly
humiliated and sold, she had glanced down at her hands,
concentrating her mind on the many lines that ran across
her palms.

When she was pushed forward and she felt thousands
of tiny needles prickling through her hands and feet, she
told herself that she would find some way to escape before
she was taken away. All the buyers looked the same to her,
all forbidding, vicious, threatening—or so she imagined—
and in her mind she robbed them of any humanity in the
same way that they denied it to the slaves they inspected.
She saw only enemies everywhere and searched for the
necessary distracting detail to stop herself from blushing
as she struggled to prevent them from undressing her. Her
eyes focused on a patch of heat haze in the distance as she
stood unflinching, derisive laughter all around her, and
hands wandered about her body: across her breasts, through
her hair, into her mouth to check that she still had all her
teeth. It almost came as a relief when she was thrown down,
shattering her brief daydream. At least she felt shielded from
view by the ground; it was during the few minutes she
was down that she dared to consider the possibility—the
smallest, most desperate possibility that she might escape.

The first buyer disappeared but was quickly replaced by
another customer. She stared directly ahead of her and tried
to slip away again, but she found it impossible to ignore the
conversation going on over her head. "Her hair is a mess."

"But how soft and luscious it is!" She almost wished
her native tongue were not so similar to theirs so that she
would not have the indignity of hearing all this. "And did
you ever see such a dazzling colour?"

The buyer used an expression Perpetua did not understand; there was more unsavoury laughter, then a hand
forced its way into her mouth again. He was a little too
rough, and the disgusting sensation of fingers almost touching the back of her throat made her retch and bite, causing
the buyer to roar with pain and back away. She had drawn

blood, she thought, with what was almost satisfaction, then she was struck down again, though at least this time she was permitted to dress herself before she was dragged to her feet. "Come on now, think how exciting she would be." In her innocence it did not immediately occur to Perpetua what was being suggested. "Could you not tame such an enchanting creature?"

It was perhaps unfortunate for Perpetua that in her mounting panic she did not catch the rest of the conversation. "I do not want her to enchant anyone; she is not fit to be anything other than a domestic."

"Oh come now, look how striking she is! What big eyes! What flaming hair!"

"She is no great beauty, and she is too old for such a purpose. She will be troublesome, cavorting about in a man's clothes. By rights she should be put to death."

All she heard in her confusion was the threat of violation, and she knew beyond doubt that she had to escape, that it was worth the substantial risk to make what might be her last chance of freedom. She realised as the men talked that she had a narrow passage of time to make a break for it whilst they were distracted, completing the payment, but she could not afford to make a mistake. The timing had to be perfect: a moment too soon and they would realise her intention, a moment too late and her new masters would have focused their attention on her again. She watched until the two men were looking away from her, passing currency one to the other, then she drew a sharp breath, gave her new master a shove, and ran.

The moment it was done there could be no going back; she threw herself forward with all her remaining energies. She knew that she could not outrun a man and tried instead to make herself disappear, slipping through the crowded streets of the market in the hope that her pursuers would take a wrong turn sooner or later and lose sight of her. She had been lithe enough once, always running from one errand to the next with the sun beating down on her uncovered head, but it felt so different now that she needed to run without slowing down for a moment. She had been kept in cramped conditions for too long, crammed aboard a ship and then in a bagno; her limbs felt stiff and sore as though she were heavily chained, and she felt giddy with the effort, but she knew she could not stop.

She had fallen into the dreamlike world again, whose sights and sounds were bewildering and intoxicating. It seemed to her that she had left the gates of hell behind her and fallen into a hinterland of spice and colour where she might still win her soul back if she could only find a hiding place, but she could not shake off her pursuers. It did not occur to her that the mop of red-streaked hair the trader had used to tempt bidders made her conspicuous even in this crowded, colourful place and she might have had a flag tied to her body bidding them to follow her wherever she went.

She lost count of how many corners she turned, how many people she pushed past. Nothing mattered except her need to stay out of reach, as though everything around her were a mere fresco she was running through, and she and her new masters were the only human beings left alive in the whole world. She looked over her shoulder again and again, but they were always there, not quite close enough to reach her but too close to lose sight of her. She was surrounded by enemies; any number of people could have stopped her, but by some miracle she simply slipped past them, as though they were too shocked to act or she had bewitched them.

She turned another corner and found herself facing a blank wall, but in her desperation she refused to believe that she was trapped. Without thinking, she threw herself at it and used her last remaining strength to climb up, avoiding their hands by inches.

"Get down!" shouted the elder of the two, then something else that she did not understand but she suspected was a warning. She did not need a warning. The wall was thick and wide enough to stand on safely, but when she looked down she could see clearly that the drop was far too steep to be jumped. If she threw herself down she would certainly suffer a broken neck. She looked back at them and realised that their demeanour had changed considerably. They were no longer simply angry and breathless; they were anxious that she would fall and deprive them of the object they had paid for. And she was not afraid of them any longer, because she knew that she had the power to escape them and the life they had chosen for her. She was still free and her life was her own. They would never touch her again; they would never, could never, do her any harm.

"I will throw myself down!" she called out before she turned her back on them once and for all. It was so easy. She had simply to do nothing, to let every muscle in her body go limp, and she would fall ... she would fall ...

Pierre Dan Remembers

It was no idle threat she made as she stood there, with hell yawning beneath her feet. It is likely she did not care that she would damn herself by stepping into that dreadful void; she was simply too tired and too frightened to live. It is hard to explain to those who have never witnessed slavery or been forced to bear it, how it must feel to know that there is no way out and that if one survived the torments that would have to be endured for trying to escape, what remained afterward was a lifetime of servitude with no hope of redemption. To such poor unfortunates, particularly one as young as that, slavery must indeed seem to be the beginnings of eternal damnation. But nevertheless, she hesitated to go through with the act, because it is a terrible thing to die at one's own hands.

They could not reach her to force her down without risking her throwing herself off simply to escape their hands. It was with some regret that I answered their request to minister to her, knowing as I did that they cared nothing for her soul, merely the loss of a chattel. I had seen her take flight and knew she would not get far—indeed I was astonished at how far she did manage to run—but she had not perhaps known the risk she was taking or was desperate enough after the horrors of the slave market to try anything.

I did not know what language people of her race spoke, so I tried several languages with her—Spanish, French,

Italian, which she seemed to recognise but refused to respond to—and it was only when I tried Latin that to my great surprise she gave me an answer, telling me that she had been taught the language when she was a child. She spoke though as if the words burnt her tongue, and I thought that it must remind her of freedom and her past life, but if I was to gain her trust I needed her to know that I belonged to her world, not that of her masters, and this was the language that bound us together.

"Come down", I said, as gently as I could, signalling for the other men to stand back a little. "Would you throw yourself into hell?"

"You ask me to choose between one hell and another", she said, coldly.

"I do, but there is redemption from this hell alone", I answered. "If you throw yourself to your death you will be beyond help."

"You look like an angel," she said, a little sadly, "all in white, with golden hair and blue eyes—an angel come to help me, but you cannot. I am already beyond your help."

I realised that her new masters did not understand the language we were speaking to one another. "Listen to me", I said, and she leant forward a little to hear what I had to say, which gave me some hope. "My brothers and I work to ransom Christian slaves. I cannot ransom you now—we have little money at this time—but I can help you if you will trust me."

"You cannot help me!" she shouted, in terrible fear that I knew all too well. "I am lost! They will butcher me in the marketplace!"

"No, they will not kill you", I said quickly. I had seen slaves put to death for repeatedly attempting to escape—the value of the slave being slightly less than the power of the deterrent as far as some were concerned—but I doubted that they would kill a young woman they must have paid a considerable sum to purchase only minutes before. "You will not die at their hands; why else would they have called upon me to stop you from ending your life?"

"I shall suffer for this."

"Yes, you will. You must prepare yourself for that, but you will not be killed. Trust me."

She looked at me in miserable resignation; I knew she felt that I had betrayed her somehow. "I cannot surrender to them", she whispered; "I am afraid."

I stepped forward and reached a hand up to her. "You must take courage; there is no other way. You cannot escape them now." She dropped to her knees on the wall; I thought she meant to come down, but she curled up into a ball and buried her head in her arms, like a little child who is afraid of the dark. It was almost unbearable to witness. I braced myself. "Come on, I know this is very hard, but you cannot stay where you are forever. If you come down now I may be able to intercede for you." *Be a good girl*, I was telling her, *do as you are told. Do as I tell you who am little better than they are.* Except that I knew if I had left her to end her life I would have been crueller than the most despotic of slave drivers, selling her into an eternal and terrible slavery in which there could be no consolation at all.

I could feel her trembling as I helped her down; it hurt my heart to have to lead her to the two men, whom I thought must be father and son. The elder must have bought her for the younger, I surmised, but it was too shameful to bear a momentary thought. "Do not leave me", she whispered; "I beg of you."

"I will stay with you as long as I may", I promised, but the futility of it haunted me. I had saved her life, but from this moment on I doubted that I would have the power to help her. There was no chance for me to offer her any words of comfort. The older man stepped forward and struck her hard across the face so that she was thrown out of my hands and onto the ground. I threw myself between them, pleading, "Stop! There is no call for that."

"Stand aside" came the only answer I could have expected. "You have done your work. What right have you to tell me what to do with my own property?"

I lowered my eyes for a moment and half-expected them to throw thirty pieces of silver at me. I am used to being constantly demeaned, working always on another's terms, but it is never easy to bear, still less to resist the temptation to hatred. And I did feel hate then, not so much for that vile, heartless man, but for myself and my own uselessness. "Will you allow me to walk as far as your home?" I asked, finally. "She will come more quietly that way."

It was as horrible as placing a rabbit into the claws of a hawk, but at least I was able to pick her up off the ground and wipe the blood from her mouth, and she did not come to any further harm for the rest of the journey with me walking by her side. Not that she would have noticed very much if she had; the girl was almost in a trance, and I had to hold her arms quite tightly to stop her from falling or simply stopping where she was until she was goaded into moving on.

I knew the signs; they all did that with unbearable haste. Virtually every slave I had ministered to fell all too quickly into that state of lethargic despair, brought on by fear and a sense that the case was hopeless. For her, it must have been the realisation that she was trapped and the shock of being struck with such violence that had brought it on. I could feel her retreating into her own mind so rapidly that if I could not drag her back she would soon care about nothing at all, even the hope of liberty.

When we entered the house, I noted that it was the dwelling place of a wealthy family, as I had known it would be. My keen eyes took in the evidence of an opulent life, the presence of other slaves, but she noted no detail of it. Worse, whereas such a short while before she would have resisted volubly, she lowered her head and made no response whatsoever as she was led unceremoniously away from my side. The words *Like a sheep that is dumb before its shearers* came into my mind as I followed them, but then I wondered whether she simply did not realise the danger she was in. I am not a man who is easily frightened, but I felt sick with anxiety, not so much because of what she might imminently have to face, but because it was far too soon for a person who had shown such courage and audacity to cease caring about her fate. In her mind she must still be standing on top of the wall yearning for death. Perhaps she did not care what they might do to her because she hoped it might still end in death.

"Do not do this", I pleaded, but the older man was already issuing orders to another slave, and my heart sank. The slave he spoke to was clearly a renegade, a man of European appearance—Italian or perhaps Spanish, I suspected—but his vast bulk was clothed in a way that signalled his change of identity. He was a man who, shortly after his capture, had "turned Turk", as we were wont to call it, either by force or because of the misguided belief that it would lead to better treatment or freedom, when what it normally led to was being despised by both sides. An ordinary slave ordered to hurt another would do so out of fear and then only with great reluctance, but renegades had loyalty to prove, guilt to torment them, and were notorious for being considerably more brutal toward Christian slaves than their own masters. If she were not granted clemency by her master she would receive no mercy whatsoever from this monstrous coward.

"Get out of my house", the master responded, turning his back on me. "What authority do you have to interfere?"

"No authority", I said. "I merely ask you to be merciful to this woman. No real harm has been done; let it pass."

He turned back to look at me. He was a fine figure of a man, I thought, far handsomer than the young man and standing very steadily on his feet for his age, but his eyes were as cold as a Flanders winter. "She deserves a great deal worse for fleeing so publicly, running around the streets in a man's dress like some whore. I could strangle her with my bare hands. I could have her killed in front of you and who on earth would concern themselves?"

"I cannot answer for why she is dressed as she is, but she ran because she was frightened and did not think about the consequences. She will not run from you again; you have no cause to do her any harm." There was something about her that tugged at my heart. I had pleaded and negotiated on behalf of others so many times, but having persuaded her to live I felt responsible for the terrible danger she was in. I should have recognised that the situation was hopeless, but instead I continued to argue with greater passion than was usual for me. As we argued, she stood with her head bowed, shaking noticeably, but she seemed simply too tired to stop herself; the renegade stood some distance away, twisting and clenching his hands together as though he could hardly bear the delay in setting to work.

"I would be a little more inclined to listen to you if her escape had not been so public and I had not suffered the indignity of running after her myself. I will not be made a laughing stock." I opened my mouth to speak again but was abruptly cut off. "Do not vex yourself, friar, I will be merciful. I will not let him do her any lasting harm, since she is a woman after all. You may trust me on that point."

I looked back at the girl, who was still making no attempt at resistance of any kind, but I could hear her breathing in short, gasping motions. She seemed so frail then that I could have believed she would shatter into a thousand pieces at the first stroke. I had witnessed and recorded so much suffering, and this would be yet one more incident to tell our people far away in their safe homes. I knew that I should leave before he began tormenting her, in spite of my promise not to leave her alone; every inner voice told me to flee from an act I could not prevent—but all the same I found when it came to it that I could not accept it. And so it was that I found myself saying, "Please allow me to take her place."

I am not certain now precisely what reaction I had expected, but both the master and the renegade burst into derisive laughter. "This is madness", said the master; "how can you suggest such a thing for a person you barely know?"

"Because I am a man and I am a priest", I said slowly, but in truth it did not seem to be I who was speaking. I did not know myself. "She did not choose to be a slave or to suffer, but I have chosen a kind of slavery, and I can choose to suffer if you will allow me to stand in her place."

More laughter; I felt myself reddening in spite of myself. "Madness, true madness."

"I would call it compassion", I responded, but to my great relief I saw the master give a nod, and the girl was pushed to one side.

She came to life in an instant. "No!" she shouted at me; "you will not suffer for me!"

"Remove her; she should not witness this", I said, unable to look at her, but she rushed forward and grasped my wrist before they could stop her. She had the pride of Simon Peter, I thought. "Come now, show a little humility", I said, a little more sternly than I had meant, but it did not occur to her that I was afraid. "Why are you fearful of an act of love?"

She was weeping. "I will not let you bleed for me. The fault is *mine*." She continued to protest as they dragged her out of sight, and in my own pride, I hoped that she was out of hearing before the first blow was dealt and I found it quite impossible to remain silent.

The Life and Times of Pierre Dan (2)

Perpetua sat in the entrance of the house and cried until her body ached. She was a proud soul, just as he had suspected, and it seemed to her then that she could have borne the agony and indignity far better than the knowledge of being in a man's debt—and such a debt, one that she could never hope to repay. When he finally appeared at her side, her physician's eye noticed immediately that he was limping slightly and the muscles in his face were taut beneath pallid flesh. "Why?" she asked him. "Why did you do that?"

You are most welcome, he thought, grimly, but fortunately it was a long time before he found his voice. "To save your soul a second time."

"I would have taken it. I can take *anything*. I am not a coward."

"No, I do not think you are, thank heaven. God has blessed you with fortitude." He got down on his knees, wincing almost invisibly. "But you were in despair again."

"I cannot help it."

"You must. The choice you made today you will have to make every day, whatever happens to you. Can I trust you to do so?"

"I will try." She could not look at him. "No one will be able to ransom me, Father; I am from a poor people. You will not ransom me either—there are too many who need it more."

He held her face in his hands so that she had to look at him. "I may not be able to ransom you," he whispered, "but if our paths cross again, I swear to you that I will find some way to help you escape."

†

That was the real madness, he thought to himself as he made his way home, his coarse habit chafing his back with every step. What in heaven had possessed him to promise such a thing? It would be quite impossible, the risk greater than a reasonable man could ever countenance. *It was of little consequence anyway*, he consoled himself; *it was unlikely that she would ever find a safe way to escape her master's house.* She had given herself the reputation of a troublemaker by trying to slip away before her master had even brought her home, and they would be watching for the slightest warning of insubordination from now on. He hoped that he had not inadvertently encouraged her to make another escape attempt, as they might well kill her after a second offence. "Whatever made me say it?" he demanded out loud. "Dear God, I am becoming a lordly fool!"

"You are a lordly fool", declared Father Jerome, Pierre's brother priest. "What possessed you to do such a thing?"

Jerome had noticed that Pierre was injured the moment he stepped through the door, and he had demanded to attend him. After a good deal of arguing, Pierre was lying on his bed facedown whilst his comrade covered his wounds with wet rags. "I cannot quite explain it", he whimpered. The pain was abominable, all the more so for his brother's ministrations. "She looked so sad and helpless."

"Will you pay the penalty for every slave who comes to grief?" Shock made him sound angrier than he felt, but he was appalled by the state his friend was in. "They cut you to the bone. This will take weeks to heal, and you will always carry the scars."

"It was some renegade who did it. There is no one quite as vicious and bloodthirsty as a European gentleman in a corner." He struggled to breathe through another explosion of pain, then relaxed a little. "That was what really hurt. The man was laughing, and all the time, all I could think was, *But he is a baptised Christian. He was carried into church long ago as a tiny infant. How many times in his youth did he kneel before a priest like me for Communion or a blessing? Did it mean so little to him in the end?*"

"You know how fear may work its wicked magic on a man. Just be thankful his mother will never know what he has become."

"In answer to your question," said Pierre slowly, "I always wish that I could take it, and today I could. It just happened. So I did."

"You have made a fool of yourself", Jerome persisted. "You have suffered for nothing. Do you honestly imagine they would have done anything quite so vicious to a woman they had bought?"

"It looked very likely to me. It was all very threatening."

"I am sure they threatened; they were probably trying to see how easily frightened she was, but she didn't break, did she? She would have gotten off much more lightly than this, I can promise you that."

All Pierre desired was to be left alone. On top of the pain, he felt an unbearably familiar sense of futility. "I was not prepared to take the risk that they would do her serious harm," he said and knew he sounded ridiculous, "or any harm for that matter. She had already been hurt and frightened by so many people, I thought, *that's enough now. Why can't you leave her alone?"*

"You should have had a care for your position", scolded Jerome, as unrelenting as any torturer. "You have lowered yourself in their eyes, allowing yourself to be beaten and humiliated like ... like ..."

"Christ?" He tried to rise but was racked with pain and fell back. "If you had been there you would have understood. It ... it just happened."

Jerome shook his head sadly. "I am the lordly fool. And you can pierce a man's soul without ever raising your voice." He distracted himself. "You have had a shock. You should rest now."

Pierre felt a thin covering being placed over him and closed his eyes. He felt tired and wretchedly guilty. A slave, he thought, would not be cared for with such diligence and allowed time to rest and recover. In the cool quiet of the room, Pierre nestled his head in the crook of his arm and gave a long, deep sigh. *There are only limits to myself,* he thought; *there are only limits to myself.*

Two Households

It is the first time since I found myself in this strange land that I have felt no pain. Perhaps they have given me something, some cordial I do not remember drinking, to make me feel warm and comfortable. Or perhaps it is the numbness of shock still protecting me. I begin to recognise the different people, not just the lady and the priest who dresses like a gentleman, but the servants—a young girl with a voice that chirps like a little bird; an older woman, fat, white-haired, who attends me at night. When darkness comes and I begin to tire, she gathers the bedclothes around me, then she makes a bed for herself nearby and puts out the candles, prattling away in her language. I like hearing people talk, even when I do not understand them; the flow of words dispels the thoughts and memories I cannot otherwise escape.

This chamber is made to be warm, a sturdy, enclosed world with definite perimeters, the strong walls lined with wood and a place for a fire when the bitter chill of winter comes. The people are dressed to be modest and strengthened against the cold that seems to come to this land whatever the season. It is a world away from the house where I was taken as a slave, an airy labyrinth of rooms built to shelter us from the blazing sun and to capture the slightest of summer breezes—a house built for a barren land, not for an island of green places, where I learnt once again what it meant to be the unwilling inhabitant of an unwelcoming household. But unlike the family home I had so easily avoided as a child, I knew already that there could be no easy ways to escape from here.

After Father Dan had left me alone there, a woman who I realised must be the mother of the household—Munira, I later discovered she was called—ordered one of the slaves who attended her to take me to the women's quarters so that I could wash and more suitable clothes could be found for me to wear. I was filthy from the voyage and the chase, covered in sweat and dirt, and it was a blessed relief to feel the cool water slipping through my hair. The woman who had taken charge of me was old enough to be my mother and, to begin with, was completely silent, gesturing to me that she wanted me to undress or lean forwards. She was quite gentle with me as she dressed me and took away my old clothes, which were already ragged, though I had owned them such a short time. *All will be well now*, a little voice told me; *the curse of a dead man will be lifted now that you have stripped off the clothes you had no right to take.* But almost as soon as I thought this, I heard Father Antonin chiding me for thinking such superstitious nonsense. It would surely take more than a change of clothes to rescue me from the most accursed predicament I could possibly have fallen into.

The woman noticed that I was so maddened by thirst that I kept trying to drink the water she was pouring over me; she commanded me to stop when I began sucking the droplets of water from my own skin in sheer desperation. When I was washed and clothed, she gave me water to drink, but I was so parched that I choked in my haste to drink deeply.

"Slowly, slowly", she said; "hold the water in your mouth a little first." A shudder of giddy ecstasy. I thought I would have taken great gulps of water for eternity if I had been permitted to, but she soon stopped me. "Enough for now or you will sicken. More later." A round of unleavened bread was placed into my hand. I thought for a moment of Marija laying out crusty, coarse, warm Maltese bread on the table, but it is hard to be hungry and wistful for very long. I offered up a prayer of thanks and ate.

†

In the days that followed I was confined to a corner of the entrance to the house. I say confined, but I was not forced to stay there; I was simply told not to stray from that place, and I was too weary and anxious to question anything by then. It must have been a way of making me familiar with the goings on of the house, allowing me to sit on a bench and watch people coming and going about their business, but I also supposed that I was in disgrace, as I never seemed to be out of some person's sight, even at night when I lay down on the bare ground with the other serving women and struggled to sleep. I sensed that I was always being watched, particularly by the renegade who stalked the house like a disgruntled sentry, constantly seeking trouble.

There were others—the master, whose name I never knew and whom I seldom saw in those early days except when my renegade friend found some way to incriminate me. Even then, it was never for more than a few moments as the renegade seemed to have the happy task of dealing with the other slaves. The master's son resembled his weaker aspects, so much so that I felt sickened by the sight of him and everything their figures stood for. I had been touched and struck by so many men on my road into slavery whose faces I could not now recall, but there

had been something especially cowardly about these men,
striking as they did when I had already surrendered myself
into their hands and there was no need for them to subdue
me in any way. Father Antonin would never have—but
even thinking of my beloved tutor in such a place felt like
blasphemy. Father Antonin would have been as lost in this
household as I was.

Then there were women; three women slaves in particular I remember: one of middling years, whom I took to be
a housekeeper of some kind, another some years younger,
of the same race as she, I thought, and very close to her.
The third was the eldest and seemed to hold a higher rank
in the almost invisible hierarchy in which we all lived. The
old mother, Munira, was housed on the upper floor and
rarely approached me after our first encounter. She was fat
with age and comfortable living, but had a faded look about
her. She was always beautifully dressed, but everything
she wore seemed almost as though it had been deliberately
spoiled before she put it on. I could not make it out, but
then nothing made very much sense to me.

In the upper apartments there also lived another woman,
a thin, pale-looking girl, whom I only rarely glimpsed if
I was sent to give her something. She was clearly not a
slave—or so I thought at the time—but she never spoke in
my presence and seemed always lost in her own thoughts.
I often wondered who she was as I lay awake at night, but
soon stopped asking the other serving women questions, as
they seemed withdrawn and a little suspicious of me, barely
acknowledging my presence even when we settled down
together at night. They would not even answer when I
asked where the sound of a crying baby came from.

A black slave, a Muslim called Abdullah, was permitted
to talk to me when he came to give me water and scraps of

bread during the day, and to teach me what I must expect of my new life. Men and women so seldom came anywhere near one another in the house, but he seemed to me to be very old, and I thought he must be trusted to behave properly to women. "You will eat better soon", he promised, because I would gobble up every crumb he gave me and could not help looking up expectantly for more. "Master is still angry with you. It will pass." But before long he was bringing portions of his own food to share with me: little pieces of fruit; morsels of couscous wrapped in my bread.

"You will get into trouble", I protested; "someone will notice."

"I do not want you to suffer where I can prevent it; I do not want you to hate my people", he whispered. "We are different races and different faiths, but God knows we belong to him."

It was from Abdullah that I learnt about the renegade, that he was an Italian they had named Ahmed after his conversion, but whose real name had been Salvatore. "A man from a good family, they say, though not of any great wealth," said Abdullah, "a passenger on board a vessel that was captured—a coward and a weakling, an indulged only son." It was rumoured that he had betrayed his own people before they had even been removed from the ship. For all his vast stature the pirates had known that he was the passenger who would be most easily broken, as he had been thrown into panic as soon as they appeared. They had held him at knifepoint and threatened to cut his throat if he did not answer their questions; he was like a lamb, bleating and trembling, his face bloodless with terror. The other travellers, his fellow countrymen, watched helplessly as he quickly told their captors which of them had the higher status and would be of most value to them, who was possessed of the greatest wealth, and which of them was a diplomat from the Vatican, a man in holy orders who was in most danger of all. There was no secret he was not prepared to divulge in exchange for his own miserable life; he was the most despised of men by the time they came ashore.

"And he has been despised ever since", said Abdullah. "Do you suppose I can respect a man who abandoned all he held sacred and mouthed the Shahadah out of ungodly fear? He is nothing. He is such a coward; the abdal told me he burst into tears and fell into a faint when they circumcised him." That was one detail I thought I might have been spared, but I struggled to suppress a giggle. "The master knows he is cruel and bitter; he uses him, knowing that he will report the least fault he can find in any of us."

I could so easily imagine him as Abdullah described him, on his knees aboard that ship, the blade of a scimitar pressing against his throat. I could see him—white-faced, tearful, a shameful wreck of a man, determined ever after to reduce anyone in his power to the same state of miserable cowardice. "I cannot be afraid of such a creature", I said.

"He will make you afraid", warned Abdullah. "He is a monster."

During the early weeks of my captivity, I thought that my life would be almost tolerable if it were not for Salvatore. When my master felt that I had learnt my lesson, I was put to work about the house. I was still fed very little, but my simple upbringing had made me strong enough to endure a poor diet, and Abdullah continued to share his food with me in spite of my protestations that he should not go hungry himself or take such a risk on my behalf. "I do not go hungry," he promised, "not really. I am given plenty to eat."

I was used to serving others, so I did not feel ashamed of the work. I would quickly have stopped resenting my unfortunate position in life if it had not been for Salvatore. In a perverse way I may have reason to thank him, as his unspeakable behaviour prevented me from accepting slavery as easily as I might otherwise have done. Almost as though I had angered him by escaping him that first time, he looked for every opportunity to settle the score. If he saw me carrying water, he would cause me to fall so that he could punish me for spilling water and breaking the vessel I was carrying. If he found me cleaning the floor, he would step all over it as soon as I had finished and moved on to the next task, covering it with dust and dirt so that it would look as though I had been too lazy to wash it at all.

Abdullah was right, of course—only a madman would not have feared a person whose only joy in life was to make misery for others—but all I can say in my defence is that I must already have been quite mad by then, as I lost my fear of him. After all, I had a weapon of my own that was more brutal than any he had at his disposal, and I used it whenever I fell foul of him. I had only to say three words to wound him to the heart: "Salvatore, you coward!" and I could say it in his own language because Father Antonin had spoken Italian; it was one more gift of his that I could abuse.

"This is madness!" protested Abdullah. "He hates you enough without you provoking his anger. Why are you tempting him like this? It is like poking a scorpion with your fingers."

"He would do it anyway", I said; "I only call him that when he attacks me. If he will do battle with me, I will be the victor."

"A bloodied victor."

"Certainly, but to whom may I complain? What does my master care if I am bullied and humiliated for no good reason? What does any man alive care? Let him behave as he will, but I will draw a little blood of my own."

It was not Christian, and I knew it was not. I would not have fancied accounting for my behaviour to Father Antonin, but the world of priests and churches and confession and forgiveness already seemed a little alien to me. "You are playing a foolish game that will cost you your life", warned Abdullah.

"He will not kill me."

"No, he may not, but if you continue to displease your master, he will soon grow impatient, and you may be sold on to who knows what kind of a life. Or much worse than that."

"But I cannot help it!" Now I was being made to account for my actions to Abdullah. "I cannot stop this; he is determined to destroy me because he could not destroy me before. I have more than made up for the blows I escaped then, I assure you!"

The only answer Abdullah could give was to look wearily at me, but what I did not know yet was that he had gone secretly to the master's son on my behalf, thinking that the young man might listen to him. Omar was very attached to Abdullah and felt great affection for him, as Abdullah had had the task of caring for him throughout his childhood. According to Abdullah, however, Omar refused to believe that Salvatore was doing anything wrong when his own father trusted him, but he swore that he would watch Salvatore's actions more closely from then on and intervene if there was a suggestion that he had behaved unjustly.

It was fortunate I did not know immediately what Abdullah was doing on my behalf, or I would have made the mistake of becoming hopeful again when I had no cause to be. There was never cause for hope, whatever Father Dan had suggested, and in a world without hope there should have been no fear either, even the fear of a violent death. I already knew that there were worse fates than death, even murder at the hands of a master who thought me too lazy, too clumsy, too insubordinate to keep alive. And remembering it all now, I still believe that it might have been better if I had been killed like that in an outburst of temper. That way I could not have lived to regret—but there is so much, so very much, that I have lived to regret.

Perpetua Becomes Warda the Physician Again

When old Munira stepped into the room, she was so startled to discover Abdullah sitting with a young girl in his arms, she barely noticed that his prize appeared to be unconscious. Abdullah was entirely distracted and did not notice her standing nearby watching him, or he would have been terrified to be caught in such a compromising situation. She opened her mouth to demand that he take his filthy hands off the girl immediately, but he so evidently meant no harm by it that she stopped herself.

The girl looked deathly white in his arms, so small and delicate that she might have been a child; he held her very carefully, rocking her back and forth as though lulling her to sleep. Munira stepped a little closer to them, causing him to look up with a start, and she saw that there were tears tracing sorry patterns down his face. "Abdullah, what are you doing?" she asked, rather more gently than she had anticipated.

"I meant no harm", he said quickly; "forgive me."

"What has happened?"

Abdullah bowed his head immediately and returned his attention to the girl in his arms. "Master can tell you", he said quietly.

"He could, but I have asked you what happened", she persisted. "Why are you weeping?" He kept his head firmly

down. In the long years Abdullah had served her household, she had never once seen him weep nor ever known
him to refuse to speak to her. "Why is that girl unconscious? What have you done to her?"

"Truly, my lady, I did not intend this!" he spluttered.
"I was trying to *help* her." His hand stroked her hair, the
gentlest, most loving of gestures. "She was hungry and I
pitied her, so I shared my food with her. Then Ahmed
caught her with a date in her hand, and she said she had
stolen it so that no one would know I had helped her."

She smiled. She knew, as perhaps even Abdullah did not
acknowledge, that the greatest deprivation he had suffered
in a life of servitude had been the freedom to father children of his own. She could quite imagine how his heart
would have ached for such a creature, who was just the
sort of age his own children would have been had they
ever existed, and how he would have allowed himself to
go hungry to give her the nourishment he believed she
needed. She felt sorrier at that moment for the lonely years
of old age that stretched out before him than for the years
the girl might never see. "Well? What did they do?"

"He struck her," he said, "only once, and she fell into
a faint." He pressed a hand against her cheek, where a red
patch was already beginning to fade. "She will wake soon.
It is hard to say this of him, but really it was not that bad;
he did not strike so hard. It was only that she was hot and
thirsty and rather tired. The sudden shock must have struck
her down."

Munira's eyes narrowed, but he was still not looking at
her. "Attend to her until she comes to herself", she ordered;
"then give her water. I will return as soon as I may."

†

What Perpetua did not know, in her state of blessed oblivion, was that someone else had spied her being held by Abdullah: a young man she already despised, but whose thoughts were a little warmer toward her. Omar had thought very little of her when he first saw her at the market, but glimpsing her now, so pale and silent, he felt the strangest stirrings of jealousy at the thought of an old slave enjoying such intimacy with her.

"Did you hurt her, Abdullah?" he asked, kneeling to take a closer look at her and noting the mark on her cheek. "Surely not!"

"No, indeed", Abdullah protested; "I could not have done such a thing."

"Of course you could not", he acknowledged, sitting next to Abdullah. It was no good; his hand itched to touch her cold, white face, and he indulged himself. "Come now, Abdullah, you are shaking! It does no harm. She does not notice." His hand strayed to her hair, which he half-expected to be hot to the touch. "Even if she woke she could hardly mind me. Everyone else is so harsh with her."

†

By the time Perpetua awoke, Omar had gone, and she would never know that he had knelt by her side and worshipped her. She became aware instead that something cold and wet was pressing against her face and distant voices were muttering around her. As the light of day returned, she looked up and noticed old Munira standing over her, whilst the slave who had helped her to wash and dress that first day leaned over her, pressing a cold cloth against her neck. She felt the slightest tenderness along one side of her face, but when she brought her hand up to her cheek to search for the cause of it, it was carefully pushed back. "It is all right; it is nothing", said Munira, patting the girl's arm. "What is your name?"

"Perpetua", she answered, but the woman looked confused. She had had so many names that the question hardly seemed important anymore, but she had to be called some name. She was about to try Ursula but thought they might not understand that name either, and in any case, she had only ever been Ursula to a family who never loved her, and Perpetua belonged to a life she had barely lived out long enough to call her own. "My name is Warda", she said, then felt the ache of homesickness all around her. The very word conjured up Father Antonin's workshop and the smell of old books and the long, happy days spent learning the physician's art.

The woman obviously recognised the name and smiled. "Warda; that's beautiful. Very well."

Warda was distracted by the sound of a baby crying again. "Baby cries a lot", she said.

"Baby is very sick", answered Munira.

Warda turned to the slave for assistance and rose to her feet. All things were clearer now. Her head was clear, and she could hear a baby close to her, who could cry and make its distress known to the world and still be safe—a baby like the one she had so lovingly saved, only for it to be savagely killed minutes later.

She walked toward the sound. That was why it was so much clearer; Munira must have ordered for her to be carried up the stairs, and the child was in the next room— a sick child with a sad, rasping, irregular cry. She stood in the doorway and looked into the room where it lay, with Munira following closely behind. She turned to Munira. "Let me care for him."

"You cannot", said Munira. "His mother cares for him, and there is no more to be done."

Warda looked back into the room. She could see the girl she had seen walking around before, holding an infant she guessed to be no more than six months old. The girl was very young, younger than she, Warda suspected, but she seemed older, moving with such a sad dignity that she barely acknowledged Warda's presence when she tumbled inside. "Forgive me", she muttered, turning to leave again, but Munira stood behind her chuckling.

"It is of no consequence", said Munira kindly. In truth it should have been of very great consequence, but Munira was curious to see how the two women would react to one another. Standing face-to-face, Munira thought they could be the two most different women in the entire world. Hala was graceful, beautiful, and careful of her every move, a girl who had submitted to slavery with little more than a whimper and had accepted everything: her role as a concubine, the need to convert, the death of her master and protector some months before the birth of their child. She had been captured young enough that little moved her now, not loneliness, not grief, not fear—even the fear of losing her child.

Warda, on the other hand, was striking but not beautiful, with her passionate features that promised a fiery soul and her quick, unpredictable manner that had an almost animal quality to it. She was a creature who could accept nothing and would have to be broken at every turn. "Child needs a physician", said Warda; "let me care for him."

"The child has seen many physicians and healers", said Munira, a little impatiently. "Come away now; leave Hala in peace. She has everything she could need." Warda hovered, drawn irresistibly toward the fretful child. "I told you to come away. You should not have trespassed."

"I am a physician", Warda persisted; Munira was amazed that she was prepared to be quite this impudent when hunger and ill-treatment had left her so weak. "Let me try."

Munira's every instinct told her to remove the girl from the room by force if necessary, but she was curious again. The child was their only link with the firstborn son who had sickened and died before the baby was delivered, and now the child sickened and had shown no signs of recovery for all the care that had been lavished on him. It was said that some Christians had the gift of healing that Jesus had, and she wondered whether this mysterious creature, who had entered her house so unwillingly, could do something to help the child where others had failed. She had some kind of power in her, wherever it came from, to compel a stranger to suffer so cruelly and so shamefully in her place, to move a hardened old slave to nourish her and weep for her, to cause such diabolical rage in another. She looked back at Hala—cool, shallow little Hala, around whom there was no mystery at all—and she wondered ... "Hala, let her hold the child for a while. You are weary."

Omar's Choice

"I will always be in your debt for this", promised Hala, when she held her baby in her arms again and the child no longer stared listlessly past her or gave the despairing wail she had become miserably accustomed to hearing. Hala could not help admitting to herself that she half-suspected Warda of sorcery, so mysterious did her healing powers appear to her. As she had prepared her remedies or attended the baby, Warda had chanted Latin prayers to herself that reminded her of home, but which Hala mistakenly imagined to be incantations. Hala had been abducted from her coastal village when she was nine years of age, and in the few short years that had passed, her early life in Spain already seemed like a bewildering dream that was never really hers. She could barely recall that her name had once been Juana, let alone the names of her mother and father, so it was hardly surprising that she found it impossible to recognise the words Warda sang. There was just enough familiarity in the sounds and tones that came out of her mouth to unsettle her.

Warda had no sense at all that Hala was disturbed or even threatened by her behaviour. She knew so little about the bond between a mother and her child, having never known such closeness to her own mother, that it did not occur to her she might be arousing jealousy in the other woman. She was too achingly close to home to notice anything, back in her role as a healer where she was treated once again with something like respect. More than that, she was powerful again. She was given whatever she needed: hot or cold water, clean cloths, the smallest item she requested would be found or bought.

Her greatest difficulty was that she mostly knew the names of herbs and medicinal substances in Latin and often had to describe precisely what she needed in tiny detail to be understood. She began to use the problem as a means of escaping the house, as it was simpler for her to accompany to the market whoever it was who had been called upon to run errands for her. That way she gained some knowledge of the layout of the town and hoped—she always hoped—that she would meet Father Dan again or one of the other friars, but she never did. *Not that they would know me if they saw me*, she thought, *covered up so that my closest friend would not recognise me. But I would notice one of them, and perhaps I could make my presence known somehow, cause a diversion* . . .

And the baby was a consolation that brought the tiniest of joys to her life: a baby, soft, helpless, with his mother's beautiful eyes, who shivered with fever in Warda's arms as though he had always belonged there. He would fall asleep in her arms, reassured by Warda's chanting; there he would stay, because Warda refused to be parted from the baby at night when the danger of death was greatest—she slept with him curled up beside her, so that she would awaken immediately if there was any change in his breathing.

It was almost painful to see the little soul recover, knowing as Warda did that when he got better she would have to relinquish the one human being with whom she could be loving and affectionate without having anything to fear. "Let me care for him always", she pleaded with Munira, when it became clear that the child had recovered. Warda thought that she might somehow learn to bear even slavery if it were for such a purpose.

"You may stay with him a little longer until it is certain that he is recovered, but he is not your child", said Munira, who by now had tired of repeating herself but could not bring herself to be angry with a girl who had nursed her grandchild back to health. "There is another purpose for you; you have nothing to fear. Indeed, you should be glad. Because you have shown yourself to be faithful in spite of your wild ways, you have earned a better life."

She did fear, certain that no life they could choose for her would be possible to bear, except freedom, which would never come. Knowing that she must soon leave the safety of the sickroom, she sought out Abdullah and summoned up the courage to ask him the question she most feared to have answered.

"You will know", he promised; "you will know before very much longer."

"Am I to be sold?" she asked. "Abdullah, you must tell me what you know!"

The silence before he spoke was almost unbearable. "You are a gift to the master's son", he said with great reluctance. "You have caught his eye."

She sprang to life. "You mean I was never meant for this?"

"Hush, you speak too loud!" He backed away from her. "No, not at all. The master did not think you a suitable possession for his son, but he has taken an interest in you."

"Then I might have escaped such a fate if he had not noticed me?" She looked so distressed that he turned his back on her and tried to walk away, but she grabbed his wrist and compelled him to turn back and look at her. "What have I done?"

"You could not help it", he began, but by the time he had finishing explaining what had happened he was shaking and stammering. He somehow managed to tell her how Omar had been so taken with the sight of her when she lay insensible in his arms that he had been unable to resist touching her; Abdullah had known, with the wisdom and knowledge of the old, that the young man was almost in love with her already. Then he had to tell her how Omar had found ways to spy on her as she sat in what she imagined to be the seclusion of the sickroom and felt intoxicated by the tender sight of her cradling a child in her arms; how he had yearned so painfully to be close to her, to touch her again as she kissed the baby's smooth round brow that he found excuses to follow at a distance when she was taken out to make her purchases, even though she was carefully covered and he saw only a shadowy figure floating before him.

"So I am to be given to him? It is as easy as that?" She was his for the taking, she thought; it was no different from her going out into the countryside and plucking a plant she thought would do well dried and crushed in a jar.

"He asked his father leave to take you as his slave. His father said—" He had to find a kind way to describe the horrible words the old man had used to describe Warda. "He said that he could find his son the finest girl ever to step onto these shores, whatever the price—a girl so young and fresh and beautiful that he would be dazzled by her and live always in the light and warmth of her presence." He had actually said: "Why would you want that creature I bought for a risible price, who is only fit to adorn a kitchen? A girl without allurements, who cannot boast of any great beauty at all and who is so wild that the trader would have *given* her to me if I had bargained for much longer, even though she is a woman and should have held some value even if just for that."

She did not need to know such things. He knew she would be distressed enough simply to hear so abruptly the purpose for which she was to be used. "I thought all along that this would be my fate", she whispered. "I knew I would be dishonoured in this way if I could not find some means of escape."

"You must not think of escape now if you value your life," warned Abdullah, "but be of stout heart. You have found favour with the master's son, and he is a good man. He will be a generous lover. You will not suffer hunger again, you will be clothed and fed with the greatest care, and he may take you as a wife if you are obedient and attentive to him."

†

Every night she prayed that she would be spared just one more night and begged God's forgiveness if she could not escape such a fate, as she would truly rather have died than submit herself to it. But they did not give her the choice of death, and they did not understand. Even Munira, who had begged her husband on Warda's behalf never to allow the renegade to touch her again, would not spare her a duty she could not see as evil. Warda knew that she owed her those few precious days of sanctuary she retained, but in the course of eternity they counted for so little. Munira's kindness counted for so little, Abdullah's tears counted for so little, except to remind her even then that there is no corner of the world where goodness may not be found. And she thought, long afterward, that she owed them her prayers and her remorse if only for that.

"Give me another night of safety," she continued to pray, "or let him change his mind. I will bear anything else. I will bear hunger and indignity and cruelty, but this I cannot bear." But when she placed the child back into his mother's arms for the last time, she knew that even a prayer could run its course and go unanswered.

Hala Remembers

She meant to harm me from the start. I knew as soon as I set eyes on her that she brought evil with her—that flaming red hair like a fire come to tear the house apart, the bringer of death and destruction. My destruction. A whispering sorceress with her muttered magic spells and potions—she put a curse on me even as she cured my child, ensuring that we would be parted. My God and I have been condemned to worse than a simple death by her presence.

A sorceress. There is no other explanation. My child was dying and the best of physicians could not save him. How could a mere girl know such things? The young master should have taken me, his brother's widow; he was bewitched by that creature—a creature, hardly deserving to be called a woman, without grace, who had the impudence to push him away. I hoped her stubborn pride would be the death of her, but he was infinitely patient, even allowing her to keep her precious faith. I prayed she would prove barren, knowing that if I found she was with child I would have to destroy her somehow for my own sake and that of my little son.

They thought me a foolish weakling, but I did not care. Let them think it, I said to myself, if it serves my purpose. Let her think it all the more, that poisonous flower that wants plucking out at the root. She was the poor fool, lost and confused in a land she did not understand, among a people whose ways were a mystery to her. Poor, credulous

153

little fool who could not tell her friend from her enemy, and yet thought herself so strong. And when it came to it, it was almost too easy to set a trap for her. I barely had to try.

We might have been friends had we not been pitted against one another—had her child not been the enemy of mine. But there can be no friendship, no mercy between two animals battling with one another for survival. That is why I cannot regret the harm I did her, though I cannot say now who the survivor of our combat was—if there was a survivor at all.

A Most Extraordinary Confession (5)

The worst fears are always realised. We were like condemned prisoners waiting to be led to the scaffold, full of anguish and fear with only false hopes to comfort us. The child recovered, and as soon as his fever had gone and he was taking nourishment again, my work was done. He had a mother of his own, as they were so fond of telling me, and I had a master of my own, who awaited me.

I remember the infant as he was the last time I held him: plump and ruddy like a ripening apple, with soft curls of dark hair and eyes so grave they seemed to hold the mysteries of the world in them. I remember him with the fond, forbidden love of a woman who could never be loved as passionately as she might have loved.

"Let me stay with him", I begged Munira; "let me take care of this child. Your son does not need me." I must have begged her a thousand times, but all the tears I could have shed would not move her.

"Enough, for the last time. Enough of this", she demanded, utterly exasperated, but she knew I was terrified. "There now, there is no need to fear. No man will harm you, I have seen to that; my husband has promised that Ahmed will not hurt you again, and my son will not do you any harm. He is a good man, a gentle man."

But I thought that only a woman who had never been forced to do anything she did not want could speak like that. I wondered what sort of a life she had led, whether she had ever feared her husband or been injured by him. I wondered—then felt ashamed for having been curious about such a thing—whether she had always surrendered willingly to him.

†

When I woke this morning, the woman who cares for me changed my clothes, helping me into a new nightgown made of a soft, plain cloth, because there was blood on the one I had been wearing. I feel closer to home dressed simply because that was how Marija taught me to dress, how they all dressed in a poor village where there was never money to be spared on finery.

But Abdullah had told me the truth when he promised I would be beautifully dressed and well fed. Never had I seen finery like it. I recall again how it felt to stand in silence, swathed in the most exquisite cloth Arabia could weave—silk, wondrously dyed and embroidered—and precious stones woven into my hair, when at home I had once known hunger for want of a morsel of bread. I must have looked just as I had imagined a princess would be dressed, yet all I desired were the rough clothes I had torn from my own body on the night I was taken.

I kept still and silent as every part of my face was carefully painted, my eyelashes covered in some tincture that made my eyes water. Then my eyebrows were plucked, which smarted so horribly that I cursed myself for submitting to this suffering simply to please a man. An invisible cloud of amber and spices and musk surrounded me, when back home I had smelt of the herbs and spices I used in my work, sweet-smelling but not so intoxicating as this. I smelt of ill-use already, I thought, and would have drenched myself in water to rid myself of it if I had had the choice. It was what Marija would have done if I had come back after a particularly bloody encounter; she could not bear me to enter the priest's house until she had personally rinsed and scrubbed the gore from my hands.

Home. Marija's kitchen and Father Antonin's work-room. Ointments and remedies and grateful patients. I should not have thought of them at such a moment and desperately tried to empty my mind, but I still felt tears tracing their way down my face to ruin their handiwork. To think that I had hoped once to cut my hair short and kneel before the bishop whilst a black, unlovely veil was placed on my head! Oh God, it was too distant; it was all too far away.

"Do not weep; look how lovely we have made you", they said; I felt lonelier than I ever had as a child sheltering from the rains or hiding from my brother's rage. I looked from one face to the next and thought that they might have been marble statues—they seemed so cold and distant, so safe. Then I turned my back and stepped, trembling, into the chamber where I would be lost. I knew that if I could not stop him I was lost to everything I had ever known: to my people, to my faith, to my calling—and to myself. There are few steps we take in life that whisper through eternity, impossible to unravel—not even death when it comes is entirely final, because the most malicious of men cannot extinguish another human soul—but this could not be undone. I could only hope as I entered the room to stand before him that by some miracle it would not have to end like this. *By the waters of Babylon, we sat and wept when we remembered ... when we remembered ...*

†

Hell could not be more beautiful and more painful. It was a room that made the poor dwelling in which I had been born seem like a stable for animals. I crushed a carpet woven of some rich thread beneath my feet, the like of which would not have adorned our church. I remember many-coloured cushions, a wooden table inlaid with mother-of-pearl where cups were laid out, and a tapestry hung across a wall embroidered with flowers I had never seen before—flowers to line my way to ruin. And he was there, waiting for me at the end of it.

He had stood and waited for me once before, when I stood at the edge of a precipice, perhaps knowing that I would eventually be persuaded to surrender. I had known then, as Father Dan had known, that I would come to harm if I surrendered, but I had done so. Now, I would have found it impossible to believe that he meant me any harm at all if I had never encountered him before. In truth he was a handsome man, not so very different in complexion and stature from my own people, with large, quite kindly eyes that seemed to look on me with a friendly gaze. I knew his name now; they had told it to me. Omar. Omar, the younger son loved by his father. And they had spoken honestly when they said that he was a gentle man. He reached out to me and took me by the hand with the greatest of courtesy, like an indulged child stretching out his hands to receive a gift he knows to be rightfully his.

"Please," I said, "do not do this to me. I am a virgin."

He smiled. "I know you are; they said so at the market." I wondered how they could possibly have taken the trader's word for it, when until he had undressed me he had not even noticed that I was a woman. Younger women than I were wives and mothers. "Do not look puzzled. For all your many faults, my father could tell you were pure from the way you blushed. A wise eye can tell such things sometimes without checking."

I blushed all over again and tried to pull away, but he drew me close to him, and I struggled to move. I began to panic. "Please do not touch me. How will I return to my people if I am dishonoured?"

"You will not return to your own people", he said, a little more sternly. "Hush now, do not fight me. You have nothing to fear from me."

"I cannot submit to this!" I cried out, kicking against his shins because I could not move the upper part of my body at all. It was no use; I could not separate myself from him at all, and he seemed almost amused to feel me wriggling and kicking in his arms. "Please let me go. I will do whatever else I may to serve you, but I cannot give you my body."

"Stop this now", he ordered, without raising his voice. "I mean you no harm, but your body is already mine. Be reasonable."

I slipped my head down as though to rest it on his arm and bit his wrist as hard as I could. I felt the triumph of release as he let go of me, shouting with pain then blind terror, and I ran headlong out of the chamber. Of all the many acts of madness I committed during my time in that place, it was surely the most absurd: I was barefoot; I knew I could not get far, and I was still reeling from the lesson I had learnt after my last escape, but I simply ran wildly, straight into the arms of a waiting guard.

"Don't!" I shouted, because the man who had laid hands on me was a good deal more violent than my master. "Salvatore, you will let me go, you *coward*!"

He slapped a hand over my mouth. "That is not my name!" he snarled. "Never call me that again."

Omar stood before us. "Ahmed, put her down." He gripped me all the tighter. "I shall deal with this. Who gave you leave to touch her; are you mad?" He threw me onto the ground in what was almost sulkiness. "Be careful; you will hurt her."

Salvatore growled something under his breath that I did not understand and glared at me. The whole scene felt rehearsed, but I could not make any sense of it and pressed my head against the cold floor, willing it to break open and hide me. I felt so completely and utterly useless.

Omar reached out a hand. "Come with me, Warda."

There was nowhere else for me to go; I was so shaken that I took Omar's outstretched hand and let him lead me back into the room. "Forgive me," I whispered, "but I cannot bear this. I was less afraid to be beaten."

"Hush now, I would not have let him hurt you", he said, gesturing for me to sit down. "Perhaps you are not ready yet. There is no need to tremble; I will take care of you." He placed a covering over my shoulders and stroked my head until I stopped shivering; it seemed to me that I was dealing with quite a different man from the one I had fled at the market.

"I am sorry", I said, and truly I did mean well toward him. I would have done anything for him, anything at all other than what I had been bought to give him. In my mad innocence I imagined that I could make myself a companion to him, caring for him as a most devoted servant, that I could look after him as his physician, that I could and would do anything for him, even if it meant never seeing my homeland again. And I told myself that he would do as I wished, that when he had asked his father for me, he had laid claim to a woman, a wife, a companion, a confidante, anything at all but not a mere body ...

A cup was placed into my hands. I tried to put it down, but he indicated that he wanted me to drink and put it back in my hands again. In my terrified confusion I could make myself believe—as I was forced to believe every day afterward—that I did not know there was anything sinister in the cup he would not allow me to push away, that I did not detect through smell or taste the drug he had prepared amongst that rich, fragrant cordial ...

†

I glance at the priest, sitting patiently at my side, listening to this sorry tale, and could so easily deny that I drank in the certain knowledge I was being drugged, because I was afraid he would take me by force and it somehow seemed easier to send myself half to sleep to avoid the horror of facing him or the need to resist—but I cannot say. With the worst memory all around me, I am afraid of myself. I cannot help but wonder if the worst sin I have ever committed was set in motion that night ... but enough now. Enough. There must be such a thing as redemption, such a virtue as mercy, but the room spins and I am thrown back into the drugged sleep where all I once was is lost forever. And I am lost.... I am alone and lost and a stranger's comforting words cannot reach me ...

†

I could feel myself falling. The whirring, sickening dizziness forced me to throw myself flat on the floor to try to put an end to it, but even sprawled on the ground I still seemed to be falling into the depths of hell. I was back at sea again, being thrown about on rising waves, then I was helpless, unmoving as though I were being held down, but I could not see who was holding me or why. A body smothered me, a face, smiling, triumphant, filled my darkening sight like a diabolic vision, and I would have torn it, but I simply could not move. I could not push him away, and the hand over my mouth was not needed to prevent me from crying out as my throat was dry and soundless.

Even now, lying in the safety of my sickbed, I find myself trapped in the memory of that terrible waking-sleeping night where I felt and heard and longed for an end, but could not move a muscle to bring it about. I remember again, but cannot find the words to say it aloud, the agony, the shedding of blood, and the wretched, wretched misery of being imprisoned within a useless body. And in the midst of this nightmare, to know that it must always be this way, that he would come for me again and again, never satisfied, night after remorseless night until I was too old or too sick to give him pleasure any longer. There were women they spoke of who died, not through injury or murder, but out of sheer despair ... but even death could not desire me after that.

†

The piercing light of the early morning sent poisoned arrows through my head. I was alone and did not move, not because I could not move now, but it served no purpose to try. *My God, my God ...* but I never finished the prayer. Lying there in the bitter light of day, bruised, dirty, I believed that God had indeed forsaken me and could no longer hear my entreaties to him. And in all the beauty of the world, why should he notice a filthy creature whimpering in the squalor of her own ruin? A body that all the

silks and perfumes of the world could not render beautiful. No, that word would not suffice. More than filthy,
leprous—covered all over in some disgusting disease that
meant a living death nobody could ever comprehend if he
had not been forced my way.

I thought of my old life, but that peaceful, innocent
world seemed so far from me now; I could have believed
that it belonged in another woman's memory. I had imagined since my capture that if I were ever to escape I could
return to my homeland and the life I had left behind, but
I knew now that there could be no return for me. Even if
my sisters accepted me back, how could I live such a life
now? How could I ever explain to those pure, sheltered,
contented women how it felt to be used in such a way? I
thought of the white cross on my curtain and knew that
I could never again hide from the world behind it, because
the world had snatched me in the night and dragged me to
the most repulsive degradation a woman can know. I could
barely imagine how I could live any life now, except the
one into which I had been compelled.

†

The priest looks me in the eye; I could swear that he is on
the verge of weeping. "If you did not choose to lose your
virtue it can be no sin", he tells me; "you did not in any
way bring that harm upon yourself."

I have somehow—and only through the greatest pain—
to explain to this good man how much I have hated and
hated those who least deserved my hate. How I have lain
in my master's arms, eyes closed, fists clenched beneath the
scented sheets and loathed the virgin martyrs of old. How
I have hated and envied those happy souls who were given

the chance to be killed rather than be forced to satisfy a man's evil desires. I must tell him the scene there was when Omar awoke and found me kneeling before him.

I see him again as he looked on that morning, smiling at me from his comfortable position, as though he had expected to wake up and find me kneeling before him. He did not seem to notice that I was still trembling. "Kill me", I said; I cannot lie and say that I was not terrified as I said the words. "Kill me in whichever manner you choose, but do not use me again."

I wonder now whether I held any belief that he would strike me dead at my own bidding, but he sat up sharply and laughed. "And what use do you suppose you are to me dead?" he demanded, as though I were a simpleton. "What good is a body that is lifeless, rotting, stinking? Do you suppose your bones are precious enough to give me pleasure?" I was so overcome that he could say such a horrible thing to me that I could barely draw breath to make an answer, still less think of anything to say to him. "It is too late anyway", he added. "You cannot preserve your virtue now; I have already taken it. Look, there is blood if you need any proof."

Of course I did not need proof; I had felt it in spite of the drug he had been so courteous as to poison me with. And I knew that he was right. It was too late for martyrdom; it was too late to plead with him—the act was irreversible, like death and the conception of life. Even if he showed remorse, which he surely never would, it was not like any other injury he could have inflicted upon me. If he never reached out a hand for me again, I could still never be what I had been just a day before.

I flew at him in terrible rage, but he held me effortlessly at arm's length, which only enraged me even further. "You deceived me, you coward!" I shouted. "Not enough for you to attack a woman, you had to ensure I could not possibly resist!"

He shrugged me off impatiently, sending me staggering back. "You are a foolish, ungrateful creature", he said, quite coldly. "I was doing you an act of kindness. Do you honestly imagine you could have prevented me even if you had been in possession of your full strength? Look at you! Look at the size of you! I could tear you limb from limb, and you could do nothing to save yourself. I could have simply taken you by brute force."

"You did! You did take me by force. I was drugged!"

"Stop pitying yourself. Would you have preferred to be beaten into submission? Would you have felt more digni-fied that way?" He stood up, and I found it impossible not to shrink back. "I did not have the heart to subdue you like that; I did not want to feel you struggling and fight-ing with me. Other men like it; they like the feeling of conquest, but I could not do that to you."

It was a long time before I could bring myself to give him an answer, and then all I could find to say was, "You speak to me of having a heart?"

He stepped toward me and placed a hand against my face, so gently that I could not bring myself to push him away. "Do you have a heart?"

It seemed such an absurd question for a man to ask a woman he had just violated, but I knew what he was doing. I reached up and moved his hand away to break the intimacy he was creating between us. "It is not for you", I said. "My body you already have. You need not drug me again. It is as you say; I am in your power, and I cannot prevent you from taking me whenever you please, but I have already given my heart to another."

"You had a lover in your country? A husband? It is not possible."

I turned my back on him. "No, I have given my heart to God."

"That is nonsense."

"I do not care what you say; you know nothing of such matters. But it is as I have said."

There was a long silence, so long that I was startled when I felt his hand on my shoulder, as though I could have forgotten that he was still there. "I could force you to abandon your heretic faith, if you were not so obstinate and so hungry for death that I believe you would let me kill you first. And then I would still have never had your heart."

†

The silences whilst the priest considers my words are almost more troubling than the telling of the tale. "Did you ever give him your heart?" he asks.

No, I never did, and I can tell him without any fear of perjury that I never loved him. And yet ... it was all so confusing. *They* were so confusing, not at all as I imagined they would be from the stories I had grown up hearing. In that house, only Salvatore seemed evil right the way through—bitter, cruel, exacting, treacherous—with no tiny remnant of a virtue to redeem him. The women slaves were cold and unkind, but they had their pain to speak for them and their lack of power to do any real harm to anyone. Abdullah had a tender and generous heart, but he was not a brave man when it came to the test, and he let me suffer in his place when he saw me falsely accused. Then there was Munira, whose life had been made easy by the toil and misery of slaves and who thought nothing of handing me over as a plaything for her son, yet who spoke for me and trusted me when she had little cause to do so.

And then there was that man, one who saw me simply as a chattel born and bought to serve him and yet who could not bring himself to use his own strength against me to begin with; a man who desired someone who could not be bought at any market, a lover who would give herself to him freely or at least pretend to; a tender rapist. It does not make sense. I cannot make myself understand.

"And what about you?" asks the priest; I know what he is asking.

"I think that in the safety of my country all might have been well," I answer, and after what I have disclosed to him I am not afraid to be truthful, "but the battle between good and evil has always been so violent within me that when I was put to the test, the battle was lost. Father Dan could not defend me against myself and the woman I was to become."

Despair

She sat near the window in a pool of light, staring blindly outward. Slaves had come with water and new clothes for her to wear, and she had washed and dressed without looking at them. But as she slipped out of her old clothes, they could not help noticing that she had made marks all over her body from tearing at her own flesh, and she was chided for harming herself. "Bad", they said. "Very bad girl. Never do that again." Then when she persisted, they bound her hands in soft strips of cloth to prevent her from injuring herself and kept a close eye on her.

Her hands felt hot under the layers of cloth. She could have fidgeted sufficiently to loosen them or tried tearing at them with her teeth, but even if she could have summoned up the strength to try, a pair of watchful eyes scrutinised her every move for signs of trouble. So she sat utterly still and let an invisible curtain come down all around her.

†

Father Dan had been right. Every morning she woke up to feel death yawning beneath her feet and had to choose to avoid it. To begin with, she prayed with every passing day that the next morning would bring her freedom, but as the days and weeks passed, she was forced to accept once and for all that she would never be set free. Then she prayed that he would lose interest in her and she would be spared the bitterness of submitting to him—only to fear that he would discard her and she would be killed or handed over to some even crueller fate. That was something else she had learnt—that there was always a worse fate to suffer. Even if she could not imagine a greater misery than whatever she was being forced to endure, Warda knew that there were no limits to how much one human being could hurt another in this world—except the boundary of death. And so she prayed for death at the very same time as fending it off, hating herself for being too cowardly to die and too miserable to make something, anything at all, out of the dregs of life they had left for her.

She was never allowed out of the house and did not know whether it was because they thought it unseemly for a woman such as she to walk the streets or, more probably, because she was behaving so strangely they suspected she might run off again if she so much as stepped into the outside world. During the long daylight hours when she was left alone, she took up her position by the window and looked out at the little corner of the world that surrounded her unwelcome home. She looked out with the impassive eyes of a prisoner whose cell window merely reveals the rest of the gaol and its unfortunate inhabitants—at the pale, stark walls of the buildings that glared at her in the harsh sunlight; at the men richly dressed in brightly coloured satins; at the poor and the enslaved in their dreary, coarse clothes, walking with weary steps as though their only purpose in life was to make the wealthy seem all the more dazzling. Here and there she saw women, covered beyond all recognition—women without faces.

†

Omar held her face in his hands. She had already learnt
to stop herself flinching when he touched her, because she
knew it would aggravate him if she seemed to find him
repulsive. It was astonishing how quickly she had learnt—
not so astonishing, she thought, drearily; she was a scholar
after all and could set her mind to anything, even becoming
a good whore. And fearful necessity was such a ruthless
tutor. The cloths were removed from her hands when she
showed herself to be so resigned that she could no longer
summon the energy to tear her flesh. She had learnt the art
of disappearing into a silent world whenever she could not
bear to exist anymore, a dark, silent world where everything that happened around her—everything that happened
to her for that matter—seemed quite inconsequential. She
was a scholar learning the art of submission.

But she could not understand Omar at all and could
only watch his attempts to gain her affection with utter
bemusement. He seemed sincerely to desire to please her
and lavished his time and wealth on her as though she were
his greatest treasure and he were a shy lover battling to
win the heart of a disdainful maiden. That was where her
confusion began. When she looked back at those months
with the clear sight of safety, it seemed so obvious to her
that she should at least have refused him any affection if
she could not refuse him anything else; that she had been
right to be so unremittingly cold toward him and to want
nothing to do with him. Even her dark melancholy seemed
in retrospect to have had a power to it as it had shut him
out and made him miserable, because no one can be glad
in the company of a woman who is too unhappy to speak
or look him in the eye.

Yet it did not always seem so simple. There was something almost tragic about his desire to make her happy, so

much so that when he tried she began to feel churlish if
she did not try to please him a little in return. He seemed
at those times like a bewildered child who yearned to do
something good with his little gifts to her and his quaint
affection, and she was callous and ungrateful with her miserable disdain for him.

A lifetime away from Omar's world, buying and selling
a woman for such a purpose could be seen in all its ugly,
bitter colours, but at the time she felt something like pity
for him. She began, without truly knowing it, to think
as they all thought, caught up in this mad, twisted world
where slavery was simply part of the tapestry of life and
some women—women such as she—were destined to be
used, but where she might prosper if she could only learn to
submit herself. And if that were the case there was nothing
wrong in what he did to her. Every inner voice could tell
her that it was all wrong, but every outer voice conspired
with him against her, and so it began. She began to break.

He had told her that he could force her to abandon her
faith, but she was too obstinate and hungry for death for
him to risk threatening her. Now it seemed that he did not
need to frighten her at all; he had simply to hold her head
gently in his hands or stroke her hair and tell her that he
loved her, though they all thought him mad for loving such
a creature as she. Father Antonin had warned Warda when
she began to grow up that the most dangerous temptations
lay in the littlest, kindliest things—an apparently friendly
smile, eloquent words, a false friendship. After all, Simon
Peter had promised that he would be put to death rather
than betray his Lord, but a mere maiden's question had
broken him.

So she was Simon Peter then, betraying everything
through the little things he did to tempt her heart. If there

had been someone, anyone to guide her away, to tell her that she owed him nothing, least of all her soul—but that only meant blaming someone other than herself for her own weakness.

"That's my good girl", he said, when she gave in to his entreaties and looked him in the eye. His relief was so evident she could hardly bear to hold his gaze. "My beautiful girl. You see, it is not so bad."

My God, why did you not keep me in my anchorhold? she thought, as he drew her effortlessly into his arms. *Why did you not keep me from any man who might desire or have need of me?* But even the name of her former home had an absurd ring to it now. She felt him shiver as her head came to rest unbidden in the crook of his arm, and she knew she was doing precisely what he had hoped she would do. *It was not too late*, she told herself; she could move away again if she could only find the will. She began to move, but she was so torn that no choice she made seemed right any longer. Omar put his hand on her head and pushed her very slightly back. "No, no, do not move", he said; "you would not be so cruel."

"*Cruel?* You use such a word to *me*?" she thought she asked but found that the words died in her throat. She sat in his arms, dressed in the clothes he had given her, eating the little round sweetmeats he fed her. The gesture he was making of placing food into her mouth reminded her somehow of the priest placing the small white host on her tongue during Mass—then she trembled. It was too far away; it was too far away. Perhaps it had never been.

"Do not weep; I will not have you sad."

It was worse—she knew it was so very much worse to submit through this mad sense of loyalty that was growing in her than to submit through force or fear—yet this felt more compelling than fear. Freedom, when it came, gave her the leisure to wish she had been courageous enough to resist until the bitter end, until death if necessary, as he would surely have killed her eventually whatever he claimed, and no manner of excuses seemed good enough to tell her confessor. It seemed so different then. *I was afraid in a way*, she could say, *afraid to offend him, afraid to seem ungrateful, unworthy; perhaps at heart I truly was afraid to try his patience after that first encounter.* She could say she knew no better, that the poverty and wretchedness into which she had been born had left her unable to refuse any who provided for her. Except that if she knew how to read and write, if she could converse easily in Latin with a bishop, if her head was filled with the words of the great philosophers—she had known how to keep her own soul.

Warda closed her eyes to stop tears falling—what purpose was there in weeping now?—and sat very still, aware of Omar's presence all around her and the sweet taste of damnation on her tongue. There were no roads out of hell.

A Most Extraordinary Confession (6)

I am on my knees on the floor of my cell, looking up through the hole that reveals the sanctuary and the priest saying Mass. I cannot see the priest's face clearly from my position, but I recognise the sound of Father Antonin's voice, intoning the so-familiar words. It is such a long time since I have felt at peace like this, without a troubling thought to burden my mind; I luxuriate in the warm sense of belonging.

> *Agnus Dei, qui tollis peccata mundi, miserere nobis.*
> *Agnus Dei, qui tollis peccata mundi, miserere nobis.*
> *miserere ... miserere nobis ...*

The call for mercy sticks in my throat. It simply will not be spoken, and I never hear the plea for peace. Before the *dona nobis pacem* rings out, I hear the tap, tap, tap of a fist knocking against the sill of my window and rise to my feet, wondering what rude person could have thought to disturb me at such a moment. I fling back the curtain with unbecoming ill temper.

Omar stands on the other side of the cell, smiling. I know he has been searching for me and feel my heart racing with fear before pulling the curtain shut again. It is absurd, like a child burying her head in the bedclothes to make the monster go away. His hands slide under the curtain, groping toward me. "Please, Sister, come to me", he whispers; "did you think you could run away from me?"

"Leave me!" I shout, flattening myself against the locked door, but his hands disappear from sight as quickly as they appeared. I can hear the Mass again, but it seems so far away now, as though I am separated from it by more than a mere wall, and my cell is suddenly too small for comfort. I have never felt threatened in this place before, but I know he has not gone away. "Father! Sister!" I call, before a terrible clattering at my side drowns out everything and I see the door handle rattling repeatedly as Omar attempts to get in. "Help me!"

But then he is battering against the door so violently I know it will never hold; I press myself up against it with all my strength, but the shock has knocked the breath out of my body and I can no longer call for help. It serves no purpose. Even if I could find the energy to scream, I know they could not stop this; they could not possibly reach me in time. And the door jolts with ever-greater violence as the man throws himself against it, until the lock begins to splinter and fail ...

"Stop struggling!" he commands, seizing hold of my wrists. "Gently now, stop this."

I have slipped from one nightmare to the next and find myself where I always was, in Omar's arms, struggling only because the woman I was then would have struggled. I stop trying to fight him immediately and close my eyes as I have done so many times as the nights have become weeks, have become months.

†

The time burned away and I was resigned to it all. It occurred to me that if I had been abducted as a child, I would have forgotten that I had ever had another life by the time one year had passed; but even as a woman, the slow passage of time transformed my most lucid memories into insubstantial dreams. Unlike the vivid, brutal present, there came a time when it was hard to imagine that any of it had ever been real.

Slavery was real. He was real. Despair was real and so very, very welcome. As my body was invaded, a dark mist would come between me and him, between me and pain and heat and sweat and fear—every horrible sensation that would otherwise have been impossible to bear. It stifled the knowledge that I was a coward and a weakling. I was being driven out of my mind, but it was easier that way, so I let it go. I let it all go.

†

Then, quite unexpectedly, the change came. One night, for no apparent reason, I found that the mist would not descend upon me. For the first time in so many months, I was aware of the crushing weight of his body and was overcome with such terror and fury that I struck his cheek with the side of my fist, screaming at him to leave me alone.

He was thrown back and glared at me. "Have you lost your senses?"

"No, I have found them", I answered, struggling to rise, but I was pushed back down and reacted more angrily than before, tearing my fingernails across his arm. "Do not touch me!" I shouted, because I was sure that the mere pressure of his body would crush me to death. "You will not touch me!"

He had his way in the end, but not without a terrible battle, and by the end we were both injured. Yet in spite of it, I responded the same way the next time and the next, my newfound fear a little greater than the fear of getting hurt. "What has happened to you?" he asked, when it became clear that this was not a passing madness. "Why have you become so troublesome all of a sudden?"

I knew he was trying to reason with me, but all I could do was beg him to leave me in peace. It served no purpose to appeal to him because even I did not know precisely why I was behaving as I was. Not for the first time, I did not know myself.

He quickly began to despair of me, and when argument failed, he tried to placate me, giving me his most careful attention. It only made matters worse, because I found it impossible to eat the food I had once accepted from him and pushed it away, saying that it sickened me. The greatest madness of all was that I knew I was driving the patience from him, as I had so recently feared to do, but I felt so strange and so confused that I simply did not care.

"You have become perverse again", he said finally, when no threat, no promise, no gift, no little act of kindness would move me and I continued to fight him whenever he approached me. "Perhaps you have become a little too comfortable."

So then I was forced to dress again in the plain clothes Munira had first given me to wear, and it was made clear to me that I was in disgrace, condemned to the shame of rejection I had already caused my master to suffer. I was given bread and water just as before, but not by Abdullah, now that I was secluded in the women's quarters, but by Hala, who certainly would not have thought to share her food with me even if she had had the courage to try. I knew that I was being starved down as I had been before, but this time I had lost any desire to eat and did not care. All I knew was that I felt faint, hot, and confused every moment of the day, so much so that I felt the need to lie flat whenever I was able, even though it meant lying on the bare ground where it was coolest.

"That is a filthy thing to do!" Hala exclaimed on one occasion, when she entered the room and found me lying with my head to one side to try to cool my temples. "What do you think you are doing? Sit up!"

I refused. All I could see was the large room lurching round and round with Hala lurching with it like a drunkard, and I knew I could not move. She reached forward and took hold of my arm. "Come now, Sister", she persisted; forcing me into a sitting position, "get up off the floor. It is unseemly." My body began convulsing in rebellion. I flung myself forward, but found it impossible to control myself and vomited violently, missing Hala's immaculate person by inches.

I was still retching as Hala called a slave to clean up the terrible mess I had made. There were loud complaints on the subject, followed by even louder footsteps fleeing the room to find the means to clean it. Hala helped me to the window, so that I could catch my breath, and sat beside me. "Do not talk until we are alone", she warned, shortly before the slave returned, then set to work as quickly as she could. "Hurry along", said Hala; "leave us in peace."

In spite of what occurred afterward, I can still declare that I liked her then. She had a quiet strength about her, without seeming to me to be haughty, that had won my respect when I first encountered her and I felt it again as she sat beside me, controlling the situation with remarkable ease. I try to remember her as she was the moment she sat at my side, smiling lightly, as beautiful as a summer morning. I remember her then because a minute later an act of betrayal was set in motion—just another betrayal in a land where masters cheated their slaves and slaves cheated one another, all caught up in the miserable, inhuman cycle of survival that pitted all men against one another—all women even more.

"You are with child, aren't you?" she asked quietly, giving me a pointed look I could not avoid. "It is all right; I knew you were. That is why you feel tired and restless; that is what made you sick just then."

I seized hold of her hands. "Do not tell another soul!" I pleaded. "I could not bear to believe it! No one knows, not even *him*."

"I will not breathe a word to anyone." Her voice was soft and grave. "What do you mean to do? You cannot hide it forever."

"I do not know. What will become of me if they find out?" I felt such a sense of relief. Here was a woman who had been my way before, a concubine who had borne a child. I knew that she could tell me anything and believed in my foolishness that she would not betray my confidence in her. How could she when I had used my own knowledge to save her sick child once? "What will happen to the child?"

She was silent, as though contemplating how to tell me what she knew; then she put a hand on my shoulder and said softly: "You must tell no one of this until you have decided what to do. You are not supposed to have children; you are a plaything for an indulged younger son. I was meant to provide an heir, and I have provided one. It was my duty to provide children, not yours."

I was so overcome with fear that the insult did not reach my ears. "But what will become of my child? It is too late; I am already with child!"

"They will treat you harshly in the hope that the child will die before birth", she said. "But if the child is born, it will be taken away from you and you will never see it again, or they might let you keep it for a few years until the child is old enough for the market. Little children fetch a good deal of money there. But more likely they will try to cause you to lose the baby in the first place. When you recover, things will be as they were before. There now, please do not cry; there is no other way to tell it. You must prepare yourself."

"I cannot lose this child!" I whispered, but I was sobbing so violently that she had to signal to me to be quiet in case we were overheard. "Sweet Jesus, what am I to do? I shall have to run away."

"That would be foolish", she warned immediately. "You have already been caught trying to escape once, and you only escaped punishment because a stranger took it for you. If you are caught a second time they will certainly kill you. They already regret bringing you into the house and will take any excuse to be rid of you."

"What choice do I have? If I stay, my child will be killed or stolen from me. If I run away there is at least a chance that I may save him."

"You will fail", she insisted; her manner was full of concern. "You must resign yourself to losing the child."

I clutched my head in my hands and tried to compose myself, but I could not stop weeping. "Please help me."

Her hand rested gently on my shoulder. "You ask me to take a terrible risk. If I am found to have aided you in any way, I will suffer the same fate."

"I will not tell a soul that you knew anything of this", I promised. It is as much as my soul is worth not to feel rage now, thinking of how she smiled at me as though relieved and said how good I was. "Even if I am captured, I swear to you on all I hold sacred that I will not tell anyone you helped me."

"You must not act rashly. You are frightened and upset. Consider the matter for a few days first. If you have concealed your condition thus far, you can do so a little longer."

†

Oh Hala, how cruel is the love of a mother! How cruel and how desperate was the love we both felt. I loved enough to risk my life; you loved enough to end my life. Oh Hala, what it means to love a child, even children neither of us asked to bear. In that, we were equals. I was not afraid of the anger I would provoke if I said that I was with child. I had been beaten so many times before I had even reached the age of reason that they had little power to threaten me by now, but I could not bear the thought of them causing me to miscarry. And I knew I could not give up the child. I remembered again the woman on the night of the raid whose little baby was torn from her arms, and I saw myself as she had been, screaming and pleading as little hands slipped helplessly away from me. My God, I could not see it done.

In the days that followed I began to dream of a life with my child, if I could only make good my escape. I imagined standing on board a ship that would carry us to safety and freedom—saw the blue arc of sky above us promising a new life in some peaceful corner of the world. I knew in my heart, for all my make-believe, that I could not return home. If my family had rejected me when I was a child, when I was an anchoress, I knew they would never allow me to enter their house now, a woman with a child and no husband.

But in the delirium of terror and hope, I thought that perhaps I could go home after all. I could somehow find a way to reach that little island I had never dreamed of leaving once, and I could take the child to Father Antonin. I told myself that he of all people in this miserable world would take pity on me. I could almost see him pouring water over the little head as the infant screamed the devil out.

I began to realise that there could be no new life for us, even if we both survived to return home. The child would make me what I had been when I was myself a child—a wanderer, begging in the streets of the town with my baby clamouring at my breast and my hand outstretched for alms. I knew we would always be hungry, always despised and rejected, that my child would survive on the morsels poor Father Antonin could spare from his own meagre table— and yet it seemed to me that any life would be paradise if, when night fell, I could go to sleep with a tiny face pressed up against mine and the sound of little breaths assuring me that she was alive.

And so it was that after days of dreaming and hoping, I asked Hala once again to help me. "Are you certain?" she asked, as I knew she would.

"Quite certain", I said. "I cannot live without the child."

"You are very brave," she said—my God, she looked me in the eye when she spoke as though she were as honest as the angels!—"and now you must listen carefully. I have been thinking up a plan. You must do precisely what I ask of you."

"Tell me all. I will do as you say."

"Very well." She sat close to me and whispered so low that I had to concentrate on her every word. "Listen. I will bring you suitable clothes to wear, which you will hide until I give you word that it is safe to go. Then you will cover yourself, and as soon as there is no one about, you will walk away. I will make quite sure that no one sees you."

"How can you possibly do that?"

"I know this household well. I know the movements of every member. Just do as I tell you. Take nothing with you; simply walk away or you will be spotted as a runaway. Keep walking, and if a stranger approaches you, do not speak with him and do not stop."

"But where am I to go?"

"Hush. There is a tavern very close to where the boats come in. It is run by a slave known as Marco. I do not know its name, but you will have no trouble finding it. If you get lost, ask for the house where the friars live, so that you will not arouse suspicion—it is very close to there. Marco helps slaves to escape abroad for a price. He will give you a disguise, pay your passage on a ship, and conceal you until such a time as the ship is to sail."

"You make it sound easy", I said; "if it were so simple to flee this land, why have you not done so?"

"Because it is not easy. If you can reach Marco, your safety is secure enough. But first you must get there; most of us are not foolhardy enough to risk our lives."

"What else can I do?"

"Nothing else, except give up on the child."

My head went into my hands again. I could feel my heart beating a frantic dance and almost wished that there was some way to make everything stop—to make the world stop, to make time and space freeze so that I could walk through the chill of the static world and carry my child to safety before everything began to move again and swallowed us up. "How am I to pay this man?"

She paused again, thinking carefully, or so I thought. "Very well. In a little while, I will be called to bring you your bread. You will find what you need there, but do not break it open. Conceal it about your person. As I have promised, I will make sure that there is no one to see you leave, then you must go. There may not be another chance."

"You mean to steal?"

"It is as I told you; I know this house well. But you must not fail. If you are captured and brought back with coins stolen from your master you will surely lose your life." She put her arm around me. "I know that your situation is quite desperate, but are you sure you can do this? If you are captured you will both die, but if you confess that you are with child, only the child will perish or be sold. You will be as you were before."

Death had stared me in the face before, hungrily, lovingly, and I had been persuaded to cheat it when I had not feared to die. Now that it came to it, I found that I felt afraid and thought it must surely be possible to die of fear, but the desire to save my child was stronger than any other sense. "Will you conceal my departure if I go?"

"I will certainly do that. It will not give you long, but long enough to take you some distance from this house."

†

A short while later, as good as her word, Hala returned to me with clothes and bread heavy with the coins she had stolen on my behalf. "God bless you for your kindness to me", I said as she hastily helped me to cover up.

"And God keep you from all harm", she said, giving me a pitying look; I saw nothing in those round, guileless eyes to arouse my suspicions. I commended my soul to God and, at her signal, walked as calmly as I could, out into the open air where the last hope I possessed lay waiting for me.

Dreams Again

I know these streets now. My veiled wanderings were more valuable than they realised, or they would never have let me out at all. I know where I am, where I am going, but I am almost overcome by fear. My pregnancy and the hunger I have suffered have left me weak and sickly; I hurry on my way, surrounded by a mist of fatigue and giddy fear. Fear, the companion of hope, searing fear. In a mad moment, I consider making for the priory where Father Dan could be found to fulfil his promise to me, but I know I must avoid involving him in my escape or I will put him in terrible danger. He has already suffered quite enough on my account.

Marco. A name so like one of my own people that it almost gives me the courage I need to push past these faces. Many faces. Faces everywhere, glancing at me in accusation. I feel naked in spite of the layers of billowing cloth and imagine in my terror that everyone I pass knows I am a runaway. I leave a trail of guilt behind for my enemies to follow. I imagine that my absence has already been noted, praying—and I can only pray now—that Hala will not come to harm for her kindness to me. I imagine that I am being followed.

I am being followed. I imagine nothing; *I am being followed.* I hear the thunder of hostile feet out of sight behind me and tell myself they cannot tell who I am in the long, dark covering that leaves me indistinguishable from any other woman. I reassure myself that they are not really looking for me, but I know it is I they are coming for. I would run. Oh God, I would run for my life, for my child's life, but then they would know for certain it was I, and I could not hope to escape. And they are coming for me; they are coming for my child.

Oh God, grant me one prayer since not a single plea of mine has reached your ears since I set foot in this hellish land! A single prayer. Will the God who saved Daniel from the lions' den not deliver me now from the hands of my enemies? Grasping, crushing hands that drag me down. But I am no longer human after all; I am a creature to be bought and sold and tormented and killed—I scratch and bite, taste blood in my mouth that is not my own. My veil is torn from my head, and there is laughter everywhere; but my screams will not be drowned out by mockery. I know I cannot let them take me. I cannot let them take me now ...

Darkness overtakes me again. I do not know where I am. I struggle against enemies whose hands hold me still and whose faces are obscured from my sight. But I do not know where I am. My God, I do not know where I am; I do not know whom I am fighting any longer.

The Judas Trial

When Warda was dragged back to the house by the two slaves who had been dispatched to find her, there was some surprise by the other members of the household that she was dishevelled and putting up a uselessly violent struggle "She has not stopped fighting us since we laid hands on her", said Ahmed to the master as they threw her at his feet. "She struggled like a wild animal. We were injured trying to restrain her." They held up bare arms that she had clearly bitten and scratched many times. "She is a savage." The other slave began handing over coins he had bundled up in a piece of cloth. "We found these coins on her, hidden in a round of bread. They were scattered, but I think we gathered them all up."

The old man looked down at the creature he had so mistakenly bought all those months ago and hardly knew whether he despised or feared her. "Wild animal" did not seem such a poor description of her, with her red hair that somehow made him think of a lioness and her mad, violent behaviour. Never had he found a slave so impossible to subdue. They all submitted to their fate eventually, most very quickly indeed, driven by the overwhelming instinct to survive. Others needed to be broken, but the strongest among them lost any desire to resist after a pitifully short time. She had seemed to be the same, but now, for no reason whatsoever, she had risen up against him by running away and stood before him awaiting judgment, battling to escape when she knew perfectly well there was no way out.

"Stop!" he shouted finally, and was almost relieved that she went quiet. He could sense Ahmed itching to respond to the assault he had received at her hands, but he was still under orders not to do her any harm and obeyed with supreme reluctance. "Bring her closer to me."

Ahmed placed a sullen hand around the back of Warda's neck and pushed her forward so that she fell to her knees. She opened and closed her mouth, trying to speak, but she seemed so breathless and distraught that the words would not come. She looked around and appeared to notice for the first time that the entire household was watching. Her glance rested on Omar, but he looked away as soon as she tried to catch his eye.

"Look at me", said the voice of her judge. She turned back to him, but found it impossible to look up. "Do you know what you are?" Warda opened and closed her mouth again, but she still could not speak and knew with some certainty that he did not intend her to. "You are a mistake. You are my only mistake. I should have taken you directly back to the market the moment you ran from me rather than let you run again. You are a thief twice over."

Let him say what he wants, she thought. In her terror and her despair, it would hardly have mattered if he had called her the Scarlet Whore of Babylon since she was more a whore than a thief, but better to be either than a woman so weak she could not protect her own child. She had been set upon so quickly that her struggle to resist had been quite ridiculous, drawing laughter from those who witnessed the appalling scene; but Hala's warning had rung in her ears, and she had known that death lay waiting if she were carried back to her master.

And so it did. As he spoke she thought she felt her baby quaking and struggling within her, though she knew it was far too early for that. She was a weak woman, dumb before her accusers, sweating, bleeding in spite of their attempts to avoid hurting her; a ludicrous spectacle to be mocked not pitied, who would be put to death because the only plea she could have made was her forbidden pregnancy. "Sell—sell me on", she finally managed to say, looking fixedly at the ground. "Then you will gain the money you lost."

"And you shall lose nothing" came the answer. She looked up with a jolt and saw him advancing toward her.

"Wait!" she demanded, placing a hand out as though she could push him away. "Only a moment. Wait and let me speak with your son."

He grabbed her by the shoulders and turned her around to face Omar, who was looking at her now. "Do you wish to speak with your little thieving whore who ran away from you? Is there anything you could wish to tell her?"

Omar blushed at the accusing tone and looked at a fixed point above Warda's head. "I do not," he said quietly, "and she was never mine." He glanced at her momentarily, and a weary smile flickered across his face. "She wanted to die. She told me to kill her once. Let her have what she desires."

She could not have pleaded if it were not for her condition. In an instant she had thrown herself at him and taken hold of his hands, whispering, "You must let me speak with you alone! Make him wait until we have spoken."

Omar shook her hands away from him with a single, unexpected gesture and pushed her with such violence that she was thrown back. "I would have given you anything!" he exclaimed. "I was surely bewitched by you, or I could never have desired such a creature."

She had no other chance. "For God's sake, have mercy; I am with child!" she cried out, not caring any longer if the whole world knew—but Omar was the only soul present who did not hear her, too distracted to note anything other than his own rage. He stepped toward her and let his foot come down once, twice, striking her directly in the stomach so that those who witnessed it believed he had done it with the deliberate intention of killing the child. He was dragged forcibly away from her, but they knew even as he was pulled back and called upon to stop that it was far too late.

Warda curled up in a ball and let out a single, shrill scream, sending everyone around her into a state of chaos she barely noticed. In the midst of the commotion, Abdullah slipped forward and knelt next to the crumpled figure on the ground. He saw, as she writhed and cried, that blood was beginning to seep through her skirts. "I am sorry, my little daughter", he said. "I am truly sorry."

Warda heard nothing. All she knew was the terrible cramping pain of her body surrendering her child and the knowledge that it had all been to no avail. In her delirium, she returned to the blood-drenched room where she had delivered a baby doomed to die. She felt again the taut flesh of the dead woman tearing under her knife, felt the tiny, folded limbs of the child slipping through her hands as she fought to drag him out. She heard the long-awaited birth cry defying the world, then the cry of another child, killed because it was not worth taking away, then Hala's child wailing and fretting with fever, the face a terrible colour. She saw and touched and smelt the sweet aroma of every baby she had ever known. She held them close to her, only to feel the wrench of the limp bodies being torn from her arms one by one. And in the midst of it all, there were tiny hands reaching ever out to her that she could not hold and the piercing cry of a baby who would never be born.

Delirium

Somebody very near me is weeping. There is grief all around me, but I feel nothing and still cannot tell where I am. I seem to be at sea again, rocking and bobbing on the open water with the mist of the early morning chilling and clouding my senses. One moment I think I can hear a man sobbing and saying the words of an anguished prayer I remember from the past, then he is gone and there are other sounds—the tears of an old woman who sits passively at my head unable to touch me, a man murmuring over and over again, *I am sorry*, when I know he has no reason to seek forgiveness from me—and in the distance, two men arguing about me.

It hardly matters which place is real and which is a dream; I am on my deathbed all the same and a familiar empty misery nestles around me. I know only that I am beyond thought now—beyond thought and sense.

Out of the depths I cry to thee, O Lord ...
De profundis. Out of the depths ... out of the depths ...
   "Father, is my baby lost?"
"Hush."
Out of the depths ... "Mistress, my baby is lost. My
   baby ..."
"Hush. Not now."
I cry to thee, O Lord. Hear my cry for mercy ... "Father,
   shall I die?"
"We must all die. Do not be troubled."

Out of the depths I cry to thee, O Lord. "Mistress Munira,
   am I going to die?"

"I cannot say, Warda. Your fate has not yet been
   decided."

No one escapes death then. Every reprieve is a mere
postponement of the hour when life is taken, gently or
with violence. I escaped the embrace of the sea only so that
I would die in the comfort of this room; I escaped cruel
murder only to discover that the sentence was still upon
my head. "Why am I alive?"

"Because God wills it so", says the priest, drawing me
back to a world without cruelty that I cannot enter again.

"Why do they not kill me now? Why wait for me to
become strong again only to be struck down? Let it end
now if I am condemned to die."

"I do not wish it so", says Munira. "I have pleaded for
your life, but my husband still wishes you dead and my son
cannot decide which way to fall." She places a hand on my
head. There is something reassuring about a simple gesture
like that. I can smell her perfume and feel protected by her
presence as though she were guarding me. "Warda, Abdullah said he saw Hala stealing the money you were carrying.
Is that true?" I cannot answer. I promised I would not betray
her for helping me. "Warda, you do not deny it."

I cannot deny it and perjure myself, but nor can I answer
her and make myself a traitor. "Please do not ask me, mistress." I raise my head, but I have lost blood and feel too
weak to move.

"Your life may depend on your answer"—my life, such
as it is now. Tears return. I know I have cried a great deal;
my eyes feel gritty and tired with the effort of weeping,
but I cannot remember it. Munira speaks again. "Why did
you not tell anyone that you were with child?"

"Because I knew you would kill it!" I should not weep like this; I do not have the strength, but I cannot help myself. I feel Munira cradling my head, but I cannot stop. "Hala warned me. I ... I wanted to save the child. I ran away so you could not hurt her."

"Hala told you that?"

"Do not be angry with her; she was trying to help me! It was my fault." I could find no words to say it then, but it seemed to me that it would have been better for me to tell them I was with child and plead for the child to be brought to birth, even if she had been taken from me as soon as I had delivered, but the wisdom of Solomon only came to me in my agony, when the baby had already been crushed to death in my womb.

Munira is gone without a word, and I am left with my grief and my confusion. I believe that I will never love again. When Hala's treachery is uncovered for the world to see, I will never trust again. I have never been a human being to them, and in my sickbed I lose the honour of feeling like one. But for now I am nothing, not alive and not yet dead, not angel or animal, but not a woman either. And yet I have been here before. In this confusion and loneliness, I am almost at home.

An Oath Unbroken

The room was as it had been before. The blood had been cleaned from the floor, leaving a lingering stain as a reminder that the demonic event truly had happened the last time a sentence had been passed. His voice was so familiar now—cold, relentless, offering not the slightest hope that he might yield—and the words were almost the same. In spite of what had occurred, nothing of any importance had changed. Death was still coming, and now there was no reason for me to fight it, but I still found myself searching for the way out.

Omar stood nearby, silent and unmoved. His face was ashen, and my physician's eye could not help but notice that the hair framing his face was a little moist and his eyes had a red tincture to them as though they were swollen. Another pair of eyes might have seen a man shaken by an unexpected blow, a man who had grieved and been starved of sleep by his guilt, but I knew that guilt was not what ailed him. I knew what terrible fate lay before him, that very soon he would sweat and tremble with fever until he believed he was burning alive, that he would be tormented by dreams and visions as the fever took control of his senses, and that his heart would finally give up the struggle to keep his body alive. We were both under sentence of death, and no matter what cruelties my master could have thought up to end my life, nature had a more lingering death planned for his son than he could have ever meted out to me.

"Answer me!" I had trembled at the sound of his voice on the last occasion I had been brought before him; but I was a physician now, studying an unfortunate patient and fought to give him my attention. "Did Hala tell you the child would be killed or abducted?"

"She was trying to help me", I told him, but I heard a tremor in my voice. The act of taking my eyes away from Omar and his sickness had made me think of my own danger. Hala, I noted, was nowhere to be seen. "Where is she? What have you done to her?" Something was wrong. I had not even heard her child. "She was trying to help me!"

"She betrayed you, you foolish girl. She told you lies. She set a trap for you, and you were wicked enough to walk into it. Even if she had not betrayed you, were you truly foolish enough to imagine that you could wander alone through the town without anyone noticing?"

He glanced wordlessly in my direction, perhaps knowing what was going through my mind. Where I came from, a betrayal of friendship was no less than the kiss of Judas Iscariot echoing across the centuries, and a betrayer of friendship the most disgusting of criminals, a filthy, wretched outcast well fitted for the loneliness of hell. I felt again the pressure of Hala's embrace before I left the house and the empty place under my heart where my baby should have nestled in safety. "You would not have harmed me? You would not have killed the child?"

"Of course we would not have hurt you, you ignorant child; do you imagine we are savages? You think evil because you are evil and will never be taught otherwise."

I opened my mouth to answer, but there were no words left for me to say. I was foolish, and all the knowledge Father Antonin could cram into my head could not have made me wise.

"Did Hala pretend to help you escape? Did she steal for you?" I could not bring myself to look at Omar again, even with the eyes of a doctor, and so glanced downward at nothing. "Impudence! I will have an answer. Abdullah said he saw her."

"Master, let me speak." Abdullah spoke now. Abdullah, who had found his courage at last and dared to interfere. "Master, she cannot answer you. She must have sworn to Hala that she would never mention her part in it. It is the sort of thing Hala would have demanded to save herself, and now Warda cannot answer you without breaking her oath."

Silence again. "Woman, you owe her nothing. She betrayed you."

I felt faint and could not tell whether it was fear or grief. I imagined Father Antonin standing at my side as he did in gentler times when I knelt before the bishop and wondered, since I had failed in every other endeavour, whether I might be able to hold fast a little now. "Hala may be a traitor, but I am not", came a voice I barely recognised as my own. "I cannot answer you."

He was not angry any longer; he was bewildered. "Can you not see that I am giving you the chance to defend yourself? Do you want to die?"

"No, I do not want to die, but nor can I live at any price." Fear had left me again. I was not a slave—I was a physician; I was a scholar. "I have let myself fall so far through fear that I barely know the difference between right and wrong any longer. But I do know what it means to swear an oath."

"Very well. So be it then." I looked into his face again, and he still did not seem angry, even as he shrugged his shoulders and gave up on me. I saw a figure by my side—not

Father Antonin, but a flesh-and-blood man who had done me harm before, reaching out to me for the last time. No, I was not afraid. I told myself that I was not afraid. *I am not, I am not afraid*—but I could not embrace death as it came to take my hand. I stepped out of his reach and fell to my knees.

"Wait! Do not do this."

"Enough, it is too late."

"Spare me one more day. In a few hours your son will be overcome by a terrible fever, and you will have need of me. Spare me until then."

"Nonsense."

But now I heard Omar's voice, weaker than usual as I had known it would be, the voice of a frightened man who was already beginning to feel the fever taking him. "Father, do as she asks. What difference may a day make?"

My master glared at me with the hatred of a man who had been cheated. "My son, this is foolishness. She merely begs time to escape her fate."

I stood on my feet and stepped a little closer to Omar, knowing that my safety lay in his danger. Death makes villains of us all. "Keep me under close guard if you wish", I told him. "Make certain I cannot escape. You shall see that I speak the truth."

This is a mad world or it had made me mad to feel joyful as my wrists were painfully bound, but there was deliverance in the act of being confined. He had done as I had asked and withheld his judgment for a day, whilst the pale, trembling man whose fate was so bound up with mine, faced a harsher judgment still.

The Physician's Prophecy

"I did not do it", said Warda.

"How could you have known?" The old man was holding her against the wall with a hand over her bare throat. "You have cursed him! He sickens as you said he would."

"I am a physician; I merely saw the signs. He ... he was trembling; he was feverish." She could never push death away. No sooner had she been granted a day's grace when the prediction that had earned it had come true and she was being accused of little better than murder. "I have seen this sickness before, that is all. I did nothing."

"Will he die?"

"I do not know." She felt his grip on her loosening and sank to the ground immediately. When Omar had awoken at daybreak in a feverish delirium, she had been beaten so severely that now it was painful to stand or draw breath. She had pleaded over and over again that she had done nothing to cause his sickness, because it did not occur to her in her panic that she was wasting her time. She had been labelled a thing of darkness the moment she first entered this house and had brought little but trouble and disorder to the family; her mysterious gift of prophecy had only confirmed her position as a monstrous harbinger of doom. All she had known was that the man raining blows on her was so distraught he might quite easily kill her this time, whether or not he intended to, and he was certainly too angry to hear a word she said in her own defence.

Eventually, Abdullah had come running. He was too frightened to intervene when his master was in such a desperate state, fearing for his own skin, but he was so terrified for the girl's life that he ran for help. Warda did not notice Abdullah's presence or his sudden flight—she was in such agony she could not even bring herself to offer it up. She could feel her flesh bruising and tearing, but even when she curled up as tightly as she possibly could, she still felt utterly helpless and knew that only his exhaustion would bring the ordeal to an end. Then just as she was beginning to slip away from the world of sense, she heard a blessed voice calling out: *"Enough!"*

He stopped. She lay on the cold floor, gasping for breath, whilst above her head she thought she heard her life being bargained for once again. By the time the master had seized Warda by the throat and lifted her onto her feet, her face was swelling so horribly that her answers were slurred and faltering.

"She speaks the truth", said Munira; "she is a physician. Remember how she cured the child. Perhaps she can cure our son."

"Well, can you?" demanded the master.

"I do not know", said Warda, when the answer should have been yes. She had slipped down again and was sitting with her head resting on her knees, so that it was a strain for them to hear her. "But it seems to me that you should let me care for him anyway, since my life is of such little consequence to you. His sickness is certainly infectious, and the whole household may otherwise be taken by it."

She was immediately dragged to her feet again and cried out with pain. "Very well," he said, "you will attend to him. If you save his life, I may consider sparing yours."

†

It was almost a kind of freedom. They gave her a key to
lock herself into the sickroom so that no one could enter
by accident and risk succumbing to the illness. She was
given one of the household slaves to bring whatever she
needed to the door: water; cloths; spices; nourishment for
herself, as he could not eat a morsel; the means to dress her
own wounds. Warda knew that she could ask for almost
anything and expect to be granted it, whatever was deemed
necessary to keep a young man alive whose existence could
not have meant less to her.

She had wanted so fervently for Hala's baby to live. She
remembered, as she nursed the man who had deprived her
own child of life, how she had loved that child, how she
had lain awake through the long hours with a frail body
curled up against hers and the tiny rasping breaths pattering
against her cheek. She had wanted the baby to live though
it was not hers—she needed this man to live.

As she set about using her skills to secure her own survival, she thanked God for the man who had so generously
given his great knowledge to her and prayed that he was
still alive, far away in his little parish church with Marija
and Giuseppe for company.

"Father Antonin, is this right?"
"The compress is tied a little too tightly about his
   head."
"He is sinking. The fever does not cool."
"You are a physician, not a guardian of souls. If God
   takes him, you cannot stand in his way."
"If God takes him, I will accompany him on the
   journey. I have caused such trouble my master will
   not spare me this time."

"Prepare yourself for the worst then, or prepare to flee."

"I cannot run again."

"It may be your only hope if you are not to lose your soul."

"I think it is already lost."

The Dark Angel's Curse

This is not a judgment. It is the curse of an infidel. I heard my father curse her for a sorceress when I could not be dragged from my bed at daybreak. It has all happened as she said it would, as she meant it to happen. In her mad, unholy hate she has conjured a spell, and I have been struck down in the midst of my youth and strength. I have been struck down by her dark ways.

My flesh prickles and burns with fever. I feel the ache of limbs too heavy to move and the dull pain in my chest every time I draw breath. He struck her and called her a vile witch, but then he had to let her live or how could he force her to undo her evil magic? If she is evil, she is worse than a sorceress; she is the darkest of angels. A witch is still a woman, and no human creature could have such wicked spirits at her command. I see her demons all around me, crawling over my dying body, shrieking in my ears as though they wish to drive me to madness before they take my life. Tiny, unearthly creatures with bloodless bodies and hair aflame, whose every touch is like a thousand pinpricks. I would cry out with fear, but the fever strangles every sound that rises in my throat.

I do not know day or night, nor can I number the hours that pass. I am trapped in a tunnel of darkness and only she can carry me from it, but I wonder if she knows how. Satan himself cannot undo his own evil. I feel the touch of her hand against my brow, gentle, as cool as a winter breeze, and I could be deceived into believing she was giving me a blessing. It cannot be; there is no good in her. I loved her and was attentive to her. I gave her every good thing, and she was so hard of heart she would not be moved. Why should I have borne such insolence when I dragged her out of nothingness? When she first entered my father's house, she was the most wretched of women, good for nothing but the drudgery of the kitchen, a thing despised who only escaped a savage beating because another man was more foolish than I came to be. Foolish priest, foolish or mad to suffer such miserable indignity without hope of gaining anything in return. Without hope, without *seeking* anything in return. Fortunate for the poor simpleton that he asked nothing of her, she would have spurned him and sent him away empty-handed as she did me.

I took her from her life of drudgery where no one took note of her or so much as touched her unless it was to hurt her in some way. I loved her though they all said I should keep my distance from her. I was blinded by desire and thought her worth more than she truly was—and I have paid.

No, this is not a judgment. Why should I have been judged for having a heart? I loved her; it was no mere carnal desire—she possessed me, bewitched me, then drove me to hurt her when I swear I never wished to do any such thing. She could not be moved by any other means, no act of love or kindness. She thought herself ill-used, yet I was the one who suffered. The child was lost, my heir, my son, lost because she hid the truth from me. It died because she was too proud and too shamefully arrogant to trust me with her secret. She killed her child through her own folly.

†

She is ever near me. Through this dizzy haze, I hear her
sing-song voice with its strange accent as she walks about
the room, pouring water, mixing her preparations. I smell
her spicy presence and know, even when so little else
is clear, that she is my sole companion, working every
moment for me. I wonder how much he threatened her for
her to be so diligent, or perhaps she wishes for me to live. If
she were truly evil, would she not kill me or at least leave
me to die? No one watches over her; they are so fearful of
catching their own deaths. She could so easily pretend I had
died of this fever and she had been powerless to save me.

I called for her in the night. I could neither move nor
see. The dark tunnel was collapsing all around me, and
I knew I would be buried alive. I called, and she held
me in her arms, rocking me to sleep. "I will not die", I
told her, and she promised I would not. She promised she
would cure me somehow. I heard my dark angel promising
to save me and knew she regretted the injury—the many
injuries—she had done me and wanted to put them right.
I felt her remorse in her tiny hands stroking my hair and
her whispered prayers. *Blessed Mother, do not abandon me
now* ... If it is not fear it is remorse, which is almost love.
If it was not a curse at all, perhaps it was a judgment.... I
am falling asleep. I am falling. I am falling, and she holds
me, swearing I will not be lost.

And I promised her. Somewhere in my feverish confusion I promised that I would free her in reparation for my
sins. I could not trust her to keep me alive for anything
other than her own profit, so I made her a promise and I
believe I meant it when it was said. I told her she would
be free.

A Most Extraordinary Confession (7)

Pain returns. It always returns when I do not wish to speak, and the priest has come to notice it. He has been sitting at my bedside with his head in his hands so that I may not be distracted, but the silence is so long this time that he sits up and looks at me. "You must not be afraid to tell me the truth", he says. "God already knows the secrets of your heart."

"That is why I am afraid." It is hard to say without sounding proud that before I was sold into slavery I never had much of any consequence to confess. Not many grave sins, that is. The most humiliating thing about kneeling in the confessional then, was saying aloud the thoughts and omissions and acts I had committed that I knew to be wrong and thinking all the time, *But how foolish all this is! My sins were neither pleasurable nor even interesting! Why ever did I waste my time with them?*

I never dreamed about my petty childhood sins, but I dream about Omar all the time. I see again his bloodless face, the only part of him that was bloodless by then; I hear the terrible silence that followed, when I knew I was all alone because he was no longer with me. "I cared for him to begin with," I tell the priest, "cared not out of love but because I had been well taught and he was in my care, in need of my help."

I felt no concern for him as I attended him, but I had been trained to keep my distance from the patient I cared for, for my own sake and for his, but I cannot pretend it would have mattered to me in the least whether he lived or died, if my own life were not so bound up with his. I felt fear not grief when he took a turn for the worse. When I thought I would lose him within the hour, I held his body in my arms and wept, pleading that our Blessed Lady would intercede for me. Anyone who witnessed it would have thought we were lovers and my heart was breaking, but my tears were entirely selfish and I wept for my own death, which crept closer to me with his every faltering breath. I felt the constant tug of a cord around my neck whenever he closed his eyes, and I could not be certain he would ever open them again.

Perhaps selfishness is better than hate, and I would have hated him if I had felt anything for him at all. All that absurd pity I had felt for him, that ludicrous sense that I should do as he wished—sweet Jesus, it seemed now so clear to me that I had given in to a man's childish whim!—that I had been bought for silks and spices and sweetmeats. Hala had deceived me in the hope of bringing about my death and the death of my child, but I had been more cruelly deceived by him. I knew little about the matters of the heart, but I knew that if he had ever cared for me, looked lovingly at me for a single moment, he could not have so coldly given me up to death.

And then there was the child—the child who never lived.

"What are you trying to tell me?" asks the priest. "What did you do?"

"My head is muddled", I answer. "I can hardly remember. I cannot make sense of what I was thinking. There were times ..."

"Yes?"

There were times. There were times when I stopped seeing him the way he had always seen me, as a mere object to be used. There were times when he was no longer an interesting problem to cure or my only hope of life. During the long hours we were alone together, I would look on his sleeping face and remember his cold glare as he abandoned me to my judge or threw me away from him as I pleaded with him not to harm me for the sake of the child. But I knew if I indulged such thoughts I would hate and never stop hating him. I occupied my mind with the task at hand, and when there was nothing much to be done, I told him stories.

"Stories?"

"Yes. When men are suffering some severe illness, they sometimes become afraid or angry because they cannot move as they normally do. Father Antonin taught me to distract attention by telling stories, so I told him stories."

I told him every kind of tale to drag his poor, selfish little mind away from his peril. I fancied that I had become Scheherazade, because we were both in fear of our lives and in need of the comfort that such voyages bring with them—Scheherazade, the woman who told stories to save her own life. Perhaps I imagined that I could win back his favour so that if he lived he would save me. And I am Scheherazade again, telling the tale of my life to a stranger who may not save my life, but may perhaps save my soul.

I return again to the sickroom, to the long, miserable nights, sitting in the half-light near his head. I tell him of the mysterious race of giants who came to the Maltese islands and built their temples there, great pagan temples built with massive stones that tower over men still. The giants have long vanished from the face of the earth, but the temples remain, like great circular footprints leading back to a time of darkness and mystery.

I tell him the tale of a saint escaping the persecution of
the Romans who sailed away from his tormentors, across
the sea to Malta aboard his own cloak—a saint miraculously kept afloat to be cast ashore on a friendlier land. All
my stories return home to those craggy shores I was torn
from on that terrible night, every single one as though my
storytelling could carry me home forever. When I run out
of stories, I reveal to him the greatest story of all, the tale
of a holy man they called Paul who was a prisoner aboard
a ship that set sail for Rome. In the silence of this room,
I tell of a mighty storm that shattered the uneasy calm of
the night, of the great ship wrecked upon the shores of an
island. The survivors discovered that they had chanced upon
a welcoming land, and the good people of Malta treated
them with the great kindness and generosity for which they
were henceforth known. In the shelter of a cave, Paul helped
to gather wood to make a fire, and as he carried a pile of
sticks to throw onto the flames, a snake slithered out and
fastened its fangs onto his arm. Then the people said, "This
man is cursed, for he escaped the dreadful storm only to
be poisoned by a snake. In a moment his body will start to
shake and swell, and he will die a terrible death."

But Paul did not sicken and die. He shook the snake from
his arm, and it dropped harmlessly into the fire. So then they
said, "Why, he must be a god for he cannot be killed!"

He told them that he was not a god, but God Almighty
had sent him to them. After that, the people brought their
sick to him for healing and listened to his message, for he was
a man of great wisdom. Then when it was time for the ship
to set sail again, the people pleaded with their beloved Paul
to stay with them, as they knew he would be put to death if
he went to Rome. But Paul was not afraid to die and knew
that he was called to go on to Rome, now that his work was

over in this place. And our most beloved father, Paul, stepped aboard the ship that would take him to Rome and death.

"I would not have been able to leave willingly."

"You miss your home very much", says Omar. He drifts in and out of confusion, but at this moment his eyes focus quite steadily on my face. "If you save my life, I will set you free."

I had dreamed that he would say such a thing to me. "You will let me go?"

"I will do anything for you if you will save me from death."

I knew he was lying. I knew it—I am certain now that I knew he was making a promise he had no intention of honouring—but yet I wanted to believe that I would be free so I took him at his word. I began imagining the journey home, as I had never dared to think of it before—the voyage across the sea, the first glimpse of the dusty, honey-coloured land where I had left my heart. I saw myself taking the road to Father Antonin's little house next to the church, and the joyous reunion there would be. In my vanity I thought I might even dare to hide behind the high altar again so that he or Giuseppe would find me after Mass. A child of the hidden places always secretly desires to be found.

And we all desire to walk the road to freedom. *Poor banished children of Eve.* It is the deepest yearning and the most anguished prayer. *After this our exile ... poor banished children of Eve. Poor banished children ...*

†

But then Omar began to recover, so much so, that he knew he would live, and he began to change his mind. "You would not choose to leave me", he said. "I am a good man, and if I set you free, it would be no liberty at all. Think of the life you would be condemned to; think of the loneliness."

"I am lonely now."

"But if you found your way back to your island home— and how indeed could you, since you would have no money to pay your passage on board a ship? Even if you did find some kindly captain who would take you, how are you to know that you would not fall into unfriendly hands again? The sea is such a dangerous place, swarming with enemies, and the worst enemy is the sea itself. Think what a torment it would be if your ship were wrecked and you ended your days beating back the waves until exhaustion overcame you and you drowned?"

"I would rather lie dead in the depths of the sea than remain a captive on dry land."

"No one would rather die—you least of all, who have tried to save your miserable life so many times." His weakness made his voice sound mercilessly cold and toneless. "Even when you asked me to kill you, you knew I would not do it."

"You said that you would free me."

"You do not really wish to be free, anymore than you ever wished to die. If you returned to your homeland you would lead a half-life. No man would want a woman who was already used, who has lost the bloom of her youth. You will end your days begging on the streets, despised by your own people. They will mock you and spit on you. They will throw stones at you."

"They are Christians. They will not abandon me", I said, though I did not even believe that myself.

"What nonsense you do speak! No living soul will ever touch you again, even those you loved once. But here, I will care for you ..."

"As you cared for my child."

I braced myself for a response, but he did not move a muscle. Instead he said quietly, "You killed your own child. It is of no consequence. There will be many others, *Inshallah*. I will take you as a wife, and you will never want for anything."

I found that I was shaking, and it was not with fear. I should not have been so wounded—I had *known* he could not be trusted—but all the same I saw my every dream of liberty crumbling all around me, an edifice built on sand, built in the greatest haste. "You know I can never be your wife. I am a Christian! There can be no marriage between the likes of you and the likes of me."

"You will convert. It only hurts for a moment."

"I will not."

That was when it happened. He looked me directly in the eye and said: "Do not give me any further reason to do you harm. You know you do not have the courage to die a martyr's death. Whether you elect to suffer or not, I will have you in the end as I always have."

I cannot explain the strange transformation that took place then; I do not entirely understand it myself. I can only say that I felt as though I were slowly freezing to death. I felt the chill in my hands and my heart as though I had been bled half to death and no longer belonged to this world at all. And yet outwardly I must not have appeared any different, for he did not seem to note any change in my behaviour.

For the rest of the day, I drifted about my duties without even fear to jolt me to attention, since I knew now that he was unlikely to die. Then when night fell, I did it.

"Did *what*?"

He needed bleeding. Father Antonin had taught me the art of bloodletting, as he himself could not draw blood since he was a priest. I prepared his arm carefully as I had been instructed to do and cut open the vein, catching the blood that spurted out in a small vessel. I watched carefully to ensure that he shed the right quantity—not so little as to have no effect, but not so much as to make him sicken again—then I reached for a bandage to staunch the wound.

But I never did staunch the wound. I found myself hanging back, paralysed at his side whilst blood poured out of his body, and I thought, *But why should I?* I sat impassively and watched as Omar lay bleeding, feeling nothing at all—not fear, not regret, not even anger. I simply watched him dying as I had watched him sleeping and sweating and convulsing with fever. It would not have seemed any different, except that he began to realise that he was losing too much blood. Perhaps he felt the giddiness and weakness creeping over him or simply knew that I had waited too long, but he began trying to stop the bleeding himself, grasping the wound with his other hand.

"Are you mad?" he demanded, looking at me in fear disguised as anger. "Bind it!"

I calmly moved his hand away from the wound. He was weaker than he had realised and was able to offer only the most pitiful resistance. "Do you mean to kill me?" he asked; now he was simply afraid.

"Yes," I answered, "you are already dying."

He writhed and struggled, but he was like a silly child, helpless and terrified in the face of death. He was as I had been when I had struggled against him, against Ahmed, against the others, but I felt no pity for him, not even when he touched my arm and pleaded: "You are a healer, not a killer. Have mercy on me!"

I shrugged his hand away, picked up the bandage I had meant to use to bind his arm, and forced it into his mouth to stop him calling for help. "I will show you a little more mercy than you have shown me. You will die presently, without ever suffering pain."

I watched and I waited. He fought to remove the cloth from his mouth, but he was almost paralysed by now and could neither spit it out nor use his hands to pull it from between his teeth. When he reached out to me again, I simply slipped back a little so that he could not touch me, and he was left to fight the air around him until he could no longer move at all. He died, frightened and unloved, drowning in his own blood. When his heart failed and he stopped breathing, I leant forward and did him the courtesy of closing his eyes, then I covered his body in a blanket and rose to my feet.

†

Cold silence. Cold house. I am trapped in that dark room again, standing near the body of a man I have killed. There is blood all around me, cold, clinging blood that cannot be hidden. They will know I murdered him—there was no other way it could have been done than by my hand—and I will pay. I must find my way out of the house and on through the streets, as far from this place as I can reach. I wonder how they will choose to kill me, what terrible way they will find to snuff out my life for this, because I know now that there is no such thing as unconditional love or trust in this miserable world, only unconditional cruelty.

I hurry away through the night with every blood-curdling vision of death hovering about my head, and I am alone. I cannot appeal to God to come to my aid because I have killed my own soul in the act of bleeding a man to death; I cannot take refuge in Eternal Goodness when there is no good left in me now. A full moon glares down at me like an unblinking eye, and I am lost. I am lost and can never be found behind the altar of my childhood because hell has already claimed me. I should not run because torture awaits me wherever I go and whatever I do—and yet I run all the same. The heartless universe stretches out above my head without hope, without hiding places, and yet I run. I cannot stop running now.

The Reluctant Accomplice

Father Dan knew who she was the moment the light from his lamp revealed her face, so he dragged her inside before anyone could see her. "Please tell me you remember who I am", she pleaded, the moment the door closed behind them.

"Of course I remember you", he said, and she could hear panic in his voice. "Whatever are you doing here? Have you fled again?"

"I have", she responded, with the weariness that a terrible shock can bring with it. "You said that if our paths crossed again you would help me to escape. I must ask you to make good that promise now."

"I did not intend you to take such a risk", he said, but he knew it was far too late to say such a thing. "You may not escape with your life if you are captured again."

"I certainly shall not. I have slain my master."

Father Dan staggered back as though reeling from an unexpected blow. "You would not do such a thing." She was stolidly, guiltily silent. "It cannot be."

"He violated me and made me lose my baby. What does it matter if I bled him to death—he thought nothing of making me bleed."

"God in heaven! You come to me with your master's blood on your hands?"

She blinked at him in surprise. "Surely you do not side with him? A virgin violator? A man who bought human lives at the market like cattle?"

"You are not a judge; his life was not yours to take!" He placed his trembling hands over his face. "If you thought nothing of the wickedness of such an act, surely you considered how they would make you pay for it?" He looked up at her, and for the first time she looked visibly afraid. "You do know what they will do to you for this?"

"I must be away from here as soon as the gates of the town open. Once the household is awake it will not take them long to discover the body." She felt her nerve giving way. The chill of despair had propelled her through the dark, dangerous streets and the belief that this man who had been her saviour once before could again deliver her from all evil. But he was filled with fear and horror at what she had done and seemed paralysed by it, so much so that she began to suspect he would baulk at the idea of helping her again. She threw herself at his feet and grasped the hem of his habit in an act of submission she could not have been forced to make to her master. "Good father, do not abandon me to my fate!" she cried out. "I do not ask you to forgive what I have done, but please help me!"

He took hold of her arms and pulled her to her feet, but before he could speak, an inner door was thrown open, and she flung herself down again. "What is the meaning of this?" demanded a man's voice.

"Jerome, we must speak", said Pierre, advancing toward the shadowy figure. He looked at Warda over his shoulder. "Get on your feet, girl, and wait for me here. We have little time."

He bundled his comrade back through the door and closed it to hide their conversation from her. "What is the meaning of this?" asked Jerome again. "Who is that woman?"

"She is an escaped slave, the girl I spoke of before who tried to escape from the market."

Jerome raised an eyebrow. "So it was on her account you were beaten, was it?"

"It was." He drew a sharp intake of breath. "I promised her that day that if our paths crossed again I would help her out of slavery, and so I must."

"Pierre, you cannot do this!" he burst out. "You had no business making such a promise. It is too dangerous, even for her."

"She needs to be away before they begin the search for her, or there will be less chance that she may escape unnoticed."

"You cannot involve yourself with her. You have been imprudent once on her account; I will not allow you to be so again."

"I cannot abandon her now!"

"Think of our work", pleaded Jerome, to his friend's covered face. "If this is discovered, we will be lost, and then what will become of the slaves we ransom and minister to? You cannot forfeit the hopes of thousands for one slave who has won your affection."

"It is too late; she has killed her master. If I do not see her safely away, she will be put to such a cruel death it does not bear speaking about."

"She has killed?" He choked on the word. "This is madness; you can have nothing further to do with her!"

"I have failed her so terribly. She was driven almost to self-murder, then to murder because I could allow myself to be tortured for her, but I could not ransom her. I had to force her to submit to a heartless master who would treat his horses with more care than a slave in his power."

"Pierre, she is a murderess. She has shed blood. It was never your fault that you could not save her from slavery; there are thousands of slaves we cannot help."

Pierre looked up; Jerome saw that his eyes were swollen with tears. "Hand her over then; I cannot do it. Stay with her and prepare her for death as best you can before they butcher her. I cannot do such a thing."

Jerome hung his head. "What do you really want me to do?"

"Nothing that will endanger you any further", came a voice, causing both men to jump in alarm.

"I thought I told you to stay still?" demanded Pierre, pushing Warda back through the door. "Can you not do as you are told?"

"If she could, she would hardly be here, would she?" Jerome put in.

Warda looked fixedly at the ground. "I did not mean to put you in such danger. Give me a man's clothes so that I may hide my true identity, and I will be gone. I will not trouble you further than that."

†

Warda sat still as Father Dan cut her hair. He was systematic and careful, holding every strand in his hand as he cut it off before placing it straight onto a piece of cloth. He would tie it up into a bundle later and burn it, knowing that a single red strand found on the ground or stuck to his clothing would be evidence that she had been there. "You failed to pass as a boy last time because you had no time to do it properly", he said; "this time you must not fail. Tell me who you are."

"My name is Pietro Contarini. I am Genoese, of humble origins."

"That is important. On no account must anyone imagine that you are of noble stock."

"I understand. I am Pietro Contarini, a Genoese, a messenger. Why am I a messenger?"

"Because messengers can be secretive without arousing suspicion. You are under no obligation to tell anyone whom you have visited and to whom you return. Your business is your own. There is something else. Your face is bruised; you will have to say that you have been in a fight if you are questioned about it."

Jerome stepped into the room carrying a bundle of clothes. "I have the things you need", he said. He turned to Father Dan. "Are you certain about this?"

"She has no other choice."

"What are you saying?" she asked.

"Nothing", said Father Dan.

"Is anything amiss?" she enquired, with growing impatience.

"Nothing at all. Hush now." He turned to face her. "We will leave you to change your clothes. Hasten, the time moves on."

Soon after, Warda stood before them, looking very much like an eager young courier about to set out on a journey. Besides the man's clothes, Father Jerome had gathered together a little money to help her on the voyage. "I am ready."

"Do you understand precisely what you have to do?" asked Father Dan again. "The tavern is not far from here. You can conceal yourself easily enough there until you discover a means to get aboard a ship. Speak to no one if you can avoid it, and under no circumstances do anything to draw attention to yourself."

"Is the tavern owned by a man named Marco?" she asked.

Pierre shook his head. "I do not believe so; I have never heard of such a man. Why do you ask?"

Warda let the memory leave her. "Nothing. I thought Hala might have said one truthful thing." Her hand went to the hilt of the dagger she had found in amongst the clothes.

"Very well. That dagger is for effect and to defend yourself if necessary. Do not kill again unless there is no alternative."

"You have my word", she said, but thought dejectedly, *Such as it is worth.* She turned to leave. "God bless you for helping me, Father."

He stopped her. "You are embarking on a perilous journey that may well claim your life. Let me hear your confession before you go."

She hesitated, knowing that there was a certain safety in this place and to make her confession to him would give her leave to remain a little longer, but that was scarcely a good reason to accept. She shook her head and turned away. "Good father, I am not sorry."

Father Dan raised one hand in blessing almost out of force of habit, but it was with a sense of overwhelming gloom that he watched her slip outside into the unwelcome darkness, where before long men would be hunting for her blood. "We will burn for what we have done on that child's behalf", said Jerome.

"God is very merciful."

"Men are not. We have taken a terrible risk—what if she tells?"

"She will never talk. I know she will not."

"What if she is captured? What if she is tortured? She will be forced to disclose who it was helped her!"

"I know she will never talk," said Pierre a little sadly, "but nor can I say for certain that she will ever see her homeland again." He could not bring himself to say it, but he wondered whether she would ever see heaven either.

PART III

Ibrahim Reis

When Warda recalled the hour she spent seated in the corner of the tavern, she could never quite describe the fear. Every other detail came alive as though she had uttered a magic spell—the overpowering smells of drink and unwashed bodies, the naked feeling of being a woman caught in a world of men, where the slightest mistake might give her away. Yet she could never again know what it meant to hide herself in the most sordid corner of a city where a man lay dead, waiting to be discovered. Omar had been right; she was not meant to be a martyr. She was not prepared to die, still less to die in agony and indignity; so she could call herself a survivor or a coward, any name at all as long as she could escape this place, where every shadow seemed to hide a predator, watching, suspecting, stripping her disguise away.

I am Pietro Contarini, she said to herself, looking down into her beaker. *I am Pietro Contarini* ... She was among slaves—bagno slaves exhausted from their labours in the quarries and building works; the proprietor himself was a slave who paid his master a fee in exchange for an almost free life—but it would count for very little if she were caught. There was no honour among slaves as she had learnt to her cost. The idea was forming in her mind that she might be able to hire herself out as a physician on board a ship or as part of a caravan travelling across the desert. She did not much care how she left the country as long as she did so quickly. They would find him in the morning. If she kept her head down she might last, disguised as she was, a few days without being discovered, but she knew she would be found eventually if she could find no way out.

That was when she saw him. Of all the faces that were to haunt her conscience, his was the most vivid and the most accusing. She saw him then for the first time, a ruggedly handsome man in his late fifties. His beard was streaked with white, and he was richly dressed in the local style, but the icy blue eyes peering out of a ruddy, sunburnt face betrayed his European identity. She noticed almost immediately that he had a badly injured arm, which he clenched, unmoving, against his body as though trying to stop it breaking off entirely. He was obviously well-known at the tavern, as a slave hurried to him bearing a drink without him having to ask for it. He took it, wheeled round, and glanced coldly in her direction. "Are you looking at me, boy?" he asked, speaking with an accent she seemed to recognise. "You beauty!"

She had done the one thing the priest had warned her emphatically not to do, but it was too late to avoid drawing attention to herself now, so she held his gaze. "If you are referring to my face, I got into a fight."

The man roared with laughter. "Well, you were soundly thrashed, weren't you?"

She bristled. "I am in less pain than you are." She recognised his voice now; he had the same clipped way of talking that Father Dan had had and must be from the same country.

It was his turn to bristle. "That is no concern of yours."

"No, indeed", she replied; "if you prefer to lose an arm, that is no concern of mine whatsoever, or you could let me treat it."

He laughed again, but a little uncertainly this time. "Are you a surgeon? The last idiot who interfered with this wound made it a thousand times worse and is still senseless from the payment he received."

She ignored the threat. He wanted her to know he was dangerous, but she could have guessed as much just looking at him. "Is it a splinter wound? You are still moving your fingers, which is a good sign. The bone will not be broken."

The man raised an eyebrow and stared at her as though trying to make her out. "Come with me", he said, finally, and clicked his fingers. The man who had brought him his drink appeared at his side; there was a whispered exchange Warda did not catch, then the injured man signalled to her to follow them. She was breaking another rule, allowing herself to be led away from a crowded place, but she was almost relieved to be taken away from the threat of so many people. *Pride*, Father Antonin would have reproached her; *you simply had to let him know you knew what was wrong with him, didn't you?*

"Where are you taking me?" she asked, as the slave stepped ahead of them up a narrow staircase. In the half-light, she saw the slave unlock the door and found herself stepping into a small room. She glanced quickly around her as the lamps were lit and noted that the room was sparsely furnished with just a low-lying table and a couple of stools. She could see no other way out except for the door through which they had entered, but the slave stood there as though guarding it.

The injured man turned to look at her more closely. "I have a few questions of my own. Who are you?"

"My name is Pietro Contarini", she said. "I am a physician; I happened to notice that you were injured. That is all."

"Do you know who I am?"

She knew she was supposed to. "I do not. I am a stranger to these parts."

"Evidently." She clenched her fists behind her back; she was being interrogated. "My name is Ibrahim Reis."

"But you are not of this land", Warda interrupted, then felt a shudder of fear. Pride again.

"I am Flemish", he explained. "I was once a privateer plundering Spanish treasure, but for nearly twenty years I have sailed under a flag all Christian mariners fear. My ship awaits me, but a crippled captain is no captain at all. Come here." She stepped cautiously toward him and watched as he gritted his teeth and stripped his arm bare for her to look at. "Can you mend this? You will be well rewarded."

She took a closer look. It was, as she had suspected, a splinter wound that had been inexpertly treated, causing the whole of the man's forearm to swell. She could smell the infected tissue and swallowed hard. "I can," she said, "but I will need assistance."

"You shall have assistance. What do you need?"

She felt the inner burst of confidence she always felt when she entered the realm of sickness and healing. She lifted herself to her full height. "I need clean water; I need bandages. I need a sharp knife and whatever spices you have to hand."

The slave stepped forward. She noticed that he was a burly man of about the Reis' age. "I shall find these things for you", he said.

"I will also need something to clean the wound. Wine or vinegar. I prefer wine."

"We have wine. It will cost ..."

"Never mind the cost", spat Ibrahim Reis, who looked a little white.

"A length of rope would be useful," she added, "and I shall need you to hold him down."

"I do not need holding."

"You will when I start cutting the wound open", promised Warda, phlegmatically. "Hurry."

†

As soon as the slave returned, she set to work. She poured a small portion of the wine into a bowl, cast an eye over the assortment of spices he had found for her, and added small quantities to the wine. Then she cut the cloth she had been given into strips and laid them out on the table, all except for one piece that she wound around the Reis' wrist. Then she secured his arm to the table, ensuring that the cloth formed a snug barrier between his wrist and the rope she was using, so that he would not chafe his own flesh when he began writhing. The slave seemed to know what to do and stood behind the patient, placing his hands delicately on the man's shoulders.

"Would you like anything before I begin?" she asked, briskly. "A strong drink, perhaps?"

"Get on with it!" he roared, clenching his fists so tightly that the nails must have been digging into his palms.

She shrugged her shoulders, picked up the knife, and began the delicate operation of removing the long wood fragment embedded in the man's arm. Even though she was not a surgeon, she had been sufficiently well taught that she was able to remove it with minimal cutting, looking carefully for small particles before proceeding. The Reis was gulping and sweating, but had somehow managed to remain silent thus far. "Your surgeon did a very poor job of dealing with this", she observed. "The wound has become infected. I will have to remove the putrid matter before I proceed or gangrene may set in."

She noted that he began screaming a moment before she started cutting away the infected tissue, but she had been trained to continue regardless and blocked out the sound. Her only concern was that the slave would not be strong enough to hold him, as she could feel the strain of the man trying to rise in spite of himself. "If you are able, hold his free hand as well", she instructed him, glancing up momentarily. "He will try to knock me away."

The wound was clear. She examined it once more then flushed it out with the wine. The Reis began screaming words at her in his native tongue, which she assumed must be obscenities. "Oh, be a man!" she snapped, turning away to pick up the preparation she had made before. He stopped abruptly and glanced at her lowered head in silent recognition. "I have nearly finished now." She was facing him again, but had not looked up and did not notice his changed expression. She was too intent on dressing the wound properly—wine and spices, then the whole area bound up with the strips of cloth, securely, but not too tightly either. Then she cut through the rope and released him.

The Reis was sitting still with his head slumped a little forward, too shaken by the intense pain to move. The slave let go of him and glanced at Warda for the next order. "Fetch the man something to eat and drink," she said, "something light to eat and nothing too strong to drink. He has had a shock."

He left the room, leaving Warda alone with her patient. She felt more unsettled by his silence than by his screams, even though she knew it was a quite natural reaction to such an ordeal. She picked up a spare piece of cloth and dipped it in the water then began bathing his head to cool

his temples. After the second or third time she touched his
brow, he raised his head and looked at her again, causing
her to back away. "You have become too hot", she said,
by way of explanation.

He took the cloth from her hand and pressed it against
his face. "Will it heal?"

"I believe so. You will have to ask your ship's surgeon
to change the dressings."

The Reis smiled bitterly. "I do not have a surgeon", he
reminded her; "or rather I do, but he will have to heal
himself before he ever steps aboard a ship again."

There was the sound of a door swinging open; the slave
appeared, bearing bread, olives, and something in a jug,
which the Reis snatched upon greedily. Warda turned her
attention to putting the room to rights and tried to forget
her own hunger, but she was interrupted by the pressure of
a hand seizing hold of her sleeve. It was the slave. "Who
did you say you were?" he asked, giving her a smile that
made her flesh crawl.

"Take your hands off me; I do not answer to you."

"You will answer to someone." She looked down and
realised that he had pulled back her sleeve to reveal the
red line across her wrist where her hands had been bound
on the day Omar had sickened. It had faded considerably,
but was unmistakably the mark left by a cord cutting into
flesh. Before she could stop him, he had pulled back the
neck of her shirt, exposing more fading red lines across
her shoulder. During the time she had been operating, he
had been watching her, noticing everything. "You are an
escaped slave."

She felt herself breaking into a cold sweat. "I am not",
she protested, but she could not possibly find another explanation for those incriminating marks. "You are impudent."

"And you are a liar."

"He is my slave", said the Reis. He had gobbled up his meal and stood up, placing himself between them. "He is young and wayward. He started a brawl and I had him punished. Is it for you to tell me how to keep my own men in order?" He gave her a light kick. "Tell him who your master is, boy."

She hung her head. The slave who had recognised her would destroy her if she did not flee. She had learnt enough from her dealings with Hala to be certain he would turn her in, even if he knew she would be killed as a result of his actions. But to accept the Reis as her master was tantamount to apostasy. He was in the service of the enemies of Christendom, and to enter into his service would be the most bitter act of betrayal. "Answer him! I do not think you are smarting enough."

It could hardly matter now; she was already numbered among the damned. It would be yet another act of wickedness to account for one day, and hell already yawned wide open for her. "He is my master", she said.

"What was that? Speak up!"

"He is my master", she said a little louder.

The slave glared at her. "But he entered the tavern alone. You did not seem to know one another …"

"I sent him ashore ahead of me", said Ibrahim Reis.

The slave swallowed audibly. He clearly knew the story simply did not make sense, but the Reis was obviously a man with whom only the foolhardy argued. "Whatever you say, Reis."

Ibrahim Reis took hold of Warda's arm and propelled her toward the door. "I will settle my account", he said over his shoulder.

Warda felt herself being pushed down the stairs. The Reis did not trust her fear of discovery sufficiently and held her in a vicelike grip as he forced her outside. After the stifling heat of the upper room, the outside air felt cool and refreshing. But hell still yawned open at her feet.

A Most Extraordinary Confession (8)

"So that was how you came to be aboard that ship", says the priest, tonelessly. "You were not a stowaway—or a hostage."

"In my heart I was", I whisper. I feel tears sliding sideways into my hair and hope he does not notice. I am still afraid to show weakness, even to a priest hearing where my most fatal weaknesses have led me. "If God is my witness, I never willingly consented to such a life. I cannot tell you what it means to feel so afraid."

He places his head in his hands again. "Continue."

"Father, please do not tell the good lady of this house what I am."

"Daughter, you know that if I tell her anything you have said I damn myself."

"I know, but it has been so long that I begin to doubt ..." The words simply will not come anymore.

"You have doubted a great deal", he tells me; "now you must have a little faith." I close my eyes and search for words again, but I am silent for so long that the priest begins to think that I have lost consciousness again and places a hand on my arm to wake me. "Wake up! You have not said all, have you?" I open my eyes and stare up at the ceiling. "You have not said all."

"If it could have ended there I should not fear so much to die, even with a man's blood on my hands. I am a coward."

"I do not believe that you are any such thing." The stern edge to his voice sets my heart racing. That is not what I expected to hear. "Do not waste your breath confessing vices that are not your own."

I close my eyes again. "It is easier this way."

"I know."

"I think it may be that I fell a little in love with him at that moment. Something happens to a person when they are rescued from a terrible fate. As soon as the slave realised who I was, I knew I was doomed. I knew that he would hand me over to my enemies for a reward and I would die—dear God, how I would be put to death! This man offered a way out. He taunted me and lorded it over me as he saved my life, but all I heard was a powerful voice making excuses for me and forcing my accuser to leave me in peace. He seemed to be setting me free."

Freedom. I took long, deep breaths as we emerged into the light of the blessed morning and he handed the slave coins for his services—and perhaps for his silence. My soul was bought for thirty pieces of silver, and yet I did not care. I thought only how powerful he was and how he had used his power to save my life.

As he marched me away, I found that I was unsteady on my feet, and he had to hold me close to him to stop me from falling. In my muddleheaded relief, I think I saw him as a protector, not as a man who had bought me out of sheer convenience and would have left me to die if I had not been of some use to him. For the moment I felt safe and wanted, pressed so close to the body of a man who shielded me from the sight of my pursuers.

"I must not be seen", I said; "I may be noticed."

"You need not fear discovery", he said. "You belong to me now. I have claimed you as my own, and no one shall take you from me."

It was almost blasphemy, but I refused to hear anything other than a promise that I would be saved from my captors. The dregs of the night had slipped away as I performed my operation, and I knew that the man I had killed would be found as the household began stirring or may even have been found already. I could believe that this one man was capable of saving me from anything, even from the blood-thirsty rage of a mob if it came to it.

And there was his ship. I was surprised at first sight how small it seemed compared with the craft that had crossed the Mediterranean to capture my people, but it was of no consequence; it was a miraculous vessel sent to take me from this godforsaken shore. He led me unresisting over the gangplank, when I had last boarded a ship by force, and this time I did not even desire to look back at the land I was leaving behind.

There were men moving about, members of the crew I supposed, still a little sleepy but busily preparing the ship, moving crates and barrels. Men. I felt myself beginning to panic again. How was I ever to conceal my woman-hood from these people for the length of an entire voyage? The very presence of men around me felt frightening and unnatural. During the long months since I had been bought at the market, I had been secluded from all but five men: a priest, Abdullah, Ahmed, Omar, and the master—and only two of them had refused to do me any harm. If they were to discover who I was ...

"You are shaking, boy", said Ibrahim Reis, pushing me down below the deck. "Not afraid, are you?"

"Must we go so far down?" I asked, but I found that when I tried to stop in my tracks, he merely nudged me forward, and I could not have resisted if I were in com-mand of my full strength. I could feel the stifling closeness

again, the thirst and the stench of the trapped bodies ...
"Please."

"You must keep out of sight", he said. "The ship is still
being prepared for its voyage. It would be more than my life
is worth if an escaped slave were found aboard my vessel."

I stumbled; my eyes unaccustomed to the poor light. He
unlocked and lifted what appeared to be a hatch of some
kind and then began pushing me through it. The smell
was overpowering, what I imagined the sea would smell
like if it suddenly turned rotten; I flailed desperately, grab-
bing hold of his cloak to stop myself from falling into the
hole. He seemed to have expected me to behave like that
and struck the back of my wrist so sharply that I let go
and fell down into the chamber beneath. "This is a cable
locker", he said, looking down at me. "It is where we store
things safely out of the way: ropes, sick people, captives.
Troublemakers."

I was thrown into confusion. "Why?" I demanded.
"Why are you detaining *me*?"

He looked steadily at me, showing no palpable emotion
at all. "It is as I said. You belong to me now, and no one
will take you from my service, not even yourself. When
we are at sea, the only way out will be overboard, and I
do not believe that a good Papist will go that way in search
of freedom. Until then, you will remain where you cannot
escape."

The hatch closed, plunging my prison into darkness, and
I heard the sound of a lock closing with a sickening snap.
I was so outraged and panic-stricken that I found my way
up the short ladder and began striking the wooden door,
shouting that he must release me at once. The confinement
was too close, the chamber so filthy and stinking that I felt
as though I had been buried alive, and I could not bear

to be left as I was. "Let me out!" I shouted, fighting for breath. "You will let me free!"

He threw open the hatch again and turned on me with such infernal rage that I was almost glad to be trapped in a place he would surely not want to enter himself. "You will be silent!" he thundered. "Or perhaps you would prefer me to shackle you as well?" I shook my head, too shocked at the change in him to utter a word. I knew that he would do it, but I had been restrained like a wild animal so many times that I could not bear to suffer such a humiliation again. "Very well then; do not stir until I return." He noticed that I was trembling with anger, and he laughed. "Do not be thinking yourself ill-used either. On board a ship there are far worse penalties an insubordinate man may face than a few hours locked up."

I was being threatened again, but managed somehow to return his glance before he closed me in a second time. Then I collapsed where I stood and wept silently into my hands until I was too weary to move even if I had desired to. The horror of the past night, the picture of my master guttering in the last throes of death, overwhelmed me at last. As sleep crept over me, I found myself shaking so violently that my limbs drummed against the ground. I slipped into dreams, haunted by thoughts of the slavery I had escaped and the terrible life that loomed before me.

The Life and Times of Pierre Dan (3)

Father Dan knelt beside the man's motionless body and listened as he made a stumbling confession. The priest had to place his head close to the man's face to be able to hear him, the voice was so muffled and rasping, but the galley slave was dying and would never speak to another human being again. Father Dan tried to be in port whenever galleys were returning, knowing that there would be some poor soul among the slaves in need of the Last Rites. Of all the fates that might befall a male slave, being sent to the galleys was perhaps the worst. Once chained to an oar, they knew that there could be no hope of liberty for them. Food was scant and the time to eat even more so, the chance to stand or lie down quite impossible. They were doomed either to drown if the ship went down or to be worked to death, rowing sometimes at full speed for hours at a time whilst the boatswain ran up and down the galley like a man possessed, shouting orders and striking their naked backs until they were driven half-mad with pain and exhaustion. Some might have been forgiven for believing that they were already dead and condemned to the worst torments of hell.

The man whose confession Father Dan was hearing was a French mariner captured at sea. His ship had been taken after a ferocious sea battle, during which the ship's firepower was defeated by a team of corsairs armed with scimitars whose boat sat too low in the water to be fired on easily. Once the pirates had boarded, both the crew and their passengers were taken with the vessel, too exhausted and terrorised to offer any further resistance. Those passengers believed to be worth a large ransom were held in the bagnos whilst their liberty was bargained for, whilst those, like this man, who had no value in the eyes of their captors beyond their physical strength, were condemned to the galleys. By the time he found himself lying on dry land under the little shade Father Dan had managed to find to cover him, his body was a twisted wreck, so badly crippled that he could barely open his hand for the priest to anoint it with oil. His flesh was covered with wounds and livid sores, making Father Dan afraid to touch him to begin with, but by the time he had made his confession the man was sobbing like an infant, and the priest found himself holding him in his arms to comfort him.

"Do not be troubled", he said; "you are going to your freedom now." *Two souls in my care on their way to liberty,* he thought. He had laid the man down facing away from the sea, knowing that it would either torment him with memories of his final months of slavery or with thoughts of his past life and the freedom that lay beyond his sight. But from where he knelt, holding the weight of the man's head on his arm, he could see a ship setting sail and moving slowly out of sight. He wondered what had become of her, whether she had put her natural cunning and ingenuity to good use and found a way out yet. *She might even be on that ship,* he thought. He spared a prayer for her too, that she was safely out of the hands of her enemies now and would reach the free world without coming to further harm—and that there would be a priest by her side to hear her confession in her final hour, if she would only consent to let it be heard.

"Where is it going?" asked the man, straining to turn his head.

"Where is what going?"

"I heard a ship preparing to leave harbour."

"You could hear it?"

"It is the last gift we lose, Father. I can barely see you now. It is as though someone has covered my head with a cloth. But I can hear everything. I could hear the anchor being raised and the sound of voices shouting commands. Just as I remember. I always thought that I would die at sea."

"I am sorry. Would you rather have had it that way?"

"No!" the mariner almost—would have—shouted if he had had the strength, then he was weeping again, great gulping sobs that must have tortured him. "Father, God has been merciful to me", he choked. "Those who died at sea were thrown overboard to be eaten by the fish. I prayed that I would not die without the consolation of holy Church—and here you are, just as I prayed."

Father Dan had never ministered to a saint before and thought that if France could have produced a dozen such men it would be the sanctuary of the world. For here was a man, who had not even thought it important to tell his own name, who had died a wretched death, broken, beaten, and starving, far from his homeland and his family, who could still speak of a merciful God.

Cast Adrift

She was falling, she was *always* falling. She was falling, falling ever further away from the light of day, down, down, always moving down toward despair and misery with no hope of rescue. When Ibrahim Reis had gone and she was alone in the terrible, foul-smelling darkness of the cable locker, she had curled up on the floor, no longer concerned that it was cold and damp, and cried herself to sleep.

A dream-haunted sleep. In the dream-darkness, bloody hands reached toward her, and she could not flee from them or fight them. Somewhere in the filthy oblivion she heard the cries and accusations of a man who had discovered that she was his murderer just a little time before his heart failed. "Have *mercy* ... mercy ..."—the stifling of a plea for help and the cry piercing her ever after. She was as helpless as she had been in the hands of Ahmed or Omar, locked into a place where every demon who had crossed her path could come for her a second time to exact payment.

"What have you done?" She could not tell who demanded to know; it might have been so many—Father Dan, her master, her new master ... A crash and creak of hinges broke her sleep in two. There were hands again, creeping across her body until they came to rest at her throat. "Answer me!"

Her eyes opened, but she believed herself to be trapped in her nightmare and struggled to awaken. "Nothing", she managed to say to the spectre that had laid hold of her. "I have done nothing."

Ibrahim Reis shook her with such violence that she struck her head against the ground. "There are people searching for a slave who has committed a murder. Is it you they seek?" She struggled to push him away, but he refused to let her move an inch. "Answer me! Have you killed your master?"

"Yes", she said, breathlessly. She felt his grip tighten on her; he was going to kill her. "It was not my fault; I had no choice."

"Did you or did you not kill the man?" He slammed her head again, deliberately this time.

"Mercy", she spluttered, as a story came to mind. "It was mercy. The man was sick, and I sought to spare him a lingering death." She looked into Ibrahim Reis' face and saw the slightest flicker of a change in the way he looked at her. She continued, less afraid. "I was so concerned for my patient that I thought nothing of what the consequences would be. But once he was dead, I thought that I could never explain to his family why I had done it, and they would have me put to death. I was afraid."

There was a tortured silence; Warda felt every muscle in her body tightening in anticipation of an assault. But the next thing she felt was the man's grip loosening, and he let go of her. "Enough said", said Ibrahim Reis. "I shall not lock you in again. Stay where you are."

He closed the hatch after himself and hurried up onto the deck, then up and over the gangplank where the group of men were assembled. "I have searched thoroughly", he said to them; "there is no one to be found, I am afraid. This is rather a small vessel for a stowaway. A ship left port some time ago; she may well have already given you the slip."

When he was sure that they were satisfied and on their way, he went down to Warda, who was lying in the position he had left her, like a stunned animal, a pink smudge tainting her throat. "Get up", he said; "they are gone." It was several minutes before she was able to move; he sensed her shrinking away from him as he helped her out. "You must remain hidden until the ship is ready to sail, but you will stay in my cabin until then. It is a fitter place. You will find clean clothes to wear and a little food to eat. You must be starving hungry by now."

"You still wish me to be your surgeon after what I have confessed to you?" she asked, but she noticed now that he took her by the arm and led her where he wanted her to go rather than pushing and chivvying her from behind.

He waited until they were safely inside his cramped cabin before answering. "It is a reassurance to know that your sex has not made you gentle", he said. "At sea, you will have to make hard choices—you may have to choose whether a man lives or dies—I needed to know that you could do so."

"Reis, I do not understand ...", she began, but he raised a hand to silence her.

"Do not try to lie to me", he said; "do not ever lie to me again. I know you are a woman. I knew it the moment you commanded me to be a man. It was a woman's reprimand." He noticed her shrinking back as far as she could. "There is no cause to be so nervous, my girl; if I had wanted a concubine I would scarcely have chosen you."

She had been the subject of so many sneering comments during her life that she could not bring herself to respond to the insult. "What are you going to do?" she asked.

"I am going to keep your secret", he said. "You have a skill that is of use to me. I have a ship that will take you from a land where you are being hunted. To my crew you will be a boy, and you will do nothing to arouse their suspicions. They are far too stupid to consider you might be anything else."

"Thank you, Reis."

"You have no reason to thank me. You know that", he retorted. "I know that you only agreed to come aboard this ship because you needed to escape at all costs. In case you consider it your sacred duty to prevent me conducting mine, there is something you should know. My men are animals who live for what they can take from others. They are controlled by fear and greed, not respect for any human life. If you cause me too much trouble, I will tell them that you are a woman and I will leave them to it. A ship full of ravenous animals in the middle of the sea is hardly a place for a creature like you, is it now?"

She turned away from him, shaking. It was the weapon they all used, the one torture that was impossible for a woman to bear. She was still a slave, and for all his talk, she was still a concubine. "When do we set sail?" she asked, finally.

"Very soon now", he promised, as though speaking to an impatient child. "Thanks to your efforts last night, we are almost ready to go."

"When will the rowers come aboard?"

He took one look at her perplexed face as she turned back to look at him and roared with laughter. "This is not a galley", he sniggered, rather girlishly considering his vast stature. "We journey by sail. No mouths to feed, no wasted space. Sails give us the freedom to journey far beyond the Mediterranean, to the ends of the earth, if we choose."

"We are leaving the Mediterranean?" Now she really was terrified. She had already begun to plan her journey home, how she might beg her passage on a ship to Malta if he could be persuaded to part with her when they docked in some friendly port. "But I want to go home to Malta!"

He shook his head, with an incredulous smile on his face. "I am taking you farther from your country than you have ever been. You will never see your island home again." He watched impassively as she sank to the floor, too shaken to make any response. If he had still been capable of pity he would have felt it then, but instead he found himself saying quite coldly, "I had almost forgotten how young you are—you are little more than a child—but younger boys than you have journeyed into the unknown with me. Take courage."

"Where will this journey end?" she whispered, her hands covering her eyes. "Where are we going?"

He hesitated then decided not to tell her yet. "Who can tell? No journey is worth taking if the end is so certain."

The Renegade's Tale

Warda lay in the cot and kept her eyes firmly closed. They were leaving port, and he wanted her out of the way, so he had told her to stay in his cabin until he instructed her further. Beyond her sight, men were raising sails and taking the ship away from dry land; she was safe from her master's revenge at last, but felt too unsettled to feel any relief. She was beginning to wonder whether the new master she had acquired might be even more dangerous than the last, living as he did beyond any rule of law. She had already seen him terrorise his servant for an offence she did not even recognise and was certain that he would be ruthless enough to carry out his threat if she gave him cause.

The ship listed so violently that she could have been forgiven for thinking it would capsize altogether, causing her to cling onto the side of the cot for dear life. *Very useful that will be if we go over*, said a mocking inner voice, but she clung on all the same. *If the ship rocked so much in calm waters*, she wondered, *how would it fare in stormy weather, dashed about on the waves like a nutshell?* She sat up abruptly, her body convulsing painfully, then vomited onto the floor.

Horrified, she threw herself down and tried to find some means to clear it up before the Reis came in and discovered it, but the smell would poison the tiny compartment even if she could remove every other sign of it. *Oh God*, she prayed, on her knees with every dizzy light flashing about her head, then she remembered she had no right to invoke his name and stopped immediately, forcing her fist into her mouth to stop herself from crying out.

†

Ibrahim Reis always felt his spirits soaring when they were safely at sea. All around him there was the reassuringly empty water and the whisper of a breeze to bathe his face and remind him that this was where he truly belonged. Ibrahim Reis had been born Johannes Peeters, a Flemish Protestant from Haarlem who had gone to sea at the age of eleven to escape the misery of a lonely, hungry childhood home. He would never know it, but he and Father Dan shared a great deal in common. They were compatriots, they had both known the loneliness and neglect that can come when a mother dies in her childbed, and they had both sought escape. But whereas Father Dan had found refuge in the Church, never knowing that it would lead him to the terrible adventure of working to ransom slaves in a foreign land, Johannes had longed for the sea and all the excitement it promised.

His childhood ended the moment he stepped on board a ship for the first time; the years that followed were a savage apprenticeship for the life of a privateer plundering Spanish shipping, an occupation that was as lucrative as it was a patriotic duty. But as the years passed, he discovered that the lure of treasure was always stronger than his ability to gain it; greed drove him to leave his Dutch wife and children for the Mediterranean, where the ships of all the nations were fair game for plunder. It was on one such voyage that he was captured by Barbary pirates and taken into slavery, but he was of a sufficiently enterprising character to turn the situation to his advantage. He converted to Islam, took the name of his master, and used his skill and knowledge to ease his way back to sea. Sailing under the command of another former Dutch privateer, Johannes (then Ibrahim) proved his worth in the search for the most precious treasure of all: people.

There had always been captives taken from the ships he had plundered, but the coastal raids he embarked upon were another matter altogether. There, people were almost all that mattered—men and women taken unawares, children from their cradles, people stolen as they ate or slept or went about their innocent business. He grew numb to it all, thinking only of what each one was worth to him, how many coins in the hand. Coins did not cry, did not plead for deliverance. It did not have to be torn screaming from the arms of a loved one.

He had been at sea far too long to allow himself to be moved by anything. And for all the gravity with which he had spoken the Shahadah, the security of material gain was all that mattered to him by then and all that concerned him now, standing exposed to the elements in a ship that he could call his home, surrounded by men who feared him and a woman who did not yet know what to make of him.

There had only been one occasion that troubled him, which he had only allowed himself to dwell on for the briefest time. On one of the early voyages after his conversion, they had sailed as far as the English Channel and attacked a Dutch ship that had the misfortune to cross their path. It was an opportunist attack, but a profitable one, though now he remembered little of the goods they took. There had been a good supply of passengers too, among them a young man, strong, strikingly handsome, who had stood out as much for his fine appearance as for the remarkable struggle he put up when the pirates boarded. They had not expected resistance, but the lad had fought with such spirit that in the end Ibrahim had been forced to deal with him himself, landing him a blow to the back of the head to bring him down.

It was only when he stooped down to shackle the boy that he realised whom he was looking at. He lay sprawling on the deck, mercifully stunned and confused, not wondering in that state why the vicious foreigner who had felled him stood over him, looking at him so intently; it was during those tortured seconds that Ibrahim realised he was looking into the grown face of his only son. He ordered another man to shackle him and did not allow himself another glimpse of the boy during the voyage. He wondered for a time whether he should take him as a prize, but then thought that there could be little purpose in claiming him now, when he had abandoned him years before to fulfil a deeper desire. The last time he ever saw him, he was being stripped and inspected at the slave market. It did not matter; he had condemned other men's sons and daughters to that hell.

Perhaps there was something about her that reminded him of his son as he had been when he was a little child. It was that curious combination of impish self-assurance and fragility she exuded that made him feel, just a little, as though one of his own had come back to claim him.

†

It was later that day when the sun was slipping slowly toward the horizon that Warda began to feel better and ventured out of the cabin she had found the strength to put to rights. Ibrahim Reis watched with barely concealed amusement as she walked uncertainly toward him, lurching awkwardly every time the ship listed. "You are an infant unsteady on your feet!" he called out to her. "You will have to learn to walk all over again." He did not notice the motion at all, but to her he thought it must have been maddening.

She had almost reached him when she lost her balance completely and fell into a heap on the deck to a chorus of laughter. "I do not remember the last ship moving so much!" she wailed, flattening herself against the boards as though she imagined she would be thrown into the water.

"That was a bigger ship", he explained through his laughter. "You would not have felt it so much—and I do not suppose you had the freedom to move around either." She showed no inclination to move, and, much to the surprise of the boy who attended Ibrahim Reis, he got up from his cushioned seat and went to her assistance. "Come on now, on your feet." He put his healthy arm around her waist and heaved her into a standing position, then held onto her to ensure she would not fall again. "There, you see. It is not so bad when you get used to it."

She could not wriggle out of his grip without risking falling again. "I should like to check your wound", she said and could have been congratulated for pulling rank at such a moment. "Will you come back to your cabin and let me look under the bandages?"

"I suppose I had better let you, or you will never find your way back alone", he teased, moving along with his arm still around her. "You look pale and sickly. Perhaps the physician needs healing?"

It was not precisely necessary to check how the wound was healing so soon, but she needed some sense of purpose to stave off the gloom of sickness and confusion, and that miserable sense of being superfluous. Kneeling beside her patient in the seclusion of the cabin, Warda was as happy as she could hope to be, her troubled mind occupied and Father Antonin's imaginary figure standing beside her, offering advice.

"Be careful to apply pressure if you are going to unwind the dressing. Do you have alcohol to attend to the wound?"

"Yes, I have everything I need."

"Who are you talking to?" protested Ibrahim Reis. "Are you mad?"

"Thinking out loud, Reis", she promised. "I have not been driven mad yet."

Ibrahim Reis grimaced with a sudden spike of pain. *Not quite mad perhaps*, he thought, *but not far off.* "What is your real name?" he asked, more to distract himself than anything else.

"I have had so many", she said, which sounded mad enough; "I hardly know what my name is now. When I was born I was Ursula; others called me Warda; then I was Perpetua. Now I am Pietro."

"Warda; that is rather beautiful. I shall call you that then."

"Please do not", she put in quickly; "my ... my father used to call me that. Anyway, it is better that you call me what the others know me as or you may make a mistake in front of them."

"I suppose you are right—" He drew in a deep breath as she bound up his arm. "Is your father still alive?"

"How should I know?" She looked intently at the man's wounded arm until her sight had cleared again, but she was afraid to blink in case tears escaped. "He is dead to me. I shall never see him again." She had finished and let go of his arm.

"You do not wish me to use a name he gave you?"

She felt his hand hovering over hers, and in the emotion of the moment it did not occur to her to push him away. "You are not my father."

"Thank God."

In what remained of her innocence, she imagined he was insulting her and fled his presence as soon as she had cleared away her things. He watched her delicate figure disappearing out of sight, still a little unsteady, and thought, *Thank God I am not. There are some sins even I would not commit.*

Two Battles

I am slipping into a nightmare again. I hear the voice of
the priest many miles away, calling me back to consciousness, and feel the tap, tap, tap of a hand against my face
determined to jolt me awake, but I cannot open my eyes.
I am sucked again into the dim, stinking confines of the
ship. I know that my slumbering body trembles and sweats
with remembered fear; a rasping voice cries out for help,
but no one can awaken me now. "No!" calls the voice—my
voice—"I will not! I will not!"

"You will stop struggling!" shouted Ibrahim Reis, twisting my arm behind my back so that it was impossible to
resist any further. "It is better this way. If you are locked
away, you will not be tempted to interfere, and no harm
will come to you. If I leave you to your own devices, you
will either be killed during the attack because you cannot
defend yourself, or you will be tempted to give the others
warning, and I will be forced to kill you myself."

I was flat on my face and could feel the painful tightening in my chest at the sound of a hatch being opened.
"Leave me alone! I will not make trouble; I will not *move*
if you do not wish it, but do not lock me up again. What
if the ship goes down?"

I imagined the chamber filling with water as the ship
sank, saw my final moments before me, battering against a
locked door and tearing at it with my fingernails, knowing
that it would never release me. He noted the terror on my

face. "Do not fear; you are in the safest place. Below the level of the water you are beneath the guns of the other ship. Can you swim?"

"No."

"Then you had better know this. If the ship goes down, you will go down with it wherever you are."

Thank God for small mercies; he had put me in part of the hold this time, which was a little more bearable. I supposed it was because they would need to drop anchor and that Ibrahim Reis could not risk my being confined in the cable locker with the thick anchor cable coiling and uncoiling so close to me. It at least smelt less appalling, but I was alarmed to notice rows of barrels on either side of me that looked ready to roll on top of me if we moved too much.

They had spotted an English ship, though I did not know whose ship it was then. I felt the change as we picked up speed and hoped that the captain of the ship we were approaching would realise he was being pursued before it was too late. So much time seemed to pass that I thought it must have slipped away into the distance, when all of a sudden the gates of hell came crashing open above my head. The roar of the guns was deafening from where I was cowering and seemed to come from all around me. I felt myself being thrown about with the movement of the cannon being fired, and clutched my head in my hands, screaming with panic, which at least could not be heard by anyone else.

The firing did not last long and was followed by a noise so terrible that I wished the guns would start again, simply to drown it out. It was the thunder of feet and the shrieking of men racing toward a prize. I curled up with my forehead battering against my knees and sobbed, remembering the hour of my own capture and the terror these men induced by their sheer appearance. I knew they were boarding the poor ship, which must have sensed danger far too late to put up any great fight. The crew would be thrown into confusion and shock—oh God, and they did not know it would be better to die in an instant than to be carried to the torment awaiting them if they surrendered. And I lay in a ridiculous heap, seeing nothing, hearing nothing any longer, simply weeping because that was all that was left for me to do.

There was a grim, uneasy silence. I might almost have been back in Gozo again, hiding behind the high altar, but even Father Antonin's sacristan would not have been so aggressive when he found me there. "Get out!" called the man who had opened the hatch. It was the boatswain, a vast, red-faced, bald-headed compatriot of Ibrahim Reis, whom I already disliked intensely. "You are needed; there are wounded to attend to."

I uncurled myself and looked up, but there were still tears streaming down my cheeks, and it took the greatest effort to move toward him. He gave me a perfunctory slap in the face. "Pull yourself together, lad! Stop crying like a girl!"

"I cannot help it."

He took hold of my arm and yanked me out into the open, dragging me toward the upper deck when I struggled to take my own weight. "You can work near the sandbox in case you need fire. Your chest will be brought to you."

I was stiff and exhausted from curling up so tightly and found it difficult to settle myself, but I was in the open air again, and there were my chest and my tools to reassure me—and the wounded. I took a quick look at the men I had been asked to treat. One was a member of our crew who had suffered cuts and grazes from what must have been unexpected resistance, whilst the other two were mariners from the other ship. The first of the mariners had a knife wound across his torso, but I noted upon a quick examination that it was a superficial injury and could be easily treated. The other mariner, however, was in such a dangerous condition I knew I would be fortunate to save him.

"Attend to our own first", commanded the boatswain; "we cannot afford to lose him." I noticed Ibrahim Reis' boy standing beside the boatswain. "The captain has offered you his servant to assist you."

"Your man is not badly injured; he will not be lost", I promised, before the boatswain walked away, focusing my attention on the captive. I suspected the young man before me had been the source of resistance that had injured our crewman. He must have either been dangerous enough in combat to make it worth their while hurting him so badly, or the wound had been an unfortunate accident, but he had been hacked across the wrist, so savagely that his hand was almost severed. He had somehow had the presence of mind to tie a cord around his arm to slow the bleeding and was holding it as tightly as possible, but he would not be able to hold on for long, even to save his own life.

I knelt by his side. "I will help you", I said, but he could not understand me, so I began taking out surgical instruments I had never used in my life. "I am going to have to amputate his hand", I said to the servant and hoped to God that my panic was not evident. The wounded man began babbling and shaking his head, but I assumed it was because of the knives I was taking out in front of him, so I ignored him.

"What do you think you are doing?" came a voice that made me start violently. The boatswain was standing behind me and had planted a hand on my shoulder. "I told you to treat our own first."

"Forgive me, I forgot", I said. I waited until he had walked away before picking out what I recognised as a cauterising iron. Dear God, I was a physician, not a surgeon! I had never dealt with a wound that bled like this before, and there was no one else on board who could, but having bled two men to death I thought that God must be giving me the chance to atone by saving this man's life, so I knew I could not fail. I handed the iron to Ibrahim Reis' servant. "Place this in the fire for me. It must be red hot."

"But the boatswain ...", he whispered, "he said ..."

"I know what he said, but I must treat this man first; he's dying." The boy looked petrified. "I will answer for this; I promise, no harm will come to you. Now for God's sake, do as I ask; there is little time!"

He turned his back on me and thrust the head of the cauterising iron into the fire whilst I made my calculations. Fortunately, the hand was so nearly severed that there was little cutting for me to do. The largest cutting instrument was clearly meant for sawing through bone, then I would need to cut through the remaining muscle and flesh, but the evidence of my own eyes told me I would have to stop the bleeding first.

A second after the servant had handed me the iron, he shrank away in alarm; I turned to find myself facing the boatswain again, his face livid with rage. "You defy me again?"

I should have been afraid, but I was a physician now, and the only thought that frightened me was the prospect of losing my patient. "This man is dying; I must treat him immediately."

"He is worthless without a hand. As good as dead."

"I will be the judge of that", I said, waving the cauterising iron in the direction of his face. "Do not touch him."

He backed away. "Do you dare draw a weapon on me,
boy?" he whispered, looking intently at the glowing red
stump of metal before him.

"I did not draw and it is not a weapon", I said, remembering a lesson from long ago; "you will leave me to treat
this man."

"I shall see you burn in hell", he said, drawing a knife
so quickly it almost seemed to have appeared in his hand
by magic. If he could move that quickly he could have the
knife in my heart before I could ever move to stop him,
as I knew nothing of combat—the men I had killed before
had been taken unawares. I clenched the iron as tightly as
I could and returned his glare, whilst all around us, the
deck and its crew and its wounded, the entire ship and
the whispering sea, disappeared without trace; we were
alone, waiting for an invisible signal to send us lunging
at one another.

A sound like a thunderclap clattered against me, throwing me off-balance. Somewhere within the nothingness
that surrounded us, a hand grasped my left wrist, dragging
my arm up and back until it felt as though it would be torn
out at the shoulder. "Put that iron *down*."

He hardly needed to shout the command. The pain in
my shoulder was quickly matched by the sensation that
he was crushing my wrist in his clenched fist; my fingers
opened up involuntarily. I heard the hiss of the iron hitting
the sandbox behind me, before the pressure he was exert-
ing on my arm forced me onto my knees. Ibrahim Reis
pushed me casually aside and faced the boatswain, placing a
hand on the hilt of his weapon. I was almost relieved that I
could not see the look on his face, because it frightened the

boatswain so evidently that he sheathed his knife without a word and took two very deliberate steps back.

"He drew first", whispered the boatswain, not looking up.

I inched my way as far back as I dared, but Ibrahim Reis reached toward me with the calm air of a man who can control anything and took hold of my hair, forcing me to stand up and look in his direction. "Did you threaten him with that iron before he drew?" he asked, tonelessly.

There was no time to explain anything, and I knew he would not be interested in my reasons. "Yes," I said, "I did."

The next thing I remember was my head hitting the side of the sandbox as I fell; the force of the blow to my face was so powerful that the moment of impact was lost in a blur of skull-splitting pain. I could feel something hard and sharp in my mouth by the time I was hauled to my feet; I just had time to spit out the broken tooth before I found myself being marched purposefully away from the scene I had caused.

Somewhere a man was slowly dying, and I was not saving him—I was not holding his life together—but all I could think of was that my head felt as though it would break into fragments and that I ought to be dead, but the sentence had been postponed again. Somewhere, in amongst the punch-drunk confusion, I had some sense that he had saved me from death again and that I should be relieved. And yet I could not possibly feel safe. I did not feel safe at all.

Another Battle Lost

"I had half a mind to leave you to the boatswain", hissed Ibrahim Reis, when he had thrown her bodily into his cabin and closed the door. "He is the finest knife fighter I have ever met." She touched the tender place where he had struck her. It felt hot and so sore at one point that she was sure the bone must have cracked. On the other side she could feel a small trickle of blood sliding down her temple like tears. "And do not pity yourself", he continued, snatching her hand away from her face. "I had no choice since you admitted your guilt; I had to be seen to restore order, or I would have lost the respect of my men. You deserved a taste of the cat." He turned his back on her for a moment, and she could hear the sound of him breathing through his anger as though trying to cool a fire.

The empty threat restored a little of her self-command. She *knew* he did not mean it. "The boatswain may have been a little surprised when I was forced to strip, and he discovered I was a woman—particularly as you were the one to bring me aboard."

She braced herself, expecting him to respond, but he did not flinch. "I said I would tell them you were a woman if you gave me too much trouble—what better way for them to find out?" he answered. "And there is always the bastinado. That way you would only have to expose the soles of your feet."

It was her turn to flinch. She had seen it done once before. The man had been forced onto his back whilst his ankles were restrained between pieces of wood, then two slaves had lifted the wood up as high as their shoulders and the soles of his feet had been struck. Abdullah had told her that he knew of a man who had writhed so violently with the pain that he put his own hip out of joint. "But the man is wounded! He will die if you do not allow me to attend him."

"Do you not realise how serious an offence it is to draw a weapon?"

"Of course I do not know. I have never been aboard a ship before. Not like this anyhow." She was thankful Father Antonin had not been present to witness her latest misjudgment, but then she was grateful he had not witnessed a great many of her actions since her abduction. "It was not a weapon; it was a tool."

"Don't play the Jesuit with me; you were using it as a weapon."

"I would not have harmed the boatswain." It was a childish argument, but she was fast running out of ways to defend herself. "I do not deserve to come to grief because I happened to be holding an instrument that might have hurt another."

"Are you deaf?"

She swallowed hard. There would always be a case against her. "No, Reis, you know I am not deaf."

"A simpleton then?"

"I am not, Reis."

"Then why," he asked, turning on her with such rage that she found it impossible to stand her ground, "why did you disobey an order? You were told—told quite distinctly—not to attend to him first."

"He was dangerously injured; it was my duty."

"Your duty is to obey!" he roared, and she knew he meant to be heard all over the ship. "You have no other duty! You will treat those you are told to treat and leave those you are commanded to leave. There was no purpose in you wasting your time with that man; he is worthless to us."

"I am a physician, Reis", she said quietly. "The only duty I know is my duty to the sick and the dying—the duty to cure. It is not for me to determine who is worthy of life and who is not." She stopped for a moment, but once she had begun down a path she found it almost impossible to turn back. "If that were the case, I would not have treated you."

His hand went to the hilt of his sword, but they both knew there was not enough room for him to draw, so he let go, raising his clenched fist so that the white, bony knuckles brushed the swelling mark on her face. "Do you seek martyrdom? Is that why you provoke me?" She found it impossible to answer. "Why must women always open their mouths when they know they cannot defend themselves against the consequences?"

"Because the consequences always come regardless", she said, but her head was becoming clouded again. "Break my head if you want to—God knows he never gave me any great beauty—but please allow me to save this man's life, if he is still alive."

He moved his hand away from her face. "I would not do that to you, but I cannot allow you to leave this cabin. The boatswain's business is not for your eyes."

It was then and only then that she became aware of the scuffle going on outside. "No," she pleaded, "stop this!" In wild, drunken panic, she tried to push past him, struggling violently when he forced her back. "Do not let them touch him!"

"Stay still!" he commanded, throwing her back. "You will not interfere!"

He seemed to fill the tiny room. In a last effort to reach her patient, she placed a hand over Ibrahim Reis' bandaged arm and squeezed as hard as she could, pressing her fingers down against the wound. By some miracle, he did not scream, but she felt him collapsing onto his knees as though she had felled an ox. In the confusion they both felt, she was somehow able to crawl out onto the deck and stagger to her feet in time to see the wounded mariner being carried to the edge of the ship, struggling pathetically with what little remained of his strength.

"Stop!" she shouted, but she was so hysterical that the word was hardly clear. "*Stop!*"

There was a despairing wail, the splash of the man's maimed body hitting the water, then nothing. He sank beneath the waves like a stone, without so much as a ripple of resistance hitting the surface of the water.

Warda could no longer see or hear or feel anything. She slumped forward onto the deck and felt blessed unconsciousness overtaking her. Her last thought before the void swallowed her was that a human being had been placed into her hands and she had lost him. She had lost another life, another battle.

The Loneliest Woman Alive

When Warda came round, her first action was to cry out at the top of her voice. Her head blazed with pain as though Satan himself had brushed up against her in her sleep; she was too confused and overcome to do anything other than writhe and cry. It was some minutes before she realised she was in the cable locker again and that a man was holding her in his arms, trying to prevent her from tearing her own flesh in her terror. "Ssh," he whispered, rocking her back and forth to soothe her, "easy now. Easy. Do not be afraid."

"I am burning, sweet Jesu, I am burning!"

"You are hurt; try to keep still. Hush now, my brave girl. Sssh."

"I cannot breathe!"

"You can; you must be calm." He tilted her head back to ease her breathing. "Quiet now. Breathe more slowly."

She concentrated on taking measured breaths, deeper and deeper until her mind gradually began to clear. The side of her head was searing, and her cheek seemed to have caved in altogether. She could feel a ragged patch on the inside of her mouth, and the taste of blood curdled at the back of her throat. In the background there was the ache of bruises from her tussle with the Reis and the queasy sense of having been unconscious for longer than was entirely safe. She noticed two men sitting close to her, one of whom had had the knife wound she had never treated, whilst a third man was holding her close to him, trying to reassure her. The rest of the English crew must have thrown themselves overboard rather than be taken ... and one ... there had been another ...

"There now, do not cry", said the third man, stroking her head. "You could not have saved him."

She looked up at him through her tears, astonished to realise that she understood him perfectly. "Where did you learn ...?"

"I have been a captive in Barbary before", he said; "that is why you understand me. Unlike these others, I know where I am going."

"A captive twice?"

"Ay. I am sorry I discovered you are a girl", he blushed. "Forgive me, you were senseless for so many hours we began to fear for your life. I loosened your clothing trying to bring you round. We will tell no one. We tried to dress your wound ..."

So that is why it hurts so badly, she thought, touching the makeshift dressing they had made out of the cleanest (and it was not very clean) piece of cloth they could find to wrap around her head. She suspected they had changed it at least once and torn the wound open in the process, rendering it a good deal worse. All said and done, she rather wished they had left her alone, but it was hardly the moment to say it. "Thank you", she said; "you have been kind."

"We owed you a favour for trying to save our comrade. My name is Thomas Payne. These others will not understand you. They are Philip Craven and John Dawson."

"What was the dead man called?"

"Kit Fraser." Her head went down. "Do not think of him. I should not have told you his name."

"Kit."

"Christopher. Yes." There was an awkward silence. "What is your name?"

"On board I am Pietro", she said. "Only the captain knows who I really am. You must not give me away."

"Your secret is safe with us." Dawson began asking him questions. He turned to her. "They want to know why you are on this ship. Are you a slave?"

She cringed, wondering whether she should feign weariness to avoid the question. Fortitude raised its persistent head. "In all but name. It is a little difficult to explain."

"Are you one of them?" he asked; she noted the sudden chill in his voice.

"Not in the way you mean", she began; "I needed to escape my master, and this was the only way out."

"Are you or aren't you?" He sounded impatient now. "It is a simple enough question. Whose side are you on? By the way you have behaved you seem to be one of us, and yet you sail with them."

"I simply sail", she put in quickly; "I have a skill that brought me aboard, but I am no more than a passenger."

"Do you know where this ship is heading?"

"No, he would not tell me."

Thomas Payne smiled with evident relief. "Of course he did not, or you might have given him trouble. That is right, isn't it?" She nodded, gratefully. "One of the Turks told me as we were being brought aboard, 'Soon there will be many of your people here.' They are going slaving to the coast of England. Do you see now why I ask you whose side you are on? No one can sit on the fence at this time. Either you are aiding their war or ours."

She lowered her head. Pain was returning to plague her, and she felt exhausted by the interrogation. "I am no apostate, if that is what you are thinking", she whispered.

"Then do something", he said softly. "This ship must not reach the coast of England, or God knows how many innocent souls will be dragged away into slavery. Even if it means destroying—" He stopped abruptly at the sound of the hatch being opened and made as much distance between them as possible.

The boatswain's cannonball of a head came into view. "So, you are alive after all", he said. "More's the pity. Get up. The Reis wants you."

She staggered, blinking, after the boatswain, too shaken by Thomas' words to consider the retribution that might be awaiting her. As she entered the so-familiar little room, she recalled that she had taken the place of a man who had injured Ibrahim Reis accidentally, in the act of trying to cure him. It made no difference. There were so many reasons to be afraid that she felt simply numb as she glanced at Ibrahim Reis, sitting up in his cot nursing his wounded arm. The boatswain, she noted, had walked away.

"Pietro Contarini", he said; she thought he sounded horribly like her old master talking like that. It was the voice of a judge. He pulled back his sleeve and indicated the wounded area. "Deal with it."

She stepped forward and began unbinding his injured arm, but she hardly needed to; the results of her aggression toward him were already evident. When she had attacked him, she had broken open his wound again, and the small quantity of blood lost had seeped through the dressing. "I need to clean the wound and change the dressing", she said, tonelessly.

"Do it then." She looked in surprise at the exposed wound. "What is the matter?"

The matter was that there was nothing the matter. A scab had formed, and the wound was healing over, though it had obviously been broken open since she had last checked it. "How long have I been unconscious?" she asked. "It cannot have been more than a few hours, judging by the position of the sun, and yet ..."

"You have been away from the land of the living for more than a day", he said; "it was rumoured that I had dealt so harshly with you that you might be dead."

"Who put that rumour about?"

"I did." She looked askance at him. "Defying the captain of a ship is sedition."

"I was acting in passion."

"This is not the confessional—do you suppose it matters here what your state of mind was at the time? The crew think I did something to you because you defied me. A man in my position must seem to settle every score with interest or risk losing everything. You know that."

Warda felt her knees giving way under her. "Stay on your feet!" he ordered. "Who gave you leave to sit?"

She braced, dug her heels in, but all in vain. She slipped onto her knees, which somehow seemed more respectful than sitting on the floor. "Are you going to tell them?" she asked.

"*That* threat is making you faint with fear, is it?" he sneered. "You, a person who appears to have no natural sense of fear left? You could have paid for attacking me with your life; if I were not protecting you, the discovery of your womanhood would hardly be a concern of yours. Skeletons on the seabed look very much alike, I assure you." She did not so much as murmur. "No one else knows precisely what occurred in this chamber. They simply heard shouting; they heard the sound of a struggle and you pleading and protesting. They may interpret what they heard however they choose."

Ibrahim Reis reached down and pulled her up so that she could sit on the edge of the cot next to him. "There now", he said, because she shuddered when his hand wandered to her face. She did not try to move, but he could sense her yearning for him to leave her alone. "Isn't that the most curious thing?" She had no fear any longer, he thought, because she had no hope. The death of the mariner had been the final straw. And yet she was afraid of him touching her, a woman who had been violated and used like so many others in this diabolical trade from which he profited. "I will not give you away, but not for your own sake. I will not share you with any other man." She blushed like a maiden. "Do you understand me?"

Warda closed her eyes. He was far too close to her. She could feel the coarse texture of his beard prickling against her face and the stinking patter of his breath against her neck. "I am a physician," she said, "not a concubine. You said as much yourself. Let it remain that way. Please."

He uncurled a strand of her short hair between his fingers. "I do not seek to use you", he said; "I am not like the man you were sold to before. You will not leave my service empty-handed." He let go of her and dropped onto his knees, signalling for her to move out of the way. She was desperately relieved that he appeared distracted and hauled herself to her feet, watching as he dragged a wooden chest out from under the cot.

"Look." He took a key and unlocked the chest, throwing it open to reveal more wealth than she had ever seen in her life. The box was partially filled with every kind of treasure—or so she thought: gold coins, crudely made ingots of gold, objects she did not recognise that sparkled in the gloom of the cabin. "Take a look at these things. Take a good look at them."

"What is this?" It was exactly what she had expected a pirate to be hiding under his bed, but all the same she found it impossible to touch anything. She had only ever seen precious stones and metals in two places before, once on the sanctuary of her parish church—and it had been scarce enough—and once again in the house where she had been a slave. She had been adorned with such things so that in Omar's little kingdom she had been among the precious objects he could claim as his own. The first time, she had had no right to touch such beautiful things; the second time, she had not wanted to and felt burned by them.

"These are the spoils of war, Warda. You have embraced the greatest freedom you will ever know. The world and its treasures are ours for the taking. You are not a slave; you are a member of my crew, subject to the same penalties and the same rewards. When this voyage is over, you will take your share of the spoils just like the others, and you will be free. Forget the nonsense you were taught as a child. Wealth is the only road to freedom in this world. If you had been born into it, you would not have been abandoned to your fate; you would never have remained a slave."

Warda had never owned a penny in her entire life. Before she had arrived in Barbary she had never seen coins exchanged. In the hand-to-mouth world of her childhood, goods had been exchanged in kind. She had begged and stolen food, tools, linen, whatever she could get her hands on; Father Antonin had given her food and knowledge; Marija had made her new clothes when the ones she wore became too patched and tight to be decent any longer. In slavery, none of the trinkets and gifts Omar had given her had belonged to her, and she had always known it. "My freedom at the expense of others?"

He took her face in his hands, and this time she was too dejected to react. "You have always known where we were going and what it would mean. Be grateful for the chance you have been given and think nothing more of it. You are a wanderer now; you know you can never go home even if I had promised to take you there myself."

If it had not been for her encounter with Thomas Payne, she wondered whether she would have given in by then, but in her mind she could not see the riches that might one day be hers; she could only see the strangers in some coastal village, sleeping peacefully in their beds whilst the ship crept up on them unawares. She saw what she had seen the night she had been taken—the families separated; the stunned, frightened people herded aboard a ship that would take them God knew where—and she heard an accusing question: *Whose side are you on?*

"You hesitate a little too long for a woman alone in the world", he said, when she had stood motionless for longer than he could bear. "You are the loneliest person alive. If I killed you now and threw your body overboard, who would know it? You have been dead to your own people since the night you were taken. There are none alive now to miss you. You would be a wanderer even in death, with no resting place among the living or the dead."

She turned her back on the chest, her eyes smarting. It was a time when she should have cried, but tears simply would not come. A Latin phrase she remembered Father Antonin chanting once came back to her: *And so passes the glory of the world ...* "Why do you taunt me like this?" she asked. "Why do you draw me toward you one moment and threaten me the next? What do you want?"

She heard the clatter of the chest being locked shut and pushed back under the cot, then Ibrahim Reis placed his hands on her shoulders, waiting for a struggle that never came. "I think it is more a question of what you want. Your fate is in your hands. It has always been. You have simply to decide what you really want."

Warda turned toward him, very carefully so that he was not forced to let go of her, and he stood with his arms around her. "I know what I want", she said, looking up at him steadily. "I want you to stop. I want you to do the first good thing you have done since you took to the sea. I want you to turn your ship around."

Ibrahim Reis looked at her in speechless bemusement. She was mad, of course, mad from ill-use—mad or possessed, with her flaming hair like some demonic baptism of fire and her *sinister* ways. He had seen that from the start, the fingers of her left hand nimbly at work mending his wound, winding bandages, waving a red hot iron in a man's face. He had heard the Latin she chanted under her breath as she worked, and though he did not understand what she was saying, he felt sure he knew which supernatural force gave her the gift of healing, and it was not the Holy Spirit.

No, she was just mad. She was not even blinking as she stared into his eyes, when there were grown men too frightened to so much as raise their heads in his presence. A derisive laugh would have been a suitable response, but he could not raise one. "You ask me to turn around? Have you taken leave of your senses?"

"Turn back or change course", she said. "I do not care about the gold you steal; it is the curse of the world. It has no body to hurt, no soul to lose—why should I concern myself with whose chest it is locked in? Human beings are different. Do you care nothing for the fate of the people whose lives you destroy? What if it was your own child being sold into a life of slavery?"

He jumped visibly but quickly recovered. "It is far too late to speak to me of such things", he said coldly. "I have stolen and ended so many lives now—women, children, whoever stood in my path. I could not stop even if I wished to. What would be the purpose?"

"Of course there would be a purpose!" she burst out; he had to put a finger to his lips to remind her to keep her voice down. "A village full of innocent people will be left in peace to live out their lives at liberty. Surely that is reason enough to turn around?"

He smiled wearily. "You misunderstand me. I meant, what would be the purpose for me? Do you suppose the God who has seen me steal, who has seen me rape, who has seen me kill without question, will care about one more sin, however horrible? I know that I am already damned to hell—so are you for all your pious nonsense. I was pre-destined to it before I was born—"

"No, that is not—"

"And if I am going to burn, I will burn whether or not I steal a few more lives to cry against me on Judgment Day." She looked away; he felt relieved, almost as though she had released him from some spell. "There now, do not be downhearted. You will see it all very differently when it comes to it; you have crossed the line already, though you may not realise it yet."

A Most Extraordinary Confession (9)

A tempest rages around me. I feel rain hammering down on my body, so heavily that I seem to have fallen overboard already with the chill waves devouring me and spitting me out again in disgust. I cling to the sides of my raft and scream with all my energy, but the howl of the wind all around blocks out my plea for deliverance, like so many damned souls shrieking in the darkness.

Hands appear from nowhere and grasp my wrists to stop me slipping to my death. "Hush!" calls a voice that is deathly clear. "Do not be afraid. There is nothing to fear."

"God is not in the earthquake!" I find myself shouting. "God is not in the storm!"

"The storm is outside; it cannot reach you!"

"God is not in the storm! God is not in the storm!"

A crash like the roar of cannon slams against my head, sending me reeling backward, but I fall against something soft and find that I am tossing and turning in no more dangerous place than my own sickbed and strong walls shield me from the storm raging outside. "You are safe from the storm", says the priest; "calm yourself."

"Oh Father, there was such a storm! We ran into a terrible storm!" I feel the chill of my sweat clinging to me and the curiously reassuring gesture of a cloth being pressed against my temples. "The storm will claim me at last."

"It would be better if it did", he says, and yet he holds me close to him to stop me being thrown about. "Let the

273

ship break apart, even if it takes us down. That will be the end of it."

"No, no, Thomas, I will not die like this!" Yet it amazes me that a ship like this can stay afloat for more than a minute with the wind churning up great walls of water to batter us down into the depths.

"Tell that to the sea!" I notice that his head is bleeding, but they all look as though they have been brawling; if the ship does not break apart and surrender us to the sea, I wonder if we will simply be battered to death by the constant movement. It is my own fault I am back in the cable locker again. When we sailed into the storm I was sent below, but I could not bear to be below decks when it seemed certain that we would sink and I would be trapped. Somehow, being swept overboard did not seem such a danger, but the boatswain clearly thought otherwise, and when I refused to go down, I was forced.

"I cannot believe it", I stammer, but I am not looking into the face of Thomas anymore. I cannot make out his features. "Wood, a few inches thick shields me from death. Water, then fire ..."

"Hush, there is no water here."

"Water and fire. I am afraid. Water and fire."

"No water and no fire yet." It is the priest again, and I am warm and dry—and I am the only object moving in the room. "Be still; the sea is far away. Do not weep."

"That was when I said I would do it. When the sea ... the sea calmed again and we were huddled up together, sick and aching, trembling with the shock of being alive."

"What did you promise?"

I feel again the groaning pain and chill of survival that we all felt when peace appeared and we knew the ship had been saved, that we had all been saved for the present.

I shook so violently that Thomas wrapped me in what I thought must have been his cloak, as though he were swaddling an infant. "God does not spare you much, does he?" said Thomas gently.

"What do you mean by that?" I asked, closing my eyes.

"I thought he might have stopped the ship, but he has not made it so easy for you." He touched my cheek so that I opened my eyes and looked at him. He looked more resigned than sad, but there was something so mournful about him that it filled me with dread. "You have to make a choice. The fate of this ship lies in your hands now, and you must stop it."

"He would not turn around", I said; "I did try."

"You did not try." Thomas lowered his voice to a whisper. "The man cannot be moved; he gave away his conscience long ago, along with his heart. The only way to stop this ship reaching the English coast is to take it to the bottom of the sea." If it had not already entered my mind I would not have been so frightened. "Do you understand what you have to do?"

"It is quite impossible!" I hissed. "I would not know how if I wanted to!"

"It is quite simple." He was a mariner again, giving instructions to his crewmate. There was no fear in him, no concern; he was simply laying out a plan. "You have to lay your hands on the key to the magazine. That is where the gunpowder is stored in barrels."

"But I know nothing about gunpowder."

"It is perfectly simple, you silly girl; gunpowder is made to explode; it needs very little encouragement. Open up a barrel and drop a flame in; a burning rag will do."

"How am I to get out?" I saw myself struggling through a smoke-filled chamber, unable to find my way.

"You will not get out; you will be killed instantly. We will all be killed."

I sat in silence, listening to the sounds of men stamping about above our heads and the distant crack of thunder echoing toward us across the water. Long ago now, I had stood at the brink of death and been persuaded to live though my heart told me to throw myself down. I stood now, staring into another precipice, and my life seemed to stand for very little. If I did as he asked, it would not be suicide because I truly did not desire to die now, but it would be the unavoidable consequence of an act of war. In the end I was still doomed to die and to die in every sense of the word. The moment a spark would hit the gunpowder, all things would come to an end—sights and feelings and memories and fears. All that had been and all that I had believed was meant to be. The explosion would break my body into hundreds of pieces, I imagined; all that would be left of my life would be fragments of flesh and bone, floating in the dark, unyielding sea. No body to bury in unconsecrated ground, and no one to regret my passing. It was as Ibrahim Reis had said: Who could mourn my death if no one lived to know that I had died? By now, the few who had ever known me would have wept their last tears over my memory, thinking me long dead, and my soul would be consigned to darkness without a single prayer to hold it.

"She did not choose to become a slave, but I have chosen a kind of slavery," I whispered, trying to remember the precise words Father Dan had said the first time we met, "and I can choose to suffer in her place if you allow it."

"What are you saying?" asked Thomas, a little impatiently. "You cannot lose your head now."

"I am not losing it", I promised; "something is beginning to make sense. I understand why he did it now."

"You must be strong", said Thomas, clasping my hand; "you cannot make a mistake this time. The captain has the key. It should be the gunner, but Ibrahim Reis is known to be a harsh, suspicious man who trusts almost no one. Take it by any means you wish and act quickly for our sakes. It is a terrible thing to sit in this prison waiting to die."

When the boatswain let me out, I looked back at Thomas and his friends, unable to bid them farewell or show any emotion for fear of betraying our plans. It was perhaps better that such a parting should have been made like that— hastily, coldly, with the boatswain chiding me for being troublesome enough to need locking up so often. I could never have found the right words, in any language, to say to them then.

Ibrahim Reis Ponders

I can feel the gentle pressure of her fingertips pressing against my arm as she goes about her work. The wound has closed over entirely now, and she tells me that there will always be a scar as though I were some prim maiden ashamed to be so disfigured. "It is better that I take the dressing off now", she states, unwinding the remaining bandage. "Does it pain you still?"

"It is of no consequence."

"Very well."

There is something about her speech that amuses me, however commonplace her information. Her way of talking sounds too rough for a woman so delicately made; her accent gives away her barbarous land of origin. And yet there is a sing-song quality to her intonation that makes her sound mischievous even when she is giving me the benefit of her pert tone. I have to make her speak again. "You have done well."

She shrugs. I would not stand for such casual insolence from anyone else. "I have been well taught."

"Indeed? Who taught you? It is rare to see a woman so accomplished."

She hesitates to answer; I might just succeed in breaking her. "My ... my father taught me everything."

"The physician's art?"

"Everything." She looks sad, and I know that the very thought of him has sent her far away from me, to a place where I cannot follow. "He was a wise man. He taught me to read and write."

"Indeed? You can read your language?"

"His languages, Latin, Greek. He taught me philoso-phy." I have never worked so hard to torture a person so gently, but it is working. I can see the tell-tale signs of a person struggling not to cry: the shiny film over the eyes, the refusal to blink, the sound of rapid swallowing. There is some warmth in her still, locked away somewhere in a happy past, and I can almost touch it.

She does not notice me slipping an arm about her shoul-ders. "What else did he teach you?"

"He taught me about mysterious things", she almost whispers, and I can hear the rasping of emotion in her throat. It will not be long now. "How to pray, how to love. Why I should—Oh Jesu—why I should do the right thing."

He was no wise man to teach her so much, but what purpose would it serve to say such a thing to her now? With the weight of her learning pressing down on her, she leans toward me until her head almost rests against my shoulder. Life would not be worth living if there were not so many risks to take, and I have taken a risk with her by evoking her past, knowing that it might remind her of a time when she believed in something other than her own survival. But it has done what I hoped it would. It has indeed reminded her of a life to which she knows she cannot return, and she turns to me because I have walked this road before her.

"Many have been our way before and found that it was a blessing", I tell her, but I no longer need to speak. She shud-ders with what I imagine to be deep emotion, and it seems quite natural to feel the soft weave of her hair beneath my hand and the warm wet tears soaking through the fibres of my shirt. I could take her now, and she would not have the presence of mind to put up a struggle, but I would gain so little from the act. Let her cling to me a little longer, long enough at least to become invisibly bound to me. I sit on the edge of the cot and hold her in my arms.

A Most Extraordinary Confession (10)

"I could not stop thinking of him", I tell the priest. "I did not know myself; I did not know where I was. So far from land and for so long out of sight of land, I did not seem to be of this world any longer. Yet I kept thinking of him."

"Whom? Whom did you think of?"

"My teacher. He brought him back to life. I—" Tears again. Dear God, will they never run dry? How can the body keep making them and not wither and die? "I have shed innocent blood. I did not even want them to die; I did not intend that they should die, but they are still dead. I cannot undo it. That is what I cannot bear. I cannot undo any of this."

"If you did not intend a man to die ..."

"But they died. They are still dead. They ... they were trapped, they—" Oh God, I cannot breathe. My head is under the water again and cannot rise. "They drowned; they were trapped. They must have died battering the hatch that would never release them, just as I had feared to die. What a death I gave them!" My head breaks the surface of the water, but it is still hard to catch my breath in the freezing darkness. "Thomas Payne, Philip Craven, John Dawson. And the other, the other I lost. Christopher Fraser. Do their names mean anything to you?"

"Only because you have told me them before."

"You do not know them? You do not know their families?"

The priest gives a sad smile. "This is a big country, much bigger than yours. There are far too many people for me to know them all, and the names are quite common. There will be many Dawsons and Cravens."

The worst pain is the pain of not knowing. The pain of Father Antonin and those who knew me who could not know what became of me after that night. The pain of Pierre Dan, who saw me walk away unrepentant into the darkness and could not know whether I lived or died. The pain these families need not suffer if they could only be found and told the truth—these strangers who are joined to me only because I was the instrument that took their loved ones into the depths of the sea. Yet it would be better if they knew the end of the story instead of being condemned to wonder all the days of their lives what became of their husbands, their sons, their brothers.

"Remember them, Father. Thomas Payne, John Dawson, Philip—"

"They cannot be found. Who knows where they came from?"

"Father, if I could only live, I would find them. I would find them all and tell them." But I will not live. I know I will not live, and I will lose their memories as I lost their lives, as I have lost everything that I have ever been given to guard—even my soul.

A Gift Given

"You are not afraid, are you?" asked Ibrahim Reis, when they had been left alone. It was a day since he had distressed her into his arms, and she looked quite changed, glancing at him with the cold detachment of a woman who has long ago lost possession of her own mind. Her thin arms were planted firmly on her hips in a gesture of defiance that seemed almost accidental. "You are not afraid of me in the least, are you?"

Her hands slipped down and swung by her sides. "Everyone is afraid of you", she said.

"You are not."

"No, I cannot help that. I am not even sure why not."

He sat perfectly still and scrutinised her again. Her mind was clearly unsettled for her to be quite so unpredictable, but he had known that much when he first set eyes on her. The previous day he had reduced her to a state of unresisting misery with barely a word. Now she was icily distant. No, it was more than mere madness. "I still cannot make you out", he said. "Sit with me."

She inched forward and sat down next to him with obvious reluctance. "There are very few heroes in this world, Warda," he said, "as well you must know by now. If I order a man to be put to torture, I can be almost certain that he will give in before he has so much as been shown the instruments. It takes courage to be prepared to submit to it at all." He traced his fingers along an invisible line around her throat and noted that she started just once when his hand came to rest there. One squeeze and she would be dead, but it either did not occur to her or she did not care and she made no attempt to move away. "Of those who are brave enough, only two kinds of man—or woman—are not broken by torture in the end. The one kind belong to a fortunate elect possessed of almost miraculous courage. The other kind are the unfortunate wretches who have already been broken and therefore cannot be broken again. To which group do you belong?"

He felt the movement of her throat beneath his hand as she swallowed with great effort. "Neither. Please do not put me to the test."

"You know that is not true."

She pushed him away with sudden panic. "Why do you ask me these things? If you want me to be afraid, there you are. What do you want of me?"

She could never have explained her transformation if she had had the slightest inclination to tell him, and he would have been horrified if he had realised what he had done. He had evoked the past to break her down, and it had called out to her across the lost months of her life. In the torment she had suffered as he had awakened her most desperate memories, she had become confused and wretched, clinging to him as though he were the only person alive in the entire world who could save her. But as he held her in his arms, promising to protect her forever, promising everything she could possibly wish for, she had felt a hand touching her head and telling her to wake up.

"Sleepyhead! You would have snored through the Agony in the Garden!"

She sat up with a start, giddy with the shock of waking from a deep sleep. She had dozed off at her books; there was a pain in her neck, and her right arm felt stiff where she had slumped forward and rested her head on it. The act of sitting up made her precious book fall to the floor with a clatter, dragging an inkwell down with it. The ink splattered against the open pages like blood spurting from a wound. "I am sorry!" she whimpered, throwing herself onto her knees to attend to the mess she had made, but the sudden downward movement made the world go black all around her and she fell forward, clutching her head.

"Steady", he said, placing a hand on her head again. "Get up slowly. You are trembling—did you have a bad dream?"

She was still murmuring her apologies as he helped her to her feet. "I was having a terrible dream. I turned into a monster and ran around destroying everything. I couldn't stop myself. I just found myself tearing everything to pieces."

"This is my fault", said Father Antonin, though she was sure it was not. "You have been inside too long today, poring over books. Your imagination is getting the better of you. Come with me."

He led her outside, into the dizzying light of the late afternoon. It was the most beautiful time of the day, with the heat haze wafting dreamily across the horizon and the cicadas playing their soft music. They walked together under an arc of sky unblemished by any cloud. "You must not be morbid", he said, after a long silence had fallen between them. "You are too old to dream about such things—monsters indeed! And no one has the power to make you destroy anything."

"It did not seem that way."

He stopped walking abruptly and turned to face her. "It is important, Warda. You have a choice. You have freedom; no one can force you to be evil. You will always have a choice to do the right thing."

"And a choice to do the wrong thing."

He was taken aback by how miserable she looked. "What is so terrible about liberty, Warda? Would you prefer God to be some horrible tyrant who forced you to do evil just to see you damned? Rejoice that there are some freedoms that can never be taken from you. You will always have the choice to do the right thing."

"Always?"

"Always!"

Ibrahim Reis was smiling at her, almost in relief. "Nothing is for always. It is a nonsense word." He reached out and pulled her toward him. "So you still have some life in you after all. Fear is the last faculty to be lost, along with the heart. Perhaps that is not lost yet either."

Warda glanced at him in cold fury. "You ask if my heart is lost? You are the second man to say such a thing to me, and neither of you have any right to it. You both bought a body, and that is all you bought—body to violate or torment or play with—but my heart was never his, and it is not yours."

He lurched at her so suddenly that she had no chance to flee before he had pushed her into the cot. "Then to whom does it belong?" he hissed, squeezing her arms so tightly that she could barely stop herself from crying out. "To whom does it belong?"

"I do not know!" It was the only answer she could give, and if she had not been so startled, she would have wept for not being sure. When Omar had asked the same question, she had been able to say quite confidently that she had given her heart to God, and it had seemed an infinitely reasonable answer, but now she could not say to whom she had given it. How could she possibly explain to such a man that no one had her heart simply because it was not worth giving, blackened, broken, unrecognisable, as her own body would be before long. "I am a physician, not a concubine. Please remember what you yourself said. I have served you well enough."

"You have served me very ill indeed", said Ibrahim Reis. "If any other member of my crew had made such an infernal nuisance of himself, I would have had him flayed alive by now. Do you imagine I would have protected you if I had seen you as a mere body?"

"Why? Why do you say these things to me now?" She stopped breathing through her nose to shut out the smell of him, or she knew she would retch. It was one of the many little tricks she had learnt in Omar's arms to suppress the instinct to fight him off, and it all came back to her now, with the weary resignation of a woman who has indeed been broken before. "You could have taken me at any time on this voyage, and you did not. Why now?"

"Because we will reach the English coast by the morning", he said, touching his knuckles against the sharp line of her jaw. It was only the faintest threat. "We will slip upon them under the cover of the murky early light whilst they sleep."

She pushed his mouth away from her neck. It was hopeless; she simply could not let her guard down. In spite of her every effort, her body rebelled against him, and she had to push him away. "You said there would be many journeys, many adventures." She was delaying him and that was all, giving herself a little more time when all she knew now was that there was no time. She had had no notion of how long a journey like this would take or even how long they had been at sea. To have only one night to act was more than she could take in.

"It changes nothing." Dear God, he would not leave her alone. His hand slipped inside her shirt, and she gave him a violent shove, throwing him off-balance. "You will soon have all the virgins you could choose from."

"Oh, I could buy or steal myself any woman I chose", he snapped. "As I have told you before, if I had wanted a concubine, I would not have chosen you. If I had, do you suppose I would not have taken you by now?" He held her face in his hands; she was aware of the moist, calloused fingers like poised claws. "I could have violated you by now; do you truly think you are strong enough to fight me off unless I choose to be pushed away? I could force you as I have forced others and will do so again—you have no right to stop me: I bought you."

"Get on with it then; why do you torture me like this?" Warda looked into his face, and for the first time, she recognised his expression. Omar had looked at her like that when he had brought her gifts and tried so hard to be kind to her. She recognised it as the look of a man who has everything he could ever desire except the one thing that cannot be bought or granted by brute force. "You do not want to take me, do you? You want me to give myself to you. I am right, am I not?"

Ibrahim Reis began unbuttoning her shirt. She grasped his wrist, causing him to pause and look at her as though trying to guess whether she could still be persuaded. "Give your heart to me if you still have one to give. I cannot demand your will or your obedience. I do not know whether you are brave or broken, but I know I cannot expect such things from you, and I do not wish for them."

We all desire to be loved, she thought, not loosening her grip on his arm for a second. *Even this feared, hated creature desires the embrace of a woman who loves him. I am less human than he is, so far beneath love now that I am not sure I can feel it or even seek it any longer.*

It would be easy enough to push him away now; she felt so utterly dejected that even the vague possibility he might turn on her if she resisted did not concern her in the least. But then she thought of the key in his possession and wondered what other possibility she would have now to take the thing, if there were to be no more days in which to divert his attention or drug his food—if there were to be no more mornings.

As she drew him toward her, she groaned under the weight of another squalid, dirty act she would have to account for before the dawn came and wished not so much that she were dead because death was coming, but that she had never been born in the first place.

Dreams of the Dead

It was time for it all to end. She crept like an insect out of the cabin, carrying her weapons in her hands. Oh God, what had she become? As she lurched toward the last disaster of her miserable life, she reeled with the knowledge that she had played her last part so well she had almost believed it herself. To steady her nerves, she told herself it counted for nothing, since in her heart she had not consented to it, and she had been forced to endure a man's disgusting demands so many times before, but it would not do. She knew this time that it had been different—a cold, calculated choice to give him what he wanted so that he would be as helpless and unguarded as possible when she came to steal the key. *My God, when did the used become the user?* she demanded to a God she could no longer appeal to. *I am a liar,* hissed her deepest, inner voice, *nothing more than a filthy liar who smiled and pretended—pretended so much I could almost have believed I wanted him.*

She could still feel him nestling in her arms, sense the frenzied rhythm of his heart calming in the aftermath, and the flush of blood in her own cheek. A man as powerful as that could never hope to find happiness, yet for those precious minutes he knew the tenderness and ecstasy of being loved. Or so he had thought. *I am the cruellest of women,* came the voice again, and no other voice than her own could be so damning; *I cheated him into believing that there was one person in the entire world who loved him, when all along I was planning his death.* His loneliness was his only weakness, and she had lunged at it with a physician's callous knowledge, as she had once pushed a knife into an unsuspecting neck.

It was better for it to end—she was too confused and too exhausted. Her broken, unsettled mind could not make any sense of her encounters with Ibrahim Reis. They passed before her eyes as she made her way to the magazine, as though her life itself was passing before her. One moment he seemed so powerful, another simply heartless, another barely a man at all. And as fast as the picture of him changed, so did hers, from slave to murderess, from surgeon to whore, from victim to tyrant. Now there was only one part left for her to play. She could not count herself a martyr when she had done such harm and her heart was as hardened and broken as so many shards of glass. And yet she thought that perhaps she could be a warrior and perform one good deed, even if it was in the act of dying.

She had taken the light from his cabin and left him sleeping. She had learnt during the voyage that when sailors rest, they sleep the sleep of the dead, and the slumbering bodies did not stir under their cloaks and blankets as she slipped down the hatch into the stores, out of sight of the watch. She thought of him fast asleep in his cabin, the blood cooling in his veins. She imagined the English mariners sitting in silent terror, knowing that every minute might be the last. For their sakes let it end quickly.

The key jangled in the lock with a noise that seemed to clatter through eternity. She stopped abruptly, listening for the sound of movement, but none came, so she carefully eased open the door to let herself in. She did not feel fear so strongly now, just the sense that it was time for it all to end. She held a light in one hand, a rag in the other. The rag she had brought to burn was his old dressing,

which seemed almost a cruelty in itself, but it had been
the first piece of cloth she had laid her hands on as she left
the cabin. She remembered a penance she had done once
for using a tool as a weapon, but Father Antonin's world
and its freedoms could not matter now that she knew as
a certainty she would never see him, never see any other
human face again.

It was all as Thomas had described it—the squat barrels
of gunpowder, the dark, acrid, close room. She felt herself breaking into a sweat that started her shivering. She
put down the light and rag. Her hands were just steady
enough to prise open the bung of one of the barrels, but in
her struggle to open it, she inadvertently scattered a small
quantity of powder onto the ground. She emptied her mind
of all thoughts and placed one end of the dressing into the
barrel so that a small length of it was embedded in the
gunpowder, then she lit the other end and let it burn.

Endings—the end of adventures; the end of hope; a violent end of fire and blood; an ending of life all alone. And
it was the loneliness that made her lose her nerve. She
looked at the flame gnawing its way along the cloth, fibre
by fibre, and was overcome by panic and grief. Shut up in
a dark chamber with only a tiny flame to draw her attention, she imagined herself in another room, a prison of her
own choosing, with the tiny light from the sanctuary lamp
flickering at her through her tiny window. She could not let
it go. The world of love and healing and learning that she
had resigned herself to leaving behind forever came back to
claim her in her final moments as it had always claimed her
when the darkness became too much to bear—the world
of companionship and peace and hope and innocence. She
could not let it go; she could not allow it to come to an
end with her own ending. The flame had not yet come

close to the powder, a length of bandage still hung over the side of the barrel with the light creeping up it so very slowly.

If she had chosen a shorter length of cloth she might not have had time for such thoughts, but the most significant moments in a woman's life can hang on a tiny detail; it was for the sake of a few inches of cloth that Warda found herself stumbling out of the magazine, closing the door behind her and hoping against all human hope that there might still be a means of escape.

And as she found her way to the front of the ship, still struggling for breath, the bandage, inexpertly positioned, was burning through and falling in a sorry glow to the ground, leaving the rest of the cloth harmlessly embedded in the powder. When it hit the ground, it ignited the small dregs of powder Warda had dropped and filled the magazine with acrid smoke and heat. Yet Warda would never know this. She stood in front of the foremast, the only place in the ship where she could feel truly alone, and cursed herself for failing. She had expected an explosion as soon as she reached the upper deck, which she had imagined would blow the lower chambers of the ship open and cause it to sink, giving her time to find something to hold onto before she was forced to throw herself into the water. By now though, enough time had passed for the flame to have reached the powder quite easily, and yet there had been no explosion; the barrel had not gone off.

She could hear voices near her, the sound of men waking up and getting to their feet. Her clumsy movement about the ship had unsettled even the sleepy men, and she knew they were searching for the cause of the disturbance. She pressed herself up against the foremast, praying that she would not be seen and all the time cursing herself for her cowardice. If she had stayed down there she could have ensured the job was finished; now she could not possibly return unseen, and it might never be. They would find out very soon what she had attempted in the magazine; Ibrahim Reis would notice that the key was missing and know she must have taken it. She would certainly be put to death, and this time there was not the slightest chance she would escape, especially when her protector realised she had betrayed him to his own death. She did not deserve any other fate, but the good people of the English coast did not deserve the fate they would suffer through her failure.

"Look!" she heard a voice shout. "The magazine has been opened! The key is still in the lock!" In the midst of the commotion this caused, Warda heard the murderous tread of a man who knew he was betrayed and the frightened scuffle of men fleeing his path. "Warda!" he called out in what was almost a scream, because he no longer cared if the crew knew what she was. "You poisonous flower, you cannot hide from me! I will tear you from this world!"

She leant back against the mast, drenched in her own sweat, hearing the sound of brutal retribution reaching her. And in her final terrible despair, she clasped her hands in front of her, raised her eyes to heaven until her head rested against the mast, and wrung out the last flicker of hope she had: "My God! My God! Have mercy on me!"

The last sound she heard before hell erupted beneath her was her own voice crying out. The explosion that followed knocked her unconscious. She did not feel her flesh burning or the sensation of falling as the ship broke open behind her and rolled slowly into the water. She would never know it, but the mast had shielded her from the worst ravages of the blast that destroyed everyone else in its path. The first thing she knew was that she was stifling under the icy gloom of the sea. She fought blindly against the water until her head broke the surface and she was able to catch hold of part of the mast.

She clung onto the driftwood and looked out at the pitiful wreckage of the ship, the burning fragments going out one by one like forgotten votive candles, the remnants of men's lives—pieces of clothing, eating vessels, a body badly mutilated by the explosion that floated past her before being dragged down to the depths. In the darkness she could not recognise the face; it could have been Thomas Payne or the boatswain or Ibrahim Reis, a man who had held her or hurt her or yearned for her. In death, it was impossible to tell.

It was becoming difficult to breathe; a weight was pressing against her chest. She felt a prickling sensation creeping down her arms, and her fingers began to uncurl. She looked up and saw a single star shining in the darkness. *Stella. Stella Maris.* She called out to the Star of the Sea, but could not hear her own voice inside her head. In her delirium, she thought she heard a woman's voice comforting her and the firm grip of hands holding her above the water.

"Mother! Mother, I am dying."

"Hush now, I am holding you."

"I am dying."

"The sea shall not claim you."

Dreams—the dream of salvation; the dream of being loved, of being wanted; the dreams of the dead.

A Most Extraordinary Confession (11)

The light is fading, and the chamber all of a sudden seems too dark for comfort. I have become a child again, afraid of the darkness—the darkness of the bagno, the darkness of the locked hold of a ship, the gunpowder magazine, the murderous waters. The darkness of despair and a guilty conscience. I have told it all now, every last terrible moment has been laid bare, and I feel a desolate sense of peace. "For these and for all the sins of my life, I ask forgiveness of God and penance and absolution of you, my ghostly father."

The priest stands with his back to me, staring out of the window. He leans forward and rests his head against the glass before saying quietly, "I hardly know what to say to you. I have sat at so many deathbeds, but never have I heard such an extraordinary confession as yours. You have sinned, but you have been tested as most of us will never be."

"Tested and found wanting. Can you give me absolution?"

He turns away from the window and moves toward me. "That question reveals everything you have been trying to tell me. You do not really believe you can be forgiven, do you? And part of you does not want to be. I am right, am I not?"

I look into his face, and he seems to want so badly for me to prove him wrong. I have been here before. "It is hard; it is such a very long time since I have felt forgiven. When I was a slave, the score always had to be settled; I have always had to pay for my actions."

"Rejoice then that you have been brought out of slavery. You have come before a judge unlike any other you have ever known, who loves you and is on your side." He reaches forward and touches the injury on my face; I find that it does not hurt any longer, but the memory of it is as raw as ever. "You do not have to bleed for your sins, because Christ has already bled for you. You must not fall into doubt and pride now."

"I am falling." The man's face has become a blur of tears again; I feel myself slipping one last time into a world where only terror and despair had the power to move me, where a man in white who seemed so like an angel it was almost a taunt, stands between me and my tormentor. And I am weeping and shouting at him. "The fault is mine! It was my fault! I will not let you bleed for me. My fault, it was my fault ..."

"Why are you so frightened of an act of love?"

I cannot tell who spoke, but through the growing darkness, I see my confessor, bowing his head as though weighing up a decision in his mind. "Do you know who I am?" he asks finally.

"How could I know? I am stranger to this land. I only know you are a priest."

"I am more than a priest; I am an outlaw. In this country, priests are under a sentence of death as soon as they arrive on these shores, simply for being ordained. I know that if I am captured I may face torture and a humiliating death, hanged and cut to pieces before a crowd."

I remember Father Antonin telling me about his friends in Rome who came to such a pass, but it seemed quite impossible to me then. Strange to think of a time when any cruelty seemed impossible. "I was told of this once."

He nods. "I am going to tell you something else. My name is Father Hugh Branton. Lady Alice, the good woman

who has taken you into her home and cared for you like a
daughter, is my late brother's wife. I grew up in this house
and take refuge here for a while before travelling back to
London. Do you understand what I have done by telling
you these things?"

I shake my head; so little makes any sense to me any
longer.

"I am placing my safety entirely in your hands. I am
trusting you with my life. You know I can never breathe a
word of what you have told me to anyone, even if I were
being turned on the rack. It is sacred, but I cannot prevent
you from talking. If you live and you choose to tell the
authorities that you met me and know my whereabouts,
you will be richly rewarded, and I will hang."

"I would never do such a thing", I would have cried
out, but the words come quietly and haltingly now.

"I know you would not. After all you have told me, I
believe that you are worthy of my trust. If I thought you
were evil all the way through, if I thought you were beyond
redemption, I would never be so foolish. And if I can see
good in you, do you imagine that God in his infinite mercy
and wisdom cannot see it?"

Mercy—true mercy that demands nothing and gives
everything, that I have simply to reach out and take. And
a prayer from my childhood returns as though my old
teacher were standing at my side again, reciting it phrase
by phrase for me to repeat and remember: "O my God, I
am heartily sorry ... I am heartily sorry ... and beg par-
don for my sins ...", but I find that I no longer have the
strength to speak. He waits for me to continue with the
act of contrition, but the words I can hear so clearly in my
head will not form on my lips.

"It is all right", he promises, after watching me fighting to spit out the words; "do not fear if speech has gone." He places a crucifix to my lips then holds it in front of me so that I can see it, then I hear the so-familiar words that I have heard whispered through the grille time and time again, but clearer now that I know I may never hear them again: "Misereatur tibi omnipotens Deus et dimissis peccatis tuis perducat te ad vitam aeternam...."

I glance at the figure on the Cross. The head is slightly bowed and the eyes closed in death. It is the tragic, haunting face of a man who has suffered; a jagged chain of thorns still encircles his head. But in death there is a sad beauty to it as though he is peacefully sleeping. My father's face looked like that all those many years ago, as he lay in that darkened room awaiting burial and my childish fears could not disturb his peace, whatever they thought.

And my peace will not be disturbed when it comes. My eyes close and I find myself drifting away to sleep or death—I do not know which, but I find myself surrendering to it all the same. And if I die my story will die with me, told as it was to the one man who cannot speak of it. But in death, the sad beauty of it all may be written on my face.